FIRST RODEO

THE COWBOY AND THE DOM
BOOK 1

JODI PAYNE

BA TORTUGA

First Rodeo: The Cowboy and the Dom, Book One
Copyright © 2019 by Jodi Payne & BA Tortuga

Cover illustration by AJ Corza
http://www.seeingstatic.com/
Cover content is for illustrative purposes only and any person depicted on the cover is a model.

ISBN: 978-1-951011-03-1

Electronic edition published by Tygerseye Publishing, LLC, October 2019
Printed in the USA

CONTENTS

As always, to our wives.

INTRODUCTION

We're all romance readers, and as authors we understand what you're looking for in a romance. We want you to know before you begin reading that each of the three books in *The Cowboy and the Dom Series* has a fully realized, romantic "happy" ending.

However, the overarching suspense element will leave readers on a cliffhanger after books one and two, to be fully resolved in book three.

With that in mind, we won't keep you waiting. Here's the full series!

The Cowboy and The Dom Series

First Rodeo
Razor's Edge
No Ghosts

1

"What the fuck are you going to do, baby brother?"
Bowie stood at the gravesite, staring down at him
like Bowie always had. *Gigantic prick.* "Do you think you're
going to fucking fix this? James is dead."

Like Sam didn't know that.

Fury flashed inside him, hot and fueled by an agony
he'd never expected, and he turned, his fist shooting out and
catching Bowie right in the uniformed gut.

Rule number two: never monologue.

That surprised Bowie enough that it doubled him over,
and Sam got an uppercut in. He had to get his shots in while
he could. His big brother outweighed him by sixty pounds
and towered over him by damn near a foot and, he had to be
honest, had ten years of being a Ranger behind him.

"Motherfucker!" Bowie reached for him, and he danced
out of range.

"You kiss my momma with that mouth, grunt?" He went
for Bowie's trick knee, thankful he had his shitkickers on.
That pointed toe was useful, and he had a chance to fell the
giant.

Rule number three: once you get them down, keep them down.

Used to be that him and James would work together to take Bowie down. That was never going to happen again.

Never.

The thought of that closed casket, that slashed-up face he'd had the misfortune to identify hidden under the oiled wood, made him gag and stumble, and Bowie took advantage, the fists on the back of his neck enough to face-plant him in grave dirt.

"Rule number one, baby brother. Don't start shit you don't have the strength to finish." The hands around his throat were strong, the tremble in them only noticeable because they were so tight.

The sound of a pistol cocking was sharp and clear, and the fuzzy image of Aunt Linda wavered in his sight. "Boys, if you upset your momma and daddy, I will be put out. Get your skanky asses off the ground. Y'all are in your Sunday clothes."

"Seriously, Aunt Linda?" Bowie muttered. "Even I didn't come to the gravesite armed."

"I know you boys. Can't trust you as far as I can throw you. Get your asses up. Now."

Bowie stood up and hauled him alongside, just as easy as pie.

"Now apologize," she demanded.

"He started it." Bowie was still a suck-up.

"Jim Bowie O'Reilly! You apologize to your baby brother for putting your hands on him right now!" God, she was a harpy—broad as a barn and fierce as any woman who had raised her own siblings had to have been.

"Sorry, asshole."

"Yeah. Me too. I just..." Sam waved one hand toward the

grave. This wasn't right. James was supposed to be in New York, living this amazing life with lights and a zillion friends. Bowie had the adventure, James had the city, and he was supposed to stay home here and...hold down the fort or something. He was the baby, and... "It should have been you, Bowie."

Everyone expected that awful phone call. Every time Bowie was deployed, they lived with that quiet fear.

James was a motherfucking school teacher. An elementary school teacher who didn't get tattoos or take drugs or—

"Sam!" Aunt Linda sounded horrified.

"What? It's true!"

"Yeah. Yeah, I know." Suddenly Bowie looked... diminished. Gray and tired and older than the seven years that separated them. "Fuck you, Sammy. I know. So what the fuck are you going to do about James? I have to report back to work."

"I'm going to go clean out his place." He was between jobs. Hell, he was between lives—college was pretty much done with him, he'd educated himself into obscurity in ranching, and God knew, no one needed a broke-dick cowboy with a master's in art history, a shattered leg from bronc riding, and a temper that tended to flare at inappropriate-at-best times. He would go clean things out and see if he could encourage the detectives to find out...anything.

"You sure you're not going to short out, Sammy?"

"Fuck you. I've been to Dallas, Austin. Hell, I went with James to Mardi Gras in New Orleans. I ain't a kid!"

"You're my kid brother, Sammy, and I only have one left now." An expression of pure agony crossed Bowie's face, and Sam turned his back so he didn't have to see it.

"I'll be fine. I've got the time, and Momma's got to take care of Daddy."

Things hadn't been good, but the news of James's murder had made the little baby strokes turn into a real one, and while Daddy wasn't crippled or nothing, no one was going to let him fly. Not yet.

"Come on. They're waiting for y'all down to the big house. You know there's food and all the Ladies Auxiliary waiting to make a fuss." Aunt Linda didn't so much as let a tear go, but she did slip her Saturday Night Special into her pocketbook. "Brother Martin will want to bless you both and lay hands."

"That son of a bitch touches me and I'll rip out his spleen," Bowie growled, and Sam had to smile. That was his big brother.

He could hear James, right now, echoing in his head.

Be good, Jim, honey. You're teaching Sammy bad habits.

God, it was never going to be right. Never.

"Come on. Let's go."

He turned and headed for his truck. James wasn't here. That was a grave, a body, a stone. He was going to go find James where he'd lived.

2

Thank God this was New York City, the only town he knew of, except maybe LA, where yellow police tape didn't slow anyone down. Aside from the cops, he was the only one there, the only one who cared. Thomas had about as much privacy as he was going to get.

He leaned against the side of the building as the NYPD took the tape down, balled it up, and stuffed it into a nearby garbage can. The evidence markers had been gone for a couple of days, the chalk lines were gone now too, and even the bloodstains in the concrete were already fading. Another day or two and there wouldn't be any evidence left that James had died here.

But Thomas wouldn't forget. He couldn't get away from it. He lived here, worked here, walked the same goddamn streets as whoever was responsible. He still carried around memories of his time with James that he'd never share with anyone. He carried around the plans they'd made and a future that could never happen now.

He hadn't received an invitation to James's funeral. This

would have to be his closure, watching the investigation into his lover's murder become routine, move on to the next "phase." Watching all the evidence disappear.

That was perhaps the most awful addition to his grief. He understood that James couldn't be wholly out to his family back home in...well, somewhere in East Texas, but understanding it while James was alive and in his arms was one thing. Coming to grips with his exile now was something else entirely. He was bitter; he was angry. Not at James, not at anyone in particular, just at a world that made them hide. He felt humiliated, and that wasn't a pill he could swallow without choking on it.

Everything about his life was deliberate, yet at the moment, he was experiencing a lack of control he'd never imagined possible.

One of the cops walked over and offered him a smoke. Colletti was his name. "Wouldn't you rather be home?"

"This is as close as I want to get right now." God, listen to him. He refused the cigarette, but just barely. Vices sounded like such a good idea.

"Dobson is going to call you, routine stuff. Did they ask you not to leave town?"

"Yeah. It wasn't an imperative, but it was strongly suggested." Insult to injury.

Officer Colletti gave him a nod. "We're done here. Take care, Mister Ward."

"Thanks."

The squad car drove off, and New York seemed impossibly quiet all of a sudden.

A man with a duffel and a cowboy hat walked up to the stoop, and for a second, Thomas's heart stopped. He closed his eyes until he could breathe again.

Fuck, tourists were everywhere in this city. He just hadn't been prepared for one in a cowboy hat. He took a breath and headed down the steps. He needed a coffee.

They passed each other, the man meeting his eyes and nodding. "Afternoon."

"Where are you going?" He knew those eyes intimately. He reached out and grabbed the man by the arm, that hazel making his heart pound. "Who are you?"

"Who the fuck is asking, motherfucker?" The little guy just popped right up into his face, those eyes flashing.

Christ, the cowboy sounded just like James too. Only James would have known better than to meet his eyes.

He stood his ground, inches away, instinct and training helping him stare the kid down. "You're an O'Reilly. Which one? Sam, right? The bronc rider? You're too small to be Jim."

"Bowie," the kid corrected immediately, even as he nodded. "Who are you?"

Nobody you'd know.

"Right. Bowie." He let go of Sam's arm. He knew he should back down, but it took real effort. "I'm Thomas Ward. I...knew your brother."

Fuck. I loved him.

"Knew him? Y'all worked together?"

What was he going to do? He wasn't going to out James now. What would be the point? It hurt, though, denying James and jumping back into a closet he'd slammed the door on as soon as he'd stepped foot in this city years ago. "No. We are...*were* really good friends. He told me all about you guys."

"Oh. I'm here to...clean up, I guess. Stuff." Sam tilted his head. "Is this your building too?"

"Uh." Well, fuck. James had always said Sam was bright. "No." He'd asked about moving in together. James had been thinking about it. "I was just missing him."

"Oh. I—come on up, huh?"

"Really? I'd appreciate that. Thank you." Just the idea made his heart ache, but he also thought maybe it could help. He just needed to keep it together.

"Sure. I never got a chance to meet any of James's friends. I always wanted to, but it never quite worked out."

Not so surprising. He followed Sam back up the familiar steps and through the breezeway doors. From behind, climbing the steps to the second floor, he might as well have been following James, as he'd done plenty of times. They were built almost the same, though Sam was a bit more compact.

Thomas could hardly believe his luck in timing. Another two minutes and they'd have missed each other completely. He wasn't sure what was on his calendar for the afternoon, but whatever it was could wait. He wanted to spend as much time with Sam as he could. He wanted to listen to his lover's brother talk, to know whatever Sam would tell him.

Sam looked for the number, then unlocked the door and stood there for a second, hand on the knob, like he was frozen.

Yeah. It was meaningless that he'd been over that threshold dozens of times. He knew just how Sam felt. He took a breath and rested his hands lightly on Sam's shoulders. "Go on. I'll help."

"Sorry. I—" The little guy shook himself, squared his shoulders, and forced himself inside. The place was so fucking normal—James's books and papers waiting to be graded, running shoes by the door. It was like James might just walk out of the bedroom, laugh, and tell him to quit ogling his baby brother.

Oh. He really hadn't meant to...Sam just felt so familiar. He pulled his hands back and crossed his arms over his chest.

He told Sam he'd help, but he wasn't sure how he was actually going to manage that. He decided he'd better sit before his knees gave out, so he slipped past Sam and sat down on James's couch. "God, it even smells like he's here."

"Yeah." Sam stood in the doorway for a long minute, swallowing convulsively before lurching to a window and working it open. He stood there, forehead on the glass as he breathed. "Warm in here."

He watched Sam's back. "I'm so sorry, Sam." The cowboy's distress made him need to get himself together. He could almost hear James asking him to look after Sam. Thomas took care of people all the time. Taking care was in his bones, part of his DNA.

He got back on his feet. "How long are you in town? Can you take your time with this?"

"As long as I need. I want—I need to know who did this. I need him to pay." Sam stood and turned, met his eyes. "Do you think he had beer? I need a beer like I need another breath."

Thomas turned and headed for the refrigerator. "You can take the cowboy out of Texas, but you can't take away his beer. Maybe he even has two." Sure enough, he pulled a pair of bottles out and used the opener stuck by a magnet to the door. "Here."

He knew about wanting someone to pay. He was losing a lot of sleep over that. He wanted to know why too, if there was a why. "I've been following the investigation. They don't have anything they can share yet."

"Yeah. That's what they told me. They're busy. I'm pissed. Maybe I can help."

He wanted to suggest that it was probably best to leave these things to the authorities, but this wasn't really the time to be discouraging. Sam could figure that out for himself.

"James loved this apartment." He wandered through the living room to a short hall and right into the bedroom. "He liked the light that came in through the windows in here, and the view of the square."

Sam followed him but didn't come into the bedroom. He stayed at the threshold, watching Thomas like a hawk.

That was like James, the way Sam watched him.

"It took him a long time to find this place. He was living in this four-bedroom monstrosity downtown with three other people when I met him. All teachers at the same school. It was chaos. Books and papers everywhere. Their dining room didn't have a table; it had a whole bunch of desks, two printers, and a TV instead. He was so glad to get out of there." He realized he'd been looking out the window, just babbling, and he shook his head. "You probably know all of that, sorry."

"It's good to hear it from someone else. You were more than his friend, I guess. I'm sorry. He hadn't told me your name yet. We had a phone call scheduled for the night he was—the night he left us."

Thomas spun around and looked at Sam. "He told you —you knew about me?" Dammit, he was supposed to be keeping it together, not losing it in front of his lover's family. But somehow the knowledge that James was going to tell Sam about him made him happy, and also twice as heartbroken. "Wow." He wiped his eyes, turned his back, and looked out the window again. He needed to breathe. He needed to get under control.

"We talked once a month, give or take. He'd texted, said there was someone special, but that was it. I was fixin' to look for something—an email or something—to tell you. I don't know. I've never done this before. I'm gonna go drink my beer. You...you take your time."

"I've never done *this* before either. I don't think there's a proper way to...it actually makes me really happy that he told you that. I just...wish we could have met under happier circumstances." He made himself look at Sam. "But we did meet, at least. We so easily could have walked right by each other." He decided to go with the joy. He'd had precious little of it in days. It felt like fresh air.

"Yeah. He must be watching over us." Sam took his hat off and turned it over and over in his hands. "I'm glad he had someone that cared for him here."

"I loved him," he said quickly. He wanted Sam to know it was more than just care, more than anything else they'd shared.

"Yeah. I'm sorry for your loss, man, and I hate that we—that I didn't know about you before we laid him to rest. He's in a good space—quiet, green, lots of horses and pecan trees." Sam met his gaze head on. "I would have invited you. I would never have dishonored James's wishes, his memory."

"Well, as far as that goes, if I'd known anyone knew—about him, about me—I'd have shown up on my own. Even if I'd had to keep my distance. It's not all on you, Sam. But thank you. That's kind."

"Me and James and Bowie—we're brothers. Bowie and me aren't as close. James was the middle of us, and we were...friends too. I think we were friends. I don't know. It don't matter no more."

The look on Sam's face, the stormy expression was so

like James. Thomas left the window and moved closer, trying to catch those hazel eyes even though he knew what it would do to him.

"Of course it matters. He loved you. I'm proof of that, if you need it. He talked about you a lot. He was proud of both of you. He had all kinds of stories."

"Bowie's a hero. Like our dad was."

Yes, and Sam had been the wild child, the one who had been smart and stupid, the one on a bronc, on a Jet Ski, living on the ranch for days, then running to the ocean until he had to go crawling back.

"And you..." Was he flirting? He felt a little like he was flirting. *God. Beer.* "James admired your free spirit. Your curiosity, your determination to live by your own rules."

Sam snorted. "They both think I'm a butthead, but thank you." Sam flopped down in the recliner, sprawling.

He nodded, laughing softly. "That too." And there, at last, was one difference between Sam and his brother. James didn't sprawl. His lover had been much too...academic. Entirely too self-aware to sprawl.

"I was going to casually leave this somewhere in the kitchen, but now that I'm officially out..." He pulled his key to James's apartment out of his jeans, set it on the coffee table, and slid it toward Sam. "He gave that to me. Ironically, I never actually used it."

"Oh." Sam looked at it like it was a snake. "Jesus. Jesus Christ. I—bathroom? Where's the fucking bathroom?"

"Hall. There." He pointed and watched Sam run. *Fuck.* He supposed that was more reality than the poor kid was ready for. Lover as a conceptual idea, fine—physical evidence still a poor choice. Noted.

He sipped his beer and picked at the label, thinking it

was probably time for him to go. The apartment, him, all of it was likely overwhelming, and Sam had only just gotten in. The kid probably needed some time. Some quiet.

He stood up and took his beer into the kitchen, at war with the part of himself that needed to make sure Sam was okay and the part that knew better than to show his hand to the dealer.

Sam came out, face damp, eyes red. "Sorry. I just...it could have been either one of us, and that would have been fair. Not James. He had a whole life."

Oh. Right. God, he could be an arrogant asshole. Sometimes it wasn't all about him.

"There's absolutely no measure on earth that can value one life over another." He took another swig of his beer, set it on the counter, and didn't ask permission before pulling Sam into his arms. "Nobody understands their own worth."

"It don't matter. I'm so sorry that y'all couldn't...that you never got to use your key." Sam shook like he was having a seizure, muscles so tight they tremored.

"It's not what...thank you." Thomas held James's baby brother close and rubbed his back, absorbing Sam's grief without question.

All the layers they'd been so carefully peeling away over the last hour were starting to weigh on him too, so this one he was leaving in place. He hadn't had any plans to move in. He only had that key because it was his due. It was symbolic. He'd never used it because he'd never needed to. But that explanation was probably a bridge too far for poor Sam. Especially today.

"I ain't never gonna breathe easy again as long as I live."

Thomas was positive the words weren't meant for him, but for James or God or maybe just Sam himself.

"I may not either, Sam." Not the way he could breathe with James. That was rare and beautiful.

"Yeah. I guess that's just how it is now. That's what Bowie would say. 'Suck it up, buttercup, and get your shit together.' " He could hear the command and growl of what must be the eldest O'Reilly brother, or a wild mockery of him.

"I take issue with that. My shit is all over the fucking city right now. I'm not sure I have a handle on everything I've lost, let alone how to put it all together again."

"Yeah. I hear that. You...shit, man. I don't know what to do. I'm not sure whether to scratch my watch or wind my butt."

"Well, we understand each other, then."

He loosened his grip on Sam and took a step back, immediately missing the contact. It was definitely time to go.

"This has been a really good and really...difficult afternoon. I can't tell you how grateful I am that you asked me to come up. But I can't imagine how tired you must be, and the apartment...it's a lot. I think I should go. But"—he ripped off the bottom half of a shopping list James had on the refrigerator and wrote down his cell phone number— "that's me. When you're ready again, call me. I can help here, or we can just take a walk. Get some coffee or a drink. Okay? When you're ready. Any time. Middle of the fucking night. Anything."

"Thank you. I'll text you my number here in a bit. I'm sure there's stuff that you want. I just...I'll holler." Sam took his number. "I'll pray for you, man. For your peace."

That was well intentioned, so he didn't make a thing of it. "Thank you, Sam. I look forward to hearing from you. Good night."

He took one step backward, getting a last look at the baby brother James had been so fond of. He honestly wasn't sure if he felt better or worse, but he wouldn't trade a second of his afternoon. It had been the next best thing to talking with James himself. He gave Sam a nod and headed out the door.

3

Sam crawled out of the drunken hell that was his week by his toenails. He wasn't sure how long he'd been sleeping on the bathroom tile, but it was long enough that every grout line was carved into his face, and the smell of his breath was enough to melt glass.

Nice.

"Lord, James, you got you an uncomfortable bathroom. I had to sit on the tub to puke into the toilet. That ain't right." He climbed into said tub, still in the clothes he'd flown in on, and sat hard, turning the water on him, taking the cold as penance until the water heater began to do its job.

Finally he was stable enough to strip off and scrub his clothes with a bar of soap before hanging them on the towel rack to dry. Okay.

Now? Food. Or coffee.

Yes. Coffee.

"I swear to God, James. If you became some weird anti-caffeine, vegan-citified type, I will...pour hot coffee and bacon grease on your grave."

He wandered into the kitchen, finding one of them cup-at-a-time pod dealies. *Jesus. Fancy.*

It only took him an hour to make a cup of froufy-assed coffee and to eat a handful of stale, dry Lucky Charms, because he'd opened the little fridge and *fucking Christ*. He needed a grocery store or a Walmart or something. Where did he find something like that here?

He sighed and went hunting for his phone. Surely he'd plugged it in, somewhere.

There were twenty-eight voice mail messages—Bowie, Momma, three of his rodeoing buddies, Sid Richardson, and four from "James's T."

Oh.

Thomas.

He started with those, and along with some scrambling and a couple of "Uhhs" and a "Was that the beep?" they all said the same thing. Thomas was checking in, seeing if he could help; one was asking if he wanted to get some food. The last one was a little longer.

"Hello, Sam...uh. This is working, right? I think it is. It's Thomas Ward again. Listen, I apologize if I've put you off. I know that was a difficult...well, it's pretty clear I didn't make a very good first impression. I just wanted to let you know that I understand that you'd probably prefer not to hear from me again. I wish you...I wish...well...I wish a lot of things, and I'm sure you do too. Be well."

Oh, damn. He shook his head and smiled. Lord have mercy, it sucked so hard that James and Thomas had been close enough to be talking about moving in together and...

The image of James's face diced up and destroyed floated up in front of him, and his fingers clenched into fists.

"Motherfucker!" He slammed his hand into the kitchen

counter, pain jolting up his arm, coffee splashing on his other hand. "Oh. Oh, ow. God *damn* it!"

He closed his eyes. *Shit.* How was he supposed to find James's killer when he didn't know where to find a goddamn Wallyworld?

Okay, ask the local.

He dialed Thomas before running his throbbing hand under cold water.

"Sam? Hello. I...well, hello."

"Hey there. How goes it?" Because this wasn't fucking weird.

"Fine. You?" Thomas snorted. "No. Sorry. Normal is... just not normal. Is everything okay?"

"I found a liquor store. I drank. A lot. Now I need to buy food and trash bags. Is there a Walmart or something?" *And a hamburger as big as my head.*

"I've been at loose ends all week myself. Did your bender help? I'm guessing not. And no, we don't have a Walmart in the city. But if you need groceries, there's a D'Agostino in James's—in the neighborhood. And I've a Trader Joe's not too far from my place if you need something special."

"I need trash bags, dish soap, hamburger meat, noodles, and a bottle of Ragu. Possibly peanut butter and bread and a gallon of milk to eat all this cereal."

"That's a respectable list. Perhaps you would prefer to join me for dinner? Or, I suppose these things don't have to be mutually exclusive."

"Yeah, I got a clean pair of jeans in my bag. I could have supper with you, if you can help me find a store after. I got to clean out this fridge."

"All right. Would you mind terribly coming up to my

neighborhood? James had a lot of favorite restaurants down your way, and I'm not sure I'm ready for that yet."

"Fine with me. You'll have to tell me where that is and what time you want me." That was good, right, that James had favorite restaurants, favorite things here? That James had a life here, and he would maybe get a few days to learn about them?

"Okay, it's so easy. You head out into the square, and you'll see the subway station right there. Take the stairs down and head for the green line uptown. Any number, doesn't matter. Take it up to 77th, and I'll meet you there. If you leave about six, that should work. James kept his Metrocard in—"

The line went silent except for Thomas's sigh.

"Sorry. The cops still have his wallet. You'll have to buy a card when you get into the station."

"Hey, you know, if you don't want to...I mean, I know that it's hard to think about him." It hurt to think about James not being here. Hell, maybe he could just find trash bags stashed somewhere here; then he didn't have to leave the house until a couple of days from now. God, where did the dumpster live here?

"I want to. I just...I mean, they have his wallet, they took his laptop and a box full of other things. Personal things. I understand why, but it makes me angry, and I hate it. I'm looking forward to talking with you again. And I'd be happy to help you with the refrigerator too. That's a lousy job."

This should be Thomas's job—not the fridge, but... everything. Knowing what was important, what was special, what Thomas wanted to take. What did he know about James anymore? What did he know about Bowie? Hell, what did anybody know about him?

"I'm sorry. This whole thing sucks." He didn't know what else to say.

Thomas sighed again. "It does. But maybe we can...have a nice dinner anyway. That wouldn't be so terrible, would it?"

"No, sir. It wouldn't. I'll try my best to get to you." He could figure this out, assuming he could remember what Thomas had said.

"I'll stay by my phone. Green line uptown to 77th. You'll be fine."

"I'll figure it. I'm a big boy." He made it here, didn't he?

"See you soon, Sam. I'm glad you called." Thomas let a little empty air settle before hanging up.

"Soon. Right." He should probably put clothes on. After one more cup of coffee and another handful of cereal. Then he'd figure this whole thing out.

If his laughter sounded false in his own ears, well, there wasn't anyone to hear it, was there?

He'd just have to fake it until he could make it.

4

Where to take a hungry cowboy for dinner? Of course the first two places he thought of were favorites of the only other Texan he knew.

Had known.

Knew.

Was someone's death just supposed to be a light switch? Thomas *knew* him; then suddenly it was *used to know* him? He didn't buy it. He'd always know James.

He did wonder if he would ever stop talking to himself about his lover, though.

It was a gorgeous night. One of those evenings when people were out, the sky was clear, Sam would have been treated to someone playing something in Union Square on his way to the subway. An inspiring night, where the air felt cleaner.

He breathed it in deeply while he waited for Sam, determined to haul himself out of his funk, if only for a few hours. Get to know Sam a little. Eat something fantastic.

He could see the cowboy hat coming his way, mingled in the crowd. James told him Sam was a pocket cowboy but that he walked like a bull rider. He got it—Sam was short and spare, but there was a confidence in his gait, a machismo.

James hadn't told him how captivating it was, however. Or what he was supposed to do with that observation either. And he had precious little time to file it away, because the cowboy had just spotted him.

He returned Sam's nod and took a few steps to intercept that walk. "You made it."

"I did." Sam looked a little like he'd been in a fight or had been sick—dark circles, lines around his mouth, one hand bruised.

He'd make a fuss over one of his own brothers for looking like that. But James had led him to believe that this was more or less par for the course for your average cowboy, and certainly for Sam, so he made no remark. He offered a hand, despite the bruises, fighting the stronger urge for a hug. "So what are you in the mood for?"

He gave Sam a minute to look around before he started walking. His neighborhood was nothing like the chaotic jumble of intersections that was Union Square. Everything up here was neat, orderly. Sane.

"I'm easy. You know what's good. It'll be my first supper here."

He squinted down the block so he didn't have to look at the dark circles dulling those hazel eyes. He didn't make a fuss, but that didn't stop him from wanting to. "Well, do you want pasta? A burger? Tex-Mex? Um...sushi?"

"How about pasta? I like all sorts of noodles, and I ain't riding right now."

"Sounds great." He was always happy with Italian himself. "You still ride? I got the impression you were done with that."

"I got my card still, so if I need to make a little money, I can." One shoulder lifted in an achingly familiar move. "I'm sorta at loose ends, I guess."

"We need to do something about that, Sam O'Reilly." He reached for the door to his favorite local Italian place. It wasn't fancy, but the food was good. They had every pasta under the sun, and it was a sweet, tiny family place.

They were hit with the smell of warm bread and garlic as he opened the door. "Mmm. I'm hungry." He smiled at the hostess as she seated them.

"No shit on that. I'm starving." Sam inhaled deep, and Thomas could hear the man's belly snarling.

His father used to say that a hungry man was an angry man, so he slid the basket of garlic bread over to Sam as soon as the server set it down on the table. He thought better of ordering wine, since his dinner guest had clearly indulged plenty in the last week, and ordered sparkling water instead.

"I fully accept that there's a certain hypocritical aspect to what I'm about to say, but if you plan to stay in the city for a while, we need to find you something to fill your time."

There were subtle ways that men with his proclivities took power and control from men who were unaware of the rewards of giving it up. Use of that gentle-sounding "we" was one of them. He knew it was a fantasy. It was unreasonable to believe Sam could or would be lulled in by such nuances, but the game distracted him, settled him. He didn't see the harm in playing it.

"I reckon I need to start figuring out how to find the man who killed my brother. That's what I've been sent here to do. Take care of business." Sam mangled the bread, working it in his callused fingers.

"Sent here?" The question was out before he could

frame it as anything other than exactly what it was, incredulity.

"Yeah—Bowie, my folks. All my people. Daddy had a stroke when he found out, you know? Bowie had to go back to saving the world. So, it's my job." Like this was standard operating procedure. One son dies, send another to find his killer.

That must be "the crazy" in the family that James used to talk about. Thomas was at a bit of a loss as to how to respond, so he left it alone for the moment. It needed a response, though. He'd return to it. "I'm terribly sorry to hear about your father. Will he recover?"

"Yeah. He's talking a little slow, and he sure as shit is in a bad mood these days, but he'll come around. Thanks for asking. It's been a weird-assed few weeks. I mean, sorry, you know that better than anyone."

"Maybe not. I don't have a corner on the market for grief." He reached over and tore off a piece of garlic bread for himself, pleasantly surprised that he genuinely felt hungry. "You know, Sam, that the NYPD is well equipped to find the person responsible, don't you? I can understand your anger. I have plenty of my own, but it's not particularly...logical to believe that you can find someone before they do."

"Yessir, but it can't hurt to have a little help." Sam's drawl was thick as syrup. "Don't get me wrong—I'm an art historian and a bronc rider, not a CSI, but...I have to do something. I have to help."

"I didn't intend to imply you were stupid. I apologize." He picked up his water and took a sip. He knew there was more to each of James's brothers than met the eye.

"Eh, no worries. Everything's all fucked up right now. I'm not all ready to be offended." Sam grinned for him, eyes rolling wildly. "Hell, I just drank myself sober, passed out on the bathroom floor, and managed a subway for the first time. I don't have the energy to be offended right now. Try me tomorrow."

"Not to worry. I'll offend you tomorrow too, I'm sure. It goes hand in hand with being arrogant and opinionated. Some of my better traits. James pointed them out regularly." He held up his glass as if he were toasting Sam and took a sip. All his relationships required negotiation, from his clients to his personal life.

"He wasn't one to keep his mouth shut when he thought you needed to know something. That was for sure. He rode my ass like a prized pony."

"I bet that was a good time." Some of the most fun they'd had stemmed from James's compulsion to speak his mind. And as much as he appreciated that image, it surely wasn't what Sam was referring to.

"Do you have big brothers?"

"I have two. I also have three younger and a baby sister."

"Wow. Wow, that's intense, but you kinda get it, right? No matter what you do, someone's right there explaining how you're either doing it wrong or how you're fixin' to get hurt or how they've already done it twice as good."

"It's the same dynamic. They just do it in teams." He laughed. "And being in the middle is its own kind of torture. James and I used to talk about that a lot." He never did anything right, but then he never really did anything wrong either. He'd been several shades of unremarkable in that herd of siblings.

"Yeah. He's like our momma—a middle child, a teacher, always fixing shit. Bowie's like Daddy—he's a hammer and the world's a nail." Sam grabbed the menu, opened it up. "What do you like here?"

He was listening. James was like Momma, Jim like Daddy. Who was Sam like? Small wonder this poor boy was at loose ends. Everyone else had a blueprint to follow. Sam was blazing a new trail, like it or not.

"If you're truly hungry, the lasagna or their spaghetti and meatballs. If you want something more delicate, the ravioli is lovely."

"I'll get the lasagna, then. I can take some back to the apartment and have supper for tomorrow, assuming I don't fall on it like a ravenous beast. That could totally happen."

If he hadn't been making sure he ate regularly, he would feel the same way. But there was a whole host of regular, normal life things he'd been forcing himself to continue despite everything. Eating regularly, running, going to work, going to bed and trying to sleep. Apart from sleeping, none of it was as difficult as it seemed. He was able to rely on habit. What was hard were the hours in his day that were less routine, the ones he'd spent with James or thinking about James.

And weekends. God, their weekends.

"You know, Mister Art Historian, you should visit the museum to use up some of that free time." He looked at Sam, realizing it was probable Sam had no idea what he did for a living. "The Met. I can get you free tickets. I work there."

"Yeah?" Oh, look at those eyes light up. That transformed Sam from grumpy, tired cowboy to fascinated, engaged scholar. "What do you do?"

"Development. I help get funding for special exhibits. Basically, I beg rich people for money." He laughed. It was a great deal more than that, but the details made the job sound dull.

"Ah. Yes. That's basically what I'll end up doing,

assuming I ever decide to get a job in my field. Right now, I'm publishing articles and doing research for people writing Westerns and making movies."

He made an effort not to say something stupid again, but he felt his head tilt a little anyway. How interesting. "I had no idea. James didn't give me the details. That must be interesting work. Do you enjoy research?"

"God, yes. I specialize in Western art, history, and culture. Mainly art, of course—Jack Wells, Russell, Remington, Glen Powell, Tim Cox—but people tend to need the other parts too. Costuming, newspapers, language even."

"We love bringing in that kind of thing. Tying the art into the culture. It's much easier for me to fund something people can relate to. Art in context, you know what I mean? So..." He thought about what he knew about Western art, which was pathetically little. "Suppose we brought in a Remington collection, paintings, sculptures. We'd also bring in something about him personally if we could, and about the time he was painting to give them context. All of that research would be valuable for us." He sat back a little and snorted. "Not that you need much context for Remington. Everything he did was so dynamic on its own, but you know what I mean."

"Well, you know he lived in Brooklyn, yes? That's where his art took off. He turned being a 'cowboy' into a career." Sam chuckled, shook his head. "Don't get me started. I can bore the most stalwart individual."

He laughed, the sound a little foreign to him, a little tentative, but it was real and made him feel the most alive he had in weeks. "I might be able to give you a run for your money." He grinned and leaned forward. "Promise me you'll come to the museum this week and test my resolve."

"Yeah. I could do that. I mean, I'm here, right?" Thomas read guilt and hunger in Sam's expression, in equal amounts.

"You're here, yes." He looked Sam over, wishing he could ease some of the guilt for him, and realized that perhaps he could. "Quid pro quo, hm? You visit the museum and teach me something I don't know, and I'll...walk you through what little is on the security cameras."

"The security cameras? You mean from James's place? Is he on it?"

"No. Well, yes, but not the attack, not up close. His building doesn't have a camera. But there are two from the square that show the guy and one from the subway entrance that shows James, and the bank has a distant recording. You can't really see much on that one. They showed them to me when I went down for—" *Damn.* Thomas had thought perhaps to omit a detail or two, but what was the point? Sam would ask his own questions, find out for himself. "When they questioned me the second time."

Sam didn't look the least bit surprised. "You're the boyfriend. Of course you were questioned. Why didn't they tell us about you?"

"They? You mean the police? Because I asked them not to. I explained that James wasn't out. I genuinely believed he wasn't. I suspect they'll consider his sexuality relevant information at some point, but they didn't then."

"They know about James. Bowie too. They're not happy, but that's more to do with lack of grandbabies than anything else. My folks aren't bad people. They love James."

"Bowie too?" Had James told him that? If so, he didn't remember the conversation. "I'm relieved to know your parents are accepting. I'm not sure why I got the impression no one knew." That wasn't true. He knew exactly why—because James never told him they knew. And he obviously made an incorrect assumption. An assumption that apparently cost him an invitation to his lover's funeral.

Goddammit. He wasn't going to think about that.

"So, is Bowie out with the Rangers?"

"No. I'm not sure Bowie wouldn't just bite the head off anyone that came on to him. Chomp." Sam clicked his teeth together. "You obviously never met him either, or you wouldn't have bothered asking."

He chuckled. "I see. That's a terrible way to live. I'm sad for him."

Sam shrugged. "He's a soldier. He loves his life, I guess. I don't know. We're not particularly close—he left home at seventeen. I was ten. He's been home...what? Three times in fifteen years? Maybe four. He's doing exactly what he wants to do. Feel sorry for him in five years when they drum him out and he's got nothing left."

Well. Nothing left, hm? "I don't actually feel sorry for him at all. Do I sense you have issues with the military, or just with Bowie?"

"Neither. I got nothing but respect, man."

That was a well-practiced, oft-said response. One he didn't entirely accept, although Sam's earnest look was lovely. "Mm. Of course." If Sam and Bowie were never close, then Sam would only feel that much more alone for losing James.

Their food arrived along with more bread and a server ready to grate fresh parmesan. He leaned back and let her cover his lasagna; then she stepped around and offered some to Sam, flirting.

"Parm?"

"Yes, ma'am. Thank you."

She smiled and watched Sam until she got the nod to stop. "Enjoy your dinner."

He waited for her to be out of earshot. "Every server in New York City flirted with James. I think it's those stunning hazel eyes you both have."

"I think it's the accent and the hat." Sam chuckled softly and shook his head. "Momma says we have baby-shit-colored eyes, you know, but thank you for the compliment."

"Oh, no. They're lovely. The way they change in the light, or shift depending on what you're wearing—or...sorry. What James would wear, I mean. Though yours are lovely too." He probably ought to be embarrassed by that slip, but he wasn't. He just watched Sam to see how he'd react.

"Oh, honey..." Sam reached out under the table and patted his leg. "I'm so sorry. My heart's broke for you. I... Lord have mercy, I'd fix this if I could."

He caught Sam's hand impulsively and held the man's eyes for a moment, not at all sure what the hell he was doing. He finally released it, thinking he should apologize, but he couldn't. He wasn't sorry. Baffled, intrigued, stunned maybe, but not sorry.

Sam stared at his supper for a long time before he inhaled, releasing the breath slowly. "Okay, first supper here. It looks amazing. I got a good friend in Austin that makes lasagna when we're both in town at the same time, but this looks better."

He knew he'd overstepped, though he didn't know why precisely. What he did know was, it wasn't well received. But rather than apologize now and make things worse, he decided it could wait while they ate and he tried to repair things.

"I think you'll like it. It's one of my favorites."

"Yes, sir." Sam began to eat, eyes on the plate. Eventually

he slowed down, looked up, and met Thomas's eyes. "It's so weird. I've never done this before. I've had buddies die on the circuit, and lots of older family, but not something like this. I don't know what to say to make you not upset."

"Sam—" He hesitated but reached out across the table and lightly rested his fingers on Sam's. "There's nothing you can say, any more than there is anything I could say to make you not upset. It doesn't make sense. It seems impossible. It's...surreal. The only thing either of us can do is breathe."

God, didn't that sound so easy? Just breathe. If only he could find air.

"Yeah. Just breathe. I can—" "The Army Goes Rolling Along" sounded, and Sam rolled his eyes. "I'm sorry. It's Bowie. If I don't answer..."

"Of course, go ahead." He understood Bowie wouldn't get many opportunities to call.

"Thanks. Hey, Bow....Yes. Yes, I'm here....Yes....No. I'm eating food....No, I haven't found...No. Dammit, Bowie, I don't even know how to start finding...Oh, fuck you, asshole. I'm trying. Don't you need to shoot someone or blow someone up?"

The voice on the other end of the line snapped out, Sam's face went ashen, and when he answered this time, his voice was dull. "I didn't forget why I'm here, I promise. I'll call home here after a bit, man. I swear."

Sam hung up without a good-bye and turned his phone off. "Sorry. I hate when folks talk during supper."

He felt like he ought to sit on his hands. There were a number of things he wanted to do right now, and not a one of them was appropriate under the circumstances. He took a deep breath and reminded himself that James's eldest brother survived on adrenaline and was grieving, and that had to be a powerful cocktail.

"Are you all right?"

"Yeah. He's just making sure I'm not slacking, you know?" Sam wouldn't meet his eyes. "I'm not here for a vacation."

He watched Sam, choosing his words carefully and speaking slowly, emotion swirling in his chest. "What exactly does he want you to do?"

"Find the man who killed James and take care of him."

Dear Baby Brother, go find a murderer in a huge city and kill him. Love, Bowie. Wow.

"That's insane. You do know that, Sam. Don't you? It's...deranged."

"It's Texas justice, I guess. I have to try to do right by him, no matter that I don't know how to go about finding a killer."

He leaned back in his chair, eyes on Sam still, stunned by what he was hearing, by what just the concept of retribution was doing to James's little brother.

"It won't bring him back."

"No, but maybe it'll help them all at home, you know? Maybe it'll help you, knowing he's not out there."

No. That was not how things were done. How he wanted them done.

"I will sleep much better when the police find him, and I know he won't hurt anyone else. Don't bring me into this. Don't do it for me. I don't want you to. Ask yourself if James would. I'm pretty sure I know the answer." He pulled out his wallet, tossed some cash on the table, and stood. "Think for yourself, Sam."

One of Sam's eyebrows lifted, that upper lip curling. "Keep your fucking money, man. I got supper. Don't let the door hit you in the ass."

He didn't touch the money. But he did return Sam's look,

evenly. "That's a lot easier than having to wonder if you might be wrong, isn't it? Good night, Sam. Thank you for joining me."

He turned and headed out the door, wishing he'd gotten that bottle of wine after all. Now he needed something stronger.

5

It took three days to clean out the kitchen, somehow. Possibly because he spent twelve hours a day bugging the police and wandering around James's neighborhood, praying for someone to tell stories on his brother, and six hours a day working.

Sam did it, though, didn't he?

Yessir.

The little gal at the Italian restaurant had helped him find a grocery store, so he had bleach and peanut butter and...

Yeah.

He called Momma once a day and checked in. He didn't answer Bowie's calls, and he didn't think about James's boyfriend. Obviously the guy didn't understand. His daddy had done had a stroke. Bowie was fixin' to be deployed. He was the only one left to make sure James's killer was found.

Ask what James would want? Had this guy seen James beat Bobby Gentry down when the bastard had knocked out three of Sam's baby teeth? Had he been there when the football team had locked him in a toolbox and left him for the weekend, and James had broken four of the quarterback's fingers until he told where Sam was trapped? No. James had been there for him, just like Bowie had been there for James. Now it was his turn. He had to be there.

He stood in the kitchen, eating a peanut butter spoon while he waited on his coffee.

Christ on a pink sparkly crutch, it was fixin' to be nine a.m. and time to wander around outside and pretend like he knew what to do.

A loud buzzing sound blared from a box by the door he hadn't even noticed was there before. It stopped, then started again, drowning out his own goddamn thoughts.

He frowned and pondered just whacking it with a broom like a smoke detector. It was altogether too early for buzzing and shit.

He jabbed the button and growled. "Whut?"

That was right, right? Fuck, if it wasn't right, who the fuck would know? This was his new motherfucking motto. Nobody knew him from Job, barring a handful of detectives, and Mr. Pissed Off, so he could fuck up all he needed to.

"Uh. Hello? I'm sorry to...my name is Kevin. I taught with James over at Reynolds Elementary School. I just...I live in the neighborhood, and I saw you coming and going yesterday. Do you have a minute?"

"Sure. Sure. I—you want to come up?" He could throw on a shirt and toss his pillow and blanket down the hall. "Or I could come down. Whatever."

He wanted to talk with someone about James, so bad.

"Oh. Well? It's kind of raining out here so...is it weird if I come up?"

"Is it? Damn. Sure, man." He managed to buzz Kevin in —and didn't that thought make him snort somehow? He felt like the world's biggest little redneck—before he grabbed his shirt and hid his bedding.

The light knock at the door was followed by, "Hey. Kevin here."

He opened the door on a short, clean-cut, solid-looking guy with dark hair and dark eyes and a six-pack in his hand. At nine o'clock in the morning.

"Hey." Kevin stuck out a hand to shake. "Thanks, it's pouring." They shook hands and Kevin pulled off his raincoat, dropping it in the hall by the door.

"I've been working with my head down some. Nice to meet you, man. You worked with my brother, you said?" *Come on. Sit. Talk to me. I'm so fucking lonely.*

"I did. And we rode in on the subway together every morning....I'm sorry, I didn't ask your name, but you have to be family."

"Sam. Sam O'Reilly. James was my big brother. Come have a sit. You want coffee?"

"Yeah. I would love some coffee."

He stepped aside, and Kevin came into the kitchen, looking around. "Oh! I brought you beer. Shiner Bock, in bottles. The bottles are hard to find up here. You have to go to this one place way up—" Kevin chuckled. "Anyway, he liked it, so I thought...I don't expect you to drink it for breakfast."

"He did. It was his favorite. Thank you. What grade do you teach? And there's all this fancy coffee; do you have a preference to type?"

"I teach third grade. It's insanity. You have hazelnut? Little cream or milk?"

"Totally. I'm on it. Third grade. Wow. You must love it, though. I know James did." He was way faster with the coffeemaker these days.

Kevin grinned, bright white teeth showing. "I can't see how you'd want to spend all day with a bunch of kids that would rather be anywhere else if you didn't."

"Right? It's a calling." Not his, but thank God for those who had it. He took Kevin the coffee and sat. "It was damn kind of you to stop by."

"I'm so sorry about your brother. He was a good guy and a gift to those kids, really. It's weird in the city to just drop in on people, but I didn't know how to call, and...I just felt like you'd like to know that. I mean, that people thought that about him."

"I do. I did. Whatever. I'm glad you came by. I miss him, and this place is...I don't know how to find him." He was losing James, seconds at a time.

Kevin looked at him thoughtfully. "You should drop by the school. His classroom. He's all over it. And the fourth grade, the kids he had last year? They did this collage memorial thing. It's a big deal. Gorgeous."

"I don't want to upset anyone. Maybe I could come after the kids go home? Just to see? Did someone pick up his personal stuff?" Could he ask any more questions in a row?

"I don't know about his personal stuff, but I could find out. Come by after school sometime. Ask for Kevin Muller. Or...you want my cell?"

"That would be great, if you don't mind." He grabbed his phone and opened up his contacts before handing it over. "I'm so glad James had friends here."

Kevin added a contact for himself—name, number, email. "There you go. Just text when you know you're headed over. No pressure." Kevin sipped his coffee. "You know Thomas, I guess."

"I've met him, yes. He loved James very much." There. That was nice, right? Hell, he wasn't even mad at the man.

He missed James, and there was all this baggage and shit. Sam was just a reminder.

"Seemed like it. I only met him one time, but he seemed like a nice guy. James was all smiles around him." Kevin put down his empty coffee cup. "Listen, I don't want to take up your time. I'm sure you're busy. It was really good to meet you."

"I...I appreciate it. Seriously. I'm glad he had people that cared here."

"Lots. Seemed like he and Thomas were always out with somebody. Thanks for the coffee. Use my number if you want."

He saw Kevin to the door, waited while the guy shrugged on his raincoat. "Ugh. This weather. Take care of yourself." Kevin jogged down the stairs and out into the rain.

He watched Kevin leave. Okay. Time to harass the detectives.

Sam caught somebody watching him from down the hall, and he lifted his hand for a wave—either a little man or a good-sized lady, he couldn't tell with all the shadows. "Mornin'."

"Hi." The figure shifted into better light. "You a real cowboy?" Huh. A kid. Maybe ten, twelve years old, by the look of him.

"Yessir." No question. It was one of the things that he knew in his soul.

The kid took a few steps closer. "Did you guys find Cowboy James yet? We're supposed to do math homework."

"He passed away, man. I'm sorry." And that was never going to be easier, was it? Probably not. He guessed it couldn't get too much worse.

"Oh." The kid frowned at him. "Are you any good at math?"

"Yeah. I sorta am. I'm James's brother. We all liked math." All of them, especially Bowie, weirdly enough.

"I'm really bad, and I have a test on Tuesday. James helps me study for my tests. Can you help me on Monday? I mean, unless you have a rodeo or something."

"Sure, if your folks are okay with it. You got a name?" God, he could ride. Something to make him feel alive.

"William. You can talk to Mom sometime, she'll say yes. Her name is Anna. She's not home; she's working. Phone is ringing. Thanks, cowboy!" The kid disappeared through a door that slammed, the sound echoing up the stairs.

"Lord have mercy." So, nine o'clock, teacher and kiddo not at school. Weekend, then. Maybe they'd have PBR on the TV today.

A guy came walking down the stairs and slipped an envelope under the kid's door, before walking right up to him and handing him one too. "Rent's a week overdue, buddy," the guy said.

"Okay. I'm still trying to figure all James's bills and all. You need a check? A money order? What?"

"Cash when it's late. Check or money order otherwise. There's a fee after Friday."

"Fair enough. Where do I bring it?" He was a little dizzy with all the complications of living life not on the ranch where everything was how it had been for years.

"Address is on the bill. The office is open Monday. Have a good one."

"Yessir." Okay. *Damn.* He needed to figure out all this stuff. There was life insurance from the bank and from the school and all. Momma had put it in a bank account and told him he could use it for this sort of thing until he figured out what he was supposed to do. He couldn't squander the money, he knew that, but this place was expensive for a broke-dick cowboy with a bunch of freelance jobs.

Lord have mercy. At least he had something to do Monday—find a bank, get money, pay James's rent, tutor William.

It wasn't something fun to do, but it was something useful, which was more than he'd managed in days.

He'd take it.

6

It was definitely Saturday night. The music was loud, the lighting provocative, and Thomas's favorite club smelled of sweat and leather.

Thomas nodded to the bartender. "Good evening, Scotty."

"Good...evening, Sir." Scotty's eyes grew wide as if the boy were looking at a ghost, and it was quite possible that he was. "Uh...single malt?"

"Fireball."

"Oh. Oh wow, okay. Coming right up, Sir."

He had no intention of appearing sorry for himself in front of a crowd on a Saturday night, but he needed to knock the edge off his funk before he could really face it. He understood Scotty's shock, and the boy wouldn't be the only one, he knew. But at some point, he had to walk back into his life again, and there was really no good way to ease into this.

He'd dressed appropriately but conservatively in all black, the smooth leather pants feeling good against his legs and the black cotton T-shirt cool against his skin. He'd get his drink and find a corner to sit in and sip it.

It was only a matter of seconds before men came up to him, offering quiet, heartfelt condolences. Nothing loud or overt—just a nod, a touch to the shoulder, a welcome, and within minutes of arriving, he felt lighter, the support woven into the fabric of his community lifting him, letting him breathe. He returned every nod and handshake he could manage, but over the next few minutes, there were many, and he couldn't be sure he'd properly thanked everyone.

He'd been there perhaps fifteen minutes, and he'd already learned a lesson. He ought to have come home sooner.

Scotty touched his hand as he reached for a pen to sign his tab. "Master says no charge tonight."

"A get-drunk-free card?" He winked. "Thanks, Scotty."

"Shibari in the red room, Sir. I know you're fond. And it's quieter."

"You're a genius, Scotty." Fireball and a show. That sounded like an excellent start to his evening. He made his way through the crowd slowly, feeling some of the tension in his shoulders release.

He took a deep breath, and there was suddenly room. Not too much. Not even enough. But room in between his ribs that made him a promise that more breaths would come.

He passed a couple of rooms, lingering for a moment in each doorway, just taking in the vibe, the sounds. The red room was comfortable with its wide couches and moody lighting, and the slightly higher ceiling made it perfect for all kinds of bondage play. Tonight, a Dom he knew well and a sub he admired were putting on a gorgeous display with ropes of several colors and complicated, practiced knotwork.

He started to sit alone, but a smile caught his eye from across the room, and he made his way over, walking behind the other couches to avoid blocking anyone's view. Coming and going, conversation, those things were expected, but it was easy enough to be courteous.

"Clint." He nodded, making an awkward effort to return the man's smile.

One solid hand reached out to him, those near-black eyes focused on him like a hawk's. "You came home."

He took the hand and let himself be pulled down onto the couch. "I...yes. I did. And I'm thinking perhaps I waited a little too long, but there's no playbook for these things. No prodigal son references, if you please."

"Oh, damn. I'd been collecting them. I'm going to have to use them on random waitstaff and the periodic librarian now." Clint never so much as hinted at a smile, but the warmth in the man's voice wrapped around him like smoke.

"I happen to know your periodic librarian enjoys your many talents." He shifted on the seat so he could look at Clint head on and still enjoy the show. "It's good to see you. I apologize that I haven't contacted you. I haven't been very... intentional in my thinking."

"The universe hasn't been particularly intentional toward you. If you hadn't come, I would have come to you." Clint did crack a smile now. "I'm glad you showed up."

"Me too." He'd been coming to this club since before James joined him, after all. It was his place as much as theirs. He knew he belonged here. "I've been doing other things, though. Working and...work has been busy."

"Of course. It's strange the way that everything is different and absolutely the same at the same time, isn't it?" Clint had lost someone years ago, and he spoke from a place of experience.

Shit. Clint was experience made flesh. It could drive Thomas out of his mind, but it was comfortable and comforting at the same time.

"That's exactly it, right? Sometimes I can't understand how the world still turns, but it does." He squinted across the room, watching without really seeing. "I met his brother."

"Is that bad?"

That was a fair question, if one he didn't want to answer. He took a deep breath and released it slowly, trying to decide the most honest way to answer that question. Clint was the sturdiest sounding board he'd ever met.

"It's confusing. It made things incredibly complicated for me. I think it might have been easier on both of us not to have run into each other. We have different...he's just so..." He looked at Clint. "He doesn't have any idea which way is up. He's just...caught in a storm. You know?"

"I can only imagine. This sort of thing devastates a family. Were they close?"

"Yes. By Sam's account they were very close. It seems like he clung to James, emotionally at least, to a pretty extreme degree. He feels guilty. He's determined to personally find James's...the person responsible. It's a little off the deep end, honestly. His brother actually called from wherever he is with the Rangers to make sure Sam was on the job. Loudly. I can't...I don't even know what to do with that."

"So...he's doing this here from Wherever, Texas?" Clint looked surprised. "Talk about culture shock, regardless, and awful pressure to do something impossible. I mean, we push subs to their limits, but that is torture."

"He's here, living in James's apartment. We literally ran into each other on the steps about five minutes after the NYPD took the police tape away." That really had been eerie. "Pushing subs is one thing. They have a net if they fall. This isn't like that at all. I told him it was insane, that he was delusional to think he could do a better job than the police. He called it 'Texas justice.' His family apparently expects him to...I don't know, hide the body. I told him he needed to think about that. He needed to think for himself. It didn't go over well." He took a breath, a lot more worked up than he'd intended. "Wow. Sorry."

"No apologies. You have been holding that back for a while." Clint watched him for a moment. "Was he cruel to you? I can't imagine James's brother being cruel, but...well, you've met my sister, haven't you?"

"No. No, no. Not at all. He was nothing but kind. Compassionate. He...gets it." He felt strangely defensive about that question. He greatly appreciated Sam's concern. It was so earnest. Sam was rudderless, lost, cracked along the edges, but still the man had been worried for him.

"Poor man. I'll see if I can't make time to go over and see him. I can only imagine how he must need a friend. I remember that James was utterly overwhelmed by the time he found us, and he hadn't been dealing with half as much."

He sighed at the little flash of indignant Dom in him that was offended at the thought that Clint might have a better rapport with Sam than he had. One of the toughest challenges in his own training had been to accept that bit of insecurity in himself and to appreciate where other's talents lay in comparison with his own. Nothing about what they did was a competition. The needs, desires, and skills at the club were as diverse as the stars. But if you wanted to get a rise out of him, that was a very good way to do it.

Clint absolutely knew that. It felt as if he had taken Thomas under his wing the moment Thomas had first walked through the door.

Thomas tried not to fall into that trap. Instead he remembered how James had been when they met. How overwhelmed he'd been by the city, the size of his school, and the scope of his new job. The way that leaving home to save his own sanity had created chaos in his family. They had gravitated toward each other naturally, but it was Clint who had suggested he take a closer look at what he could do for James. What James could offer him. It wasn't even that long ago, really, but it felt like forever.

"He has James's eyes." He hadn't meant to say that out loud, and blinked himself back into the room, back to reality and away from all the thoughts of Sam that wouldn't let him be. He cleared his throat. "I'm sure he'd appreciate the company."

"I'm sorry, Thomas. That has to be excruciating. I mean, honestly, what about this isn't?" Clint had a knowing look on his face. "I'll make sure that he's not on a downward slide, perhaps encourage him to go home, hmm?"

"Asshole." He crossed his arms and kicked back in his seat. "Don't do that. That's not..." Was he really about to say it wasn't fair? Oh, Clint would love to sink teeth into that one. "What is it you want me to say, Clint? He's beautiful, and he's broken, and his need calls to me? I don't even know how to look into his eyes."

"I simply want you to be honest with yourself. I want you to ask yourself why you're angry at me for suggesting something as reasonable as encouraging him to leave." Clint was as inscrutable as always. "Lie to the world; tell yourself the truth."

What was the truth? Being close to Sam made him feel closer to James, and Thomas worried that their grief could lead to something unhealthy between them. But he'd already convinced himself it was more than that. Words, even thoughts, were incapable of expressing how much he missed James. But it wasn't thoughts of James that had interrupted his workout or left him daydreaming at his desk.

And there was an answer to Clint's question. A very coherent one. "He can't go back there. Not yet anyway. He couldn't face his family."

That was crystal clear to him suddenly. He leaned forward again, forehead wrinkling into a frown. "I owe him an apology."

Clint ducked his chin once—less of a nod than an expression of approval. How many times had he looked for that simple motion, that acknowledgment that he had worked through another tangle? "I do love how the white ropes look on Kristoph's skin, don't you?"

"Beautiful. I've always admired Kristoph. I'm also enjoying the look on Armond's face." He glanced over at Clint. "And yours."

Clint's eyes smiled, the wrinkles at the corners deepening. "Now, Thomas, you know that I am well known for my lack of expression."

7

If he stared at the whiskey bottle long enough, he thought he could see things in there. Little flashes of dreams, shadows. Every now and again, he thought he saw faces of people who he couldn't quite remember.

Sam was fairly sure he wasn't even tipsy anymore. He'd had a couple of shots at noon to help him maybe sleep. Now it was four in the afternoon, and he was still awake.

He thought he was awake.

Maybe he was asleep and he didn't know and he was dreaming about sitting here on the floor and wishing he could rest.

God, what fresh hell was that?

"Why can't I sleep, James? Why is this so fucked up?" He wasn't helping. Officer Colletti made that clear enough.

Actually the man had offered to throw Sam in the drunk tank for a night to give himself some peace.

Fucker.

"I don't know what to do, man. I keep on trying, but this ain't like home. There ain't a good-ole-boy network that I can tap into 'cause I'm one of the O'Reilly boys. This ain't the same."

James had come here and made a life. A real life, with friends and neighbors and coworkers. Sam was so fucking proud and jealous at the same time. His life was the one that had been handed to him: Here is the ranch, here is the town and the family and the same room you have had since the day you were born. This is yours, and you have to take it because you have no other purpose.

"Oh, stop it. Christ, you're a self-indulgent prick." The sound of his voice snapping out surprised him. Okay, so he was awake.

And if he wasn't, the door buzzer from the seventh level of hell would have taken care of that for him. This time he really was going to beat that thing with a broom handle.

If he could get up off the floor.

The buzzer went off again in short little pulses that stabbed into his brain like...that guy in that hockey mask...Jason.

The buzzer went off again.

"Leave me alone!" he screamed, but the effort to do that had him crawling across the floor to slap that fucking thing hard. "What the fucking hell do you want?"

"I...uh. To apologize?"

"You're forgiven." Who was that? No one had done anything to him that warranted an apology, right?

"Are you...? Can I come up? Are you drunk?"

Was he? Nowhere near enough. He knew the voice now, though. James's lover. Mr. Fucker. The sad guy with the gorgeous jaw and pretty eyes. "Sure, honey. Come on. I'm decent."

Or he would be once he threw a shirt on.

He let Thomas into the building, then went to find his

cleanest dirty button-up and run his fingers through his new beard. Momma would be so pleased.

There was a knock at the door. It sounded friendly enough, unlike that godforsaken buzzer. "Hey, it's me." *Mmm.* The voice was smooth too, like caramel.

He unlocked the door and offered Thomas a nod. "Hey, man. Come on in. Give me a second to move this shit. You want a beer?"

He grabbed his blanket and pillow and tossed it down the hall.

"No, thank you. I hope I didn't wake you up?" Thomas was looking around curiously. What was up with that?

"Nope." He wished. "I was navel-gazing. Have a seat."

Okay, you be nice to this guy. He's all wigged from missing James and mourning. You be decent and polite and all. No losing your temper. Zen. You are the Zen. Like yoga and namaste *and pastoral and shit. Fucking ohm.*

"Thanks." Thomas settled into the couch like it knew him. "I don't want to take up your time..." The man looked at him, brown eyes thoughtful. "Actually I do. I was rude to you the other night and disrespectful and...wrong—just being very honest. I don't want to make any excuses. I just I want to apologize to you. I'm sorry."

"No worries. This whole thing sucks, and shit gets intense. No hard feelings." He meant it too. He'd figured out that most folks around here didn't just beat the fuck out of each other and let it go. Thomas had to let his evil out somehow.

Thomas nodded. "I appreciate that. So, I thought about everything you said, and that phone call from Ji—Bowie, and I guess I'd like to know if there is anything I can do to make this easier on you."

"Well, unless you happen to know who killed James,

which seems unlikely..." He found a grin for Thomas, a wink. "Seriously, I'm not even sure what I'm doing, but thanks."

Like he'd ask this guy for help. *Shit.* He wasn't a bad guy, at least he tried not to be, and this man was hurting, and he wouldn't make it worse.

"Okay. Well, maybe there is something else I can help with?" Thomas stood, stepping closer. "What can I do? You look so tired, Sam. This city can be hard on new faces. It's nothing like home, I know. I remember what James used to say about things not making sense. People, transportation, food, work. It's ironic, right? Feeling alone in a city packed with millions of people."

He caught himself nodding because Thomas was saying what was in his heart. No one touched him here. Everyone knew him at home—everyone. Buddies slapped him on the shoulder, waitresses hugged him, Momma kissed him every morning. These last few weeks had been the longest he'd ever been alone, and he was starving to death for someone to see him, meet his eyes.

What? You're going to add your load to his? Buck the fuck up, man.

"James managed okay, huh?"

Thomas nodded slowly, and Sam could see the wheels turning. "James found...like-minded friends. And learned some very effective coping skills." Thomas took another step toward him, reaching out to rest a hand on his upper arm. "I'd like to be a friend to you, Sam. Help you sort some of this out. And really, you'd be doing me a favor. I'm a little aimless myself right now."

"I don't want to be something that hurts you. I'm sorry I look like him." Sam didn't think he did, really, any more than he looked like Bowie. He was the little one, wiry where

James had been lean. Scarred and tanned where James had been finer, pointed and angular like Papaw where James and Bowie had Daddy's wider features.

"It's a little startling when you're in your hat and your face is shaded. And there's no denying the resemblance in your eyes, but you don't look like him so much as...remind me of him. But Sam, tacos remind me of him. And beer. And the Sunday crossword. And truthfully, the more I get to know you, the more I see how different you are. Don't ever apologize for being you."

He waved the words off, making sure to use the hand that Thomas wasn't touching, because that felt so solid. "It's cool to see how you loved him."

"I did. I'll always love him. And I feel the same way when I see you. You admired him, you were proud of him, and it's obvious how much you loved him. You miss him.... You're allowed to miss him." That hand moved up his arm to his shoulder and caught there. "I can't explain how much I appreciate that you see that hole in me, in my life, and I want you to know that I see it in you too. I want you to honor that. Acknowledge it. That, I can help with for sure, right? I understand."

He swallowed hard, trying to make himself breathe, but fuck, he wanted to... *No, cowboy up.* He felt himself shaking, and he couldn't stop it, and all he could do was pray Thomas ignored it. "Th-thank you, man. That's..." Quite possibly the kindest thing he'd heard in a long time. "...dear."

"Oh, Sam. You're trying so hard, aren't you? To hold it together, to do what's expected? You can let it go for a minute. I will catch you. Just let it go."

He couldn't breathe. He couldn't. It hurt so bad. He hurt so fucking bad, and if he had any sense at all, he'd excuse himself and go into the bathroom and bash his head into the tile until all this shit stopped. But he couldn't. He couldn't move.

Sam stared at Thomas, utterly fucking panicked.

The man stood steady as a rock, eyes on his. "Trust me," Thomas said softly, all authority and strength. "Breathe in and let it out. You're safe, Sam. I promise."

"I'm sorry." He drew in a shuddering breath, and the exhalation huffed out like he was a little kid who'd been caught by a baseball. "God, I'm sorry."

Thomas shook his head. "Why? What are you sorry for? Tell me."

"Huh?" The answer to "I'm sorry" was "It's okay."

"I'm not clear what you're apologizing for, Sam. Why are you telling me you're sorry?"

"For all this..." Hysteria. Drama. Emotion. Stupidity. "Shit. I'm just real tired, I think."

"Don't ever apologize for being you."

Hadn't the guy already said that?

Thomas put an arm around his shoulders. "You do look pretty tired. Why don't you lie down and get some sleep? You look a little like my nephews who know damn well it's bedtime but always fight to keep their eyes open."

He found himself sitting on the couch, not entirely sure he'd gotten there under his own power. "This is where you've been sleeping? That's your bedding?" Thomas retrieved it for him.

"Yeah. I bought a pillow and comforter." Thank God for Amazon. He leaned into the pillow, his head so heavy he couldn't hold it up. "I'm not being a good host."

"Nonsense. You forget I've spent many more nights here than you have." Thomas covered him with his blanket like he was a child and rested a warm hand against his cheek. "Can't handle his bed yet?"

"Haven't gone in his room. Seems disrespectful."

"I understand. Get some rest." Thomas stepped back from the couch. "You can't do right by him if you don't do right by yourself. Sleep."

"I want to. God, I want to." He turned his head because his eyes were watering now, leaking. What would Bowie say to him? Such a baby. Always the baby.

This time if Thomas noticed, he didn't acknowledge it. "I'm just going to use the bathroom, and I'll let myself out. No worries."

"No worries." He heard the bathroom door close, and he melted into the sofa, the sounds of someone else familiar, welcome, and easing him right down.

If he dreamed this time, he didn't care.

———

THOMAS BRACED both hands on the bathroom sink and stared at himself in the mirror, just breathing.

Breathing in, breathing out, in...and out.

He felt...good. Lighter. Stronger.

He'd said something that Sam appreciated, other things that had made the man thoughtful, and finally something that had struck a raw, terrifying nerve. He saw all of it on Sam's face. He was confident he'd read everything well, given Sam what he needed in the moment.

And he'd managed to set his own emotions aside and not push Sam too far.

He knew tonight would be pure hell. Subjugating his own pain for Sam, giving of himself, being what the man needed and not getting the break, the gift he craved from Sam in return would haunt his dreams, rip and tear at his soul. It was the price he paid for being what he was. It was like detox. Right now he felt like he could fucking fly. The dreams that woke him later would threaten to drown him.

But he'd built a solid foundation for Sam, and he'd set his lover's brother on a path to complete truth, real freedom, and ultimate trust.

He pushed off the sink and rubbed his face. Okay. This was a good beginning. But God, they had so much work to do, assuming Sam would let him. It was going to be a road as rough as it was rewarding.

He left the bathroom quietly and went into James's room, completely out of habit, and was reminded instantly how fleeting hope and joy could be. Reality was a bitch. He sat on James's bed, not feeling the kind of disrespect that Sam felt at all, or the depth of sadness he had expected either. He belonged here. He believed that with his whole being.

He reached for James's journal, a book he'd reminded James many times that he had every right to read and yet never had. He opened it, telling himself he'd only admire the neat penmanship, he'd only read a sentence or two, he'd just read one more page.

He did close the book finally, but held on to it, thoughtfully considering its contents. He took it with him as he left the room, admired Sam, who was peacefully sound asleep on the couch, then set the journal on the coffee table and let himself out, making sure the door locked behind him.

One of James's neighbors, a long, lean man with a junkie's stare and a shaky hand came up to him. "Dude. Dude, did they re-lease Tex's place?"

What the hell was this about? "No," he said flatly. "Excuse me." He tried to step around the man, but the guy stood square in his way.

"There's someone in there. A squatter?"

"What? No. It's all perfectly legal, thank you for your concern. What apartment are you in again?" He recognized the guy, or thought he did, but it would be worth warning Sam about him at some point.

"Right there." He pointed next door. "He needs any handyman work, I'm totally available."

"You knew James?"

"Yeah. Yeah, he was a good guy. He—he was nice. He liked to talk."

That was true enough. James could talk to anyone. He knew a little bit about essentially anything.

"Did you—" *Ask. What can it hurt? Just ask.* "Did you happen to see anything the night—"

"Whoa, man. Are you a cop? Shit."

"No. No, I'm not with the police at all. I was his lover."

"Oh. You're Thomas?"

James really did talk. "Yes. I am."

"Oh. Oh man. Oh man, I'm sorry, man."

"What's your name?"

The guy had started to tremble. Vibrate. "Skip."

"Thank you, Skip. I've got to run. You take care of yourself."

"Don't forget, if he needs any handiwork..."

"I will be sure to let him know. Thank you. Please excuse me." He was fairly sure Sam was at least as handy as James was. This time he simply put out a hand and shifted the man aside to walk past him.

He needed out. He needed to process.

He grabbed his phone, texting Clint. *You have a minute?*

It took seconds for the answer to come. *I have many. Coffee?*

Yes. Coffee. *Starbucks? Your place? Home?* And by home, he meant the club; that was understood.

Come home. We'll chat. Clint would have a room for them, coffee, a safe space for him to let go.

Give me 20. Thanks, Clint.

He got right on the subway at 14th and headed uptown. By the time he arrived at the club, his high was fading, and he felt like he might be rebounding as the adrenaline dropped.

It was also possible that perhaps he simply needed that coffee.

8

It took Sam ten days to read the journal.

Ten.

Ten days of wondering if he should. Ten days of staring.

Ten days of telling himself it wasn't any of his business and of following James's daily steps and of helping with math homework.

Ten days of dear texts from James's Thomas. Just checking in. Did you manage to sleep? Would you like to come to dinner Saturday?

He answered every text but turned down supper. He couldn't face that. He'd been a fucking tittybaby when Thomas had shown up, and he couldn't look the man in the eyes. Christ, he'd *cried*.

Eventually he was going to have to man up. He knew this, but he'd been...he'd acted a fool.

Finally he'd sat down to look at the journal and...

God, he didn't know what to do.

Did he call Bowie and ask? Did he throw the journal away so no one knew? Did he take it to the police?

James was...had been...the things he'd written.

Oh God.

He'd been awake all night, reading, then researching this club, this whole thing.

Sam would have gone to the police first thing, but...but he could see—read, whatever—how much James had been into...this thing.

Headspace.

They were O'Reilly boys—did they have headspaces? Was that genetically even a thing?

And there was the care that James had, the joy.

The idea that his big brother had sex—ever, much less weird sex—made him want to gag. His brothers used their dicks to write their names in the dust. That was it. Sam had no doubt that was what Bowie would say about him too.

Why on earth would anyone write this down?

Why would anyone let someone...? His brain skittered from the thoughts.

He'd researched, and he wasn't sure what was worse— the wild things he'd seen or the terribly intimate things James had written down.

Sam didn't know how to process any of this, didn't know how to swallow around how this made him feel. Didn't know how to stop thinking about it.

He sure as shit didn't know how to hide the shame he felt when he'd sprung wood. *Christ.* It was like he'd taken three too many Reds and the heart was buzzing in his chest.

When his phone buzzed with a text from Thomas, Sam didn't even read it. He just called.

"Why on earth did you leave that here for me to see?"

"Good morning, Sam. You've read James's journal?"

"That...that's not for me to have read. That's personal shit. Deeply. You wanted me to read it?"

"Yes. And you wanted to read it, clearly. What drew you

in?" Thomas's tone was even, his voice smooth. He didn't sound the least bit ashamed of himself.

"I didn't. I—you should have it. Take it. With you. I could mail it." He wasn't going to answer that question. No way. There was no answer to that question that wasn't obscene— from prurient curiosity to— *No. Nope. Stop it. No more thinking.* He was Bowie's baby brother. He could totally have no thoughts.

"Sam, if you hadn't wanted to read it, you wouldn't have. We needn't say another word about it, but you—and I— both know it's that simple, don't we? I appreciate the offer of the journal. That would be a lovely gift if you're sure you can part with it. Why don't you meet me for drinks tonight at the club?"

"What? No. No, I have...I couldn't. I should go." His cheeks were on fire. "You can have it. Seriously. This wasn't meant for me to see."

That thought stopped him, settled him all of the sudden. Everyone discovered secrets when someone died, and he wasn't sure what Thomas wanted him to know, why Thomas wanted him to know, but it wasn't for him to see. "This was something for a lover, not me. James wouldn't have let me see it."

Surely James would have been ashamed to have him read that. Thomas was just trying to...connect, he guessed? There. Connect. Right. All the connection, just without orgasms and ropes and lube and leather things and...

Would you stop it?

"No, it wasn't meant for you specifically. You're probably correct in that assumption. But you needed to read it. Let's be honest, Sam. If I had told you about the nature of a large part of my relationship with your brother, if I had said that I was his Master and he was my submissive, what would you have done? Assuming you even knew what that really meant, as opposed to some fetishized TV version of the lifestyle, would you have believed me? Would you have understood what it meant to James? To us?"

He didn't even know how to answer any of those questions. Not even one. So he went with what he did know, and what was the best thing to say. "I can tell he loved you very much."

That was decent, right? Not pervy or weird or mean or nasty. Just decent and also the truth. James had been lucky to have found someone to be with.

"I want you to come to the club, Sam. Meet his friends. Our friends. Come have one drink. You don't have to stay long. I would be very pleased to see you."

He shook his head. He couldn't. He just couldn't. What if he embarrassed himself? What if he embarrassed Thomas? What if...?

"I—" He coughed, his words caught in his throat.

"Hm? Why don't we say seven o'clock? It will be quieter at that hour. I'll text you the address."

"What? Tonight? But I have—" *Something. Come on. Come on, Sam Houston O'Reilly! Herpes. The plague. Plumbing issues. Crippling fear.* "—laundry."

Thomas chuckled. "I'm guessing the machines won't care if you stand them up. See you at seven. Come as you are, hm? Looking forward to it."

Thomas hung up the phone.

What had just happened?

Seriously. What the actual fuck had just happened?

He wasn't going to go to some club and get embarrassed to death. He wasn't going to be able to even look Thomas in the eye. No way.

He wasn't going.

He would simply text at seven with "Caught the flu" or maybe tomorrow with "Sorry, fell asleep."

His phone lit up with a text from Thomas. The address of the club, followed by, *I've arranged an Uber for you. It was nice to finally hear from you. I was getting worried.*

Oh man. That was so cheating. He hated disappointing. Hated it.

So fucking cheating.

You want to know, that awful, curious little voice whispered inside him. That voice had encouraged him to get on his first bull, had told him to drag race Paulie Marquette on the Nueces Bay Causeway, had encouraged his first cigarette, his first bottle of Cuervo, and his first spliff. It had also been there when he'd applied for grad school, when he'd published his first article, and when he'd tried bronc riding and found his event.

He did.

He wanted to know.

"Goddammit. What's wrong with me?"

Too bad Sam knew the answer to that. He needed to know. He'd never once told that little voice no.

Not one time.

9

By the time the car dropped Sam off, he'd decided to hand Thomas the journal and make some dumb-assed excuse. That way he knew the book was in safe hands, knew no one else on earth would ever know it existed; then he would find a biker bar and get into a fight.

He stood on the sidewalk, looking at what was apparently the entrance but really wasn't much more interesting than most of the apartment building entrances back in James's neighborhood.

The door opened, and a young man wearing a lot of leather gave him a wave. "Sam O'Reilly? You're in the right place. Master Thomas is waiting for you."

"Uh. Evenin'. I just...I mean, I brought him his book and all." *Shut up, Sam. Stoic. Cowboy up. Think Sam Elliott. Slow and steady and calm.*

Right. Calm. He'd done three hundred crunches to try and make the zooming in his mind go away. There wasn't enough beer on earth.

"I'm Mark. Come on in. He asked me to keep an eye out for you." Mark held the door long enough for him to catch up and brought him inside. "Master told me not to make a big deal of it, but...I just have to tell you, I'm really sorry, really sad about James. We miss him around here."

"Thank you, sir. I appreciate it. He was a good man, and it's good to meet all y'all." He offered one hand to shake. Just because he was nervous was no reason to be rude.

Mark shook briefly and gave him a quick smile, and a few steps later, he approached a round table, where Thomas was sitting with several others, and went right to his knees next to one of the men without a word.

Thomas gave him a smile and stood. He was also wearing leather, though just pants. His black button-down shirt was made of something rich and expensive-looking, and Sam smoothed his own dress shirt, hoping his pressed jeans were sharp enough. "Sam. Hey, you look great. Glad you could make it. Please take a seat." Thomas pointed to an empty chair.

Fuck-a-doodle-goddamn-do. He hadn't intended to sit. "Thank you. Evenin', y'all."

He sat, leaving his hat on. He could hide under the brim with the best of them.

The place wasn't...skeezy. In fact, it looked like a nice hotel bar, like a place that was meant for little groups to chat.

No bowls of peanuts on the tables or Bud Light neon signs, of course. He guessed kneeling on the floor with peanut shells would be gross as fuck.

"No one expects you to remember names right now, but I'll do quick introductions anyway. I wanted to get together the men who knew James best for you. This is Clint, and you already met Mark, that's Adam and Rick..." Thomas went around the table and introduced nine men, only five of whom were sitting at the table. The others stood as they were introduced, then knelt again.

"Mark met James at the gym. He's one of the reasons James came to the club to begin with."

"Pleased to meet y'all. I appreciate y'all meeting me." *Dear God, please let me survive tonight without having to eat my own fist to not say something stupid. Somewhere James is laughing his ass off at this. Smite him with fire. Amen.*

Thomas rested a hand on his knee. "What would you like to drink?"

"I'll take a light beer, please." No chance of even getting a buzz, but polite. He caught his thigh tensing, and he forced himself to relax. One beer.

Thomas gave his knee a squeeze and let him go. Thankfully, his beer arrived quickly, giving him something to do with his hands.

"So, Sam, what do you do in Texas?" That guy's name was...Ron? Rick? Something with an *R*.

"Little bit of everything, I reckon. Rodeoing, some ranch work, a little research. Just whatever needs doing." That was true enough, if simplified down to the lowest common denominator.

Oh, go math tutoring.

"He's also overly humble." Thomas winked at him. "In addition to braving the rodeo and running his family's ranch, Sam's an art historian, and he does research for authors writing Westerns and movie-makers."

Rick smiled. "An academic, like James."

"Our momma was a teacher. Schooling's important to her." And he loved it. He'd loved being in school. Loved learning new things. Loved the whole idea of Western art, of the cowboy way preserved in the fabric of America.

Sometimes he ached to be able to paint, to sculpt, but his talents were with sharing it with other people.

"Remember that kid James got into college?"

"Oh, yeah. How did that story go, Thomas? Something about the SATs."

"It was more than the one young man." Thomas nodded and looked at Sam. "James ran into a handful of high school kids on the subway one afternoon riding home from school. Kids that lived in his neighborhood. They were all talking about studying for the SATs, how unfair they thought it was that some kids could afford those expensive prep courses to help them do better and they couldn't."

"James set up regular weeknight study sessions with the group of them for a few weeks at the library," one of the men added. Thomas was right; he wasn't remembering names.

"Every single one of them got into college."

"It was remarkable and generous," Thomas added.

"But he was always doing stuff like that." That was Mark, from his knees. "I'm a disaster with plumbing. He came over one time after work and fixed my toilet when it was leaking." Mark wasn't the only one with stories.

"Right? He helped me move, and all he asked for was pizza and beer. Carried all my shit, including this big-ass couch with me down three flights of stairs."

"This one time, James brought me soup and movies when I had the flu."

"I remember that. Did you know he made it himself?" Thomas sounded proud.

"He told me that. I wasn't sure I believed him."

Thomas grinned. "Believe it."

"Was it porn?" one of the men on his knees asked.

"Huh?"

"The movies—were they porn?"

"One totally was. The other was *The Lion King*."

The whole table started laughing.

The Lion King had been James's favorite movie as a kid. They'd had to watch it every single time it was his turn to pick before Daddy came home.

Sam felt like a tornado was spinning behind his eyes. All these thoughts just running like mad, and he didn't have time to look at any of them. Not now.

Later. If he looked now, God knew what he'd do.

Other than some men on their knees, there wasn't anything about this group that shouted deviant at him. They were laughing, talking sports, James, food, all normal guy talk, except the teams were different and he didn't know any of the restaurants they'd mentioned. He'd somehow gotten to the bottom of a second light beer as the conversation started winding down close to two hours later.

Two hours to drop off a book.

Clint, one of the few names he remembered, stuck out his hand to shake and stood. "Very good to meet you. I think Thomas has a tour planned, so we're going to give you some room. Have a great night."

He stood as well, offering the man a smile and a nod. "Thank you, sir. It was something else, to hear all y'all telling stories on James."

James was ten times the man he was, Lord knew.

"We miss him. It felt good to share them with you." Everyone at the table agreed, and there was a flurry of handshakes, nods, pats on the back, and suddenly Thomas put a hand on his shoulder.

"I'm sure you're a little overwhelmed by all of that, but I want to give you a quick tour, and we'll get you home."

Thomas picked James's journal up off the table. "Are you sure you want me to have this?"

"I am. It ain't mine to have, and I sure as shit won't be giving it to Momma." He chuckled softly, shook his head. "Everyone loved him. That's good to hear. Y'all honor him well."

"You worry a lot about me, Sam, I know. I wanted you to see how much support I have. Some of these men know me better than they know their own brothers. The safety net here is wide, and it's reliable. I might not be standing here without it; that is the very honest truth. I want that for you. If not here, at least with me."

"You're a dear man. James was lucky to know you." And he meant that. James had figured shit out, Bowie had figured shit out, so maybe he'd be next. One way or the other, these people had been James's new family.

"Thank you. I can be a lot more than that if you let me." Thomas's brown eyes pinned him for a second, almost long enough for him to panic about what the hell it meant. "Come on, quick tour."

"Sure. Then I'll get out of your hair." Sam needed to...he wasn't sure, but he knew he needed privacy to figure out his shit. He wasn't ever going to look like he couldn't manage in front of Thomas again. Once had been enough.

"I like you in my hair." Thomas tossed that off over his shoulder like he was talking about the weather. He handed off James's journal to the bartender. "Scotty? Can you please put this somewhere safe for me? It's private."

"Yes, Sir." Scotty took the book, then nodded to Sam.

Sam nodded back, smiled, keeping his hat low enough that he stayed in the shadows. Lord help him get through this without hitting someone in the face, getting a boner, or embarrassing James's memory.

"From the bits I read in James's journal, I think he mentioned most of what you're going to see. Did anything stand out for you? Feel free to ask anything you like." Thomas made it sound like James's journal was a textbook or something. What stood out for you, have any questions— like this was a field trip for Kink 101. "Oh. So in the main room, starting about nine—" Thomas looked at his watch. "So any minute...there's usually a floor show and dancing, kind of alternating all night. The club is twenty-four seven, by the way. Never closes."

Sam had a sudden image of a drill team and the high school band on this terribly classy barroom floor, a bunch of Aquanetted blondes in short skirts doing high kicks while the band played Sousa marches, and near-hysterical laughter tried to bubble out of him.

Stop it. Right now.

One-two-three, kick. One-two-three, kick.

"I didn't think bars could be open all night." Oh, good on him. He sounded interested but not like he was fixin' to lose his shit.

"This isn't a bar. It's technically a private club, open to the public for certain hours. After hours is members only."

They headed up a long hall that went back much farther than he'd expected, given the subdued entrance and the size of the main bar. There were some open spaces with couches and mirrors, and some closed doors, and a handful of rooms that didn't have doors on them at all. Thomas stopped by one of those to let him look in.

"Anyone is welcome in the rooms with open doors."

This room was empty at the moment, but was lined with heavy-looking drapes, had some suspicious-looking furniture in it, and had neatly placed restraints all over. Literally all over—floor, walls, ceiling, every sturdy-looking...apparatus. Good Lord and butter, it was like looking into the weirdest tack room on earth.

Sam had looked at Bing over the last day, had seen things that made him gasp and more than one thing that had made him curl over his hand, because he'd catch himself rubbing off, but this was different.

This confused him.

He knew these scents—musk and leather—and they were the smell of good things, of home and adrenaline and men. The visual, though, was totally unfamiliar and uncomfortable.

"Rooms like this are all about imagination, Sam. Sometimes it's a shared aesthetic, sometimes it might be just about one or two people, sometimes it's loud...depends on the night, the vibe, and members' needs. I can take the time to demonstrate how some of these things are used at some point, but you can find out more on the internet if you're curious in the meantime."

Thomas stepped aside. "You go ahead, have a look in anywhere you like."

"You're a good tour guide, Mister Thomas. I don't think I'm comfortable just having a look. This seems—" *What would Bowie say?* "—above my pay grade." He chuckled softly, letting his wildly swinging emotions out as carefully as he could. "My imagination is a...well, it never thought of this kind of deal."

He couldn't imagine how much it had to cost to be a member here. Hell, there was overhead, supplies, utilities, paying off the cops because there was no way on earth this was legal.

"Works for me, cowboy. I do work in a museum, after all." Thomas walked him past another room so quickly he didn't get a good look, but he sure as shit knew the sound of a whip when he heard one. "This is one of my favorite rooms down here."

"Right. You have to show folks around quite a bit." He wasn't fucking acknowledging that sound at all, but he remembered the whip-crackers at a few of his events. Those men were something else, the sound snapping out, ringing through the air.

And best of all, watching the two of them fighting at the biker bar that night.

Jesus. That had been wild without the tequila, and Christ knew the tequila had made it better.

They stopped to look into a fairly full and yet mostly quiet room, where a man, naked with his butt turned to show and muscled to heaven and back, was being carefully bound with complicated and kind of pretty knots, the red rope standing out against pale, bare skin.

"I spend a fair amount of time in here. It's quiet, it's deliberate, it's art and skill. It appeals to me."

"I bet that takes some patience, for both of them." He wasn't sure he could handle that—having to be still and all. It looked beautiful as all get-out, but he'd have a screaming fit or shake apart or just hit somebody. He envied that guy, though. He looked like he was pretty well happy.

"There's an art to being patient too, isn't there? Learning how to be still is a skill, an important one. Being able to tap into that spot inside that's at peace."

"I bet there is. Like in hunting. Fishing, even." That was why he didn't do either of those things. He didn't have any still to him, precious little wait. Even when he'd drunk so much he couldn't move, his soul was still running itself into the ground, looking for something to occupy it.

"Like that, and not." Thomas didn't clarify.

The bound man moaned softly, the sound content and

warm, and the man tying the knots stopped what he was doing. They talked quietly, their voices just murmurs; then they kissed, gentle and slow, and got back to work.

"I have to go. I'm sorry."

His heart was broken.

All this—all of it, from understanding that he could never be the man James was to the kneeling guys to the whip sounds to the cuffs and all—was nothing compared to that kiss.

He would never have that, and he knew it, and it was cruel of God to dangle it in front of him.

Thomas looked at him, the man's expression turning serious. "Sam? Sam, don't go yet. Why don't we go sit somewhere private for a minute."

He took Thomas's hand and patted it, willing the man not to notice how he shook. "This isn't about you, honey. You have to know that. This isn't about anything bad. I just have to go. We'll have supper in a couple three days. Thank you for loving him. That's the best thing."

Thomas caught his hand and covered it, as if just that gesture could make it better instead of worse. "I'll walk you out."

"Thanks." He found Thomas a smile because he didn't want anyone to misunderstand. He wasn't offended. He was cracked down the center, and he needed to figure out what to do with himself.

Thomas let go of his hand with a sigh and led him back through the much more crowded bar to the front doors. "Just, uh...text me sometime, I guess."

Dork. He nodded, then offered an olive branch to prove what he'd said. This wasn't about Thomas. This was about him and his personal bullshit. "How about a late lunch tomorrow? After the church people are done."

"All right. Tomorrow." Thomas nodded, though his expression didn't change. "I'll come down your way about one?"

"If that's good with you, surely. I know it burns a bit, being in his neighborhood." He wasn't stupid. He got that.

"Less and less. Thanks. And thanks again for the journal. You know how to get ho...uh. Home?"

"Yessir." He waved and called himself an Uber as he walked. As soon as he got into the car, he asked the man, "Are there any cowboy bars around here? Somewhere I can get fucked up and won't nobody care?"

"I can find you something, bud."

"Good."

He could go see how many men it would take to kick his ass. He understood that sort of hurting.

This emotional shit could kiss his ass.

N *ope. No. No way.*
        Thomas waited for the doors to close behind Sam, then stormed back to the bar. "Fireball. No. No. Tequila."

"Everything okay, Sir?" Scotty pulled out a shot glass.

"I'll take the glass. And the bottle. And...an empty room."

"Will six do, Sir?"

"Whatever, just give me the key."

Scotty handed him a key, the shot glass, a bottle of Patrón Silver, all of which he scooped off the bar, then headed straight for room six. He needed to think.

He didn't see Clint coming his way until it was too late. He smacked shoulders with his mentor but shook it off and kept on walking.

"Sorry."

"Thomas?"

"There's no way." He needed to extract himself from this. He needed a graceful way out. And what the fuck was this feeling in the pit of his stomach?

He passed the boy in bondage rope and ducked into room six, letting the door slam behind him.

Okay, breathe. Breathe. Fucking breathe, you idiot. Think.

He knew it wasn't him. It wasn't him, it wasn't his choices, it wasn't home. Sam wasn't judging anyone at the club.

Sam was only passing judgment on himself.

Of course, a beautiful, broken boy was enticing. Yes, there were times that just looking at Sam made his fingers itch for a paddle or a flogger. Thomas longed to carefully claim power from Sam, help the boy dig deep, help free him from the burdens he carried of family obligation, of personal pride.

That task would be hard enough, he'd already learned. Herculean. Sam was a master at buttoning down, dismissing and discounting his own emotions. Even his own worth.

But...

It would be impossible to free the man from any of those things without first freeing him from the deepest, most ingrained, most basic kind of shame. He'd have to free Sam from the closet.

"No. No, that undermines everything. I won't do it."

He bent over and poured himself a shot and threw it back. God, that burned just right.

Fine. Lunch tomorrow would be easy. They'd talk about art and the weather. They'd talk about horses maybe, or the military, something else they had in common. And over the next couple of weeks, he'd just fade out of Sam's life or... fade Sam out of his.

Sam was some other Dominant's perfect disaster. Perhaps a woman's. Someone who wouldn't cause Sam so much drama.

Clint didn't knock. He came in, locked the door behind him, and sat.

And waited.

Thomas could have protested. He could have tried to throw Clint out, tell him it was a party for one, tell him anything he liked, but he already knew what a waste of hot air that would be.

"Drink?"

"I brought my own." He had no idea what was in the glass, but he knew there wouldn't be any alcohol in there.

For that matter, he'd had his one shot. He wouldn't touch his bottle again either. But it made him feel better that it was there.

"Over an hour of friendly conversation with men in leather? No problem. Bondage room? Eh. Barely a hint of a reaction, right?" He got up and paced across the room. "Big whip? Completely ignored that as if he'd never even heard it. It's possible he may have actually enjoyed the ropes to a degree, but what sends him into a tailspin? As in, 'I have to go now because my hands won't stop shaking'?"

He looked at Clint, who didn't seem at all inclined to help him with the punch line.

"A kiss. One lovely kiss between Master and sub, and he ran."

Clint winced. "God, poor boy. Was it his first time?"

"I have no idea. I thought he was straight."

"James never mentioned?"

No. James had said he had brothers. *I have two brothers. One is a rodeo cowboy, one a soldier.*

Not, *I have this terribly conflicted brother who is the very definition of "try too hard."*

"James never explained, no. And you know what Sam

said? Sam told me his eldest brother, Bowie, is gay. He did not add, 'and I am too.' No, he left that out."

Poor boy. Yes, poor boy. Of course. Just not his poor boy. No way. He had no idea how to make that work.

"I'm sorry, Thomas. I know you were hoping for...some closure? A connection? He seems like a dear man but incredibly lost."

"There's only one way I know to coax a man out of the closet, Clint." There was no way. He'd only just lost James.

"Have you asked him?"

"Clint." *Breathe. He meant that to be funny. Breathe.* "I..." He needed to sit down. Now.

Clint moved like lightning, easing him down, head pressed between his legs. "Breathe, Tommy. In and out."

Clint's hand was solid between his shoulder blades, keeping him where Clint wanted him.

He didn't fight. He tried to relax, concentrate on getting air in and out. "I don't know what to do."

"You're here with me. You don't have to. This is your safe space. You don't have to know anything but that."

Right. That was better. Let Clint worry about things for a minute. He could just breathe. He would just stay like this so he didn't vomit or black out, and breathe. "Okay."

"Good man." Clint stroked his back, touched him like there was nothing else on earth that needed doing. He knew if he looked up, Clint would be right there with him.

When he finally attempted to sit up, he was relieved to discover he did feel better. He leaned into the sofa and glanced at Clint. "Thank you."

He studied his fingernails, trying to figure out what he wanted to talk about. "I don't want anyone else right now. Is that wrong? I mean, in this context, is it wrong? I don't think it should be."

"Do you feel wrong? About him?"

"I feel like we make each other's lives very complicated." To say the least. "Yeah. Yeah, with this new information, I feel...like it's wrong. I can't go ahead with what I was hoping for him without dealing with this first. He couldn't be honest. Not really. And I don't think I'm...I don't think I..." Even if he found a way that didn't involve...*Jesus*. He couldn't even think the words without James's name attached.

"If this is wrong, don't see him again. He will go home and heal. You will heal. He's not your responsibility, Tommy. He's a very nice kid doomed to a world that isn't ours. James escaped; not everyone does."

He nodded. He was right, then. He needed out of this. "I'm heartbroken for him, Clint."

"I am too. He seems like a genuinely good man."

But that didn't matter. He could almost hear Sam saying that to him. Not James, Sam.

"I'm supposed to meet him for lunch tomorrow. I'll talk to him, I guess. I don't know what I'll say, but...I'll think of something. I don't know that it matters what I say. I'm not sure he'd understand. I don't think he understood that I know now."

"I know you think I'm ridiculous, but you might just ask the man. He may not know how to tell you." Clint's lips quirked. "I swear, James had some odd ideas about what was polite, what wasn't. I remember how challenging answering a question like 'How are you today?' was for him."

He looked at Clint. "Sam couldn't tell me why he was apologizing to me the other day."

"Sam seems to me like a man who might be apologizing for daring to express an emotion." Clint waved one hand. "Seriously, there is no guilt in walking away and never looking back. He is not your responsibility."

He sighed. "Are you being serious, or are you doing that thing again, Clint? I'm a little off my game."

"You are my friend. As much as I cared for James, his brother is a little cowboy who managed to be very polite and open-minded in an incredibly stressful situation. I have nothing against him, but you're my concern."

"I wouldn't have gotten through that first week without you. Honestly. You have no idea the things I was thinking... or maybe you do. I suppose you know exactly." He sighed. Of course Clint knew. "I suppose just asking Sam outright might be something to try. What have I got to lose? What have either of us got to lose, right? If he doesn't tell me, then I can walk away and feel like I did what I could."

"You do what your gut tells you. You can trust it. I trust your gut, implicitly."

He took a deep breath and sat up straighter. That was exactly what he needed to hear. He could trust himself. Right wasn't necessarily easy. He'd figure out what right was. "Thank you, sir."

"Anytime, dear one. Anytime." Clint winked at him. "I don't suppose you'd like to go get a milkshake. I have the strangest craving."

Clint was a wonderful man. Odd sometimes too. Eccentric. But loyal to a fault, and the Dom knew him so damn well. "My treat."

11

F uck, Sam hurt from his bruised jaw to his cracked rib to that swollen bit on his thigh where some asshole caught him with a crowbar.

Damn, it had been just what he needed.

He felt like a rainstorm had passed through and made things easier.

Creaky, but easier.

Sam laughed softly, groaning at the deep ache inside him.

"Took eight guys, James. Eight. Not bad for your little bro."

By the grand finale, he had ended up drinking with four of the bikers he'd fought with and had got himself an invite to come back for fight night anytime.

Fucking A.

God, he should have done this before last night.

His phone chimed, and he reached for it, grinning even as he winced. *Just got off the subway, be there in a few.*

Thomas.

I'll come down. After he wrapped his ribs and got a shirt

on. He felt like he could think again for the first time in forever, like he could—well, breathing was a little hard, but it was the same basic idea.

When he got outside, Thomas was waiting for him, though not outside the building. The man gave him a wave from about halfway down the block.

"Hey, man. How goes?" He didn't wave back, but he smiled. God, he couldn't stop worrying his split lip with the tip of his tongue. It was like a bright itch.

"Hey, sorry. I couldn't take standing on the stoop—oh my God, Sam! What happened to you? Are you all right?"

"Bar fight. I'm a little beat up but not broke, much." He grinned at Thomas, rolled his eyes. "You having a decent day?"

"Sam, you...you left the club last night and got into a bar fight? That was better than staying and talking with me?" Thomas was looking at him a little sideways like he was an alien or something.

He got that. Not everyone understood needing to blow off steam. "I was all caught up in my soul, man. Hearing all those stories about James, seeing all that stuff—I wasn't going to be a good guy, you know? I had hurt and all sorts of bullshit inside. What I needed wasn't talk."

He'd needed to lose his shit, be handed his ass, and hurt in a way he could handle.

One of Thomas's eyebrows climbed halfway into that sandy hairline, and the man nodded slowly. "I see. I do understand some of that. I believe I know a similar, saner, and possibly more productive solution, but the results appear to be more or less the same."

"This one was hard, but I got an invite back for the next time. They fuck each other up on purpose once a month. Crazy." He started moving them away from James's place.

"I'm sorry for running out so fast. I should have done this earlier. I need to do stupid shit to restart myself sometimes. Where do you want to eat?"

"There's a place around the corner that has the best french toast." Thomas turned and started walking. "You could have just asked me to paddle your ass pink for you." He was fairly sure he heard a chuckle.

"Butthead! Can you imagine me just being all 'here's my backside' like that?" He had to laugh, though, just at the thought.

Of course, laughing was bad, and he had to pant a little at the end of his chuckle. *Damn.*

"Actually, I can." There was no chuckle that time. At all. "Do you like french toast?"

"Yessir. I don't love it with the powdered sugar, but there's nothing that goes with maple syrup that I don't crave. When I'm dieting, they're the things that call to me."

"Dieting for riding?" Thomas steered him around a corner.

"Yeah. You got to be lean and have core strength. If I was riding, I'd have to lose five pounds to be at the perfect weight." He was still doing his crunches, just because.

"Huh. I wasn't aware of that. Interesting. Here we go." Thomas stopped, opened a door for him. The place smelled like coffee and comfort-food heaven.

His belly snarled, and he hummed. "Oh, this seems like a good place."

He could eat here.

They were seated quickly, the hostess giving Thomas a hug before they sat down. "Fresh omelets, good coffee, James used to get this ham steak thing. It's all good."

"Are you okay here? It's cool for you?" He could come

back later, if not, because Jesus Christ, this place smelled so good.

Thomas gave him a sheepish grin. "It's not my first time. I came here a few days after James died. I...really wanted the french toast."

"There you go. That's what I'll try. French toast and bacon and cup of coffee." Easy enough.

He stretched out in the booth, finding the best place to sit.

"Good. Great." Thomas waved someone over and ordered for them, two of the same, and they had their coffee just a minute later. "Sam, we need to talk a little about last night. Just a short conversation, but would you rather wait until after breakfast or get it out of the way?"

"I can talk. No problem." He was floating on the endorphins, the world crystal clear for today. "What do you want to know?"

"Well, Sam. Very frankly, I'd like to know if you're gay."

He arched one eyebrow. What a ridiculous question. Surely James had said. Maybe Thomas just didn't believe it. "Well, duh. I mean, I know that I'm not supposed to be, and God knows what James told you, but I tried being with girls, and I can't get it up." Both Bowie and James told him he was just copying them, and Momma kept saying how glad she was that he was going to give her grandbabies, but he knew better. He'd have to jack off in a cup and find some lady willing to do the turkey-baster thing.

"Okay." Thomas was watching him. He knew that look; James had it sometimes. That look meant Thomas was trying to figure how to say something he wasn't going to like. "Why did you leave the club when you did? And let me be clear, I know why you left. I want to know why it made you so upset."

"Envy is a terrible thing, isn't it? I never got to see that before, two guys kissing like it was easy—not ever. Not for real. And I'm ashamed of that, bad, that envy. It was better to go and deal with my demons."

"I'm sorry, Sam. That scenario never occurred to me. Thank you for trusting me with that. But envy is... unnecessary now. You're in a diverse city full of single, kind, openhearted gay men. Those are demons you could let go of if you let yourself."

He didn't know how to answer that—everyone was waiting on him to fuck up, and he didn't know how not to. "It's hard. I want to make everybody proud. James was... amazing, and he had a life, and he should be here. Not me."

He didn't understand how to explain, and he rocked against his bruised thigh, letting the jolt clear his mind.

Thomas sighed. "You've said that before. You actually believe that? That it ought to have been you that your family buried? Do you think your family would have missed you less than James?"

"I don't know. Maybe. Maybe not." He chuckled because it was a moot point. "It doesn't matter now. James is gone... and wishing won't bring him home. I do wish I could talk with him again. We had good phone calls."

Thomas reached over, rested a hand on his forearm with a smile. Kind of a sad smile maybe, but still a smile. "Me too."

They kind of breathed that in together; then Thomas leaned back in his seat. "Have you been to the top of the Empire State Building yet? Have you seen a show? Have you walked through Central Park?"

"Shit. I been to see you twice, I been to a bar fight, and I've walked every fucking inch I could walk here." He snorted. "I swear to God, I never been so lonely in my life as here. I didn't know it would be hard to learn to sleep all alone for days and days." Even on the road with the circuits, they'd all share a hotel room or a tent. There were always people wanting to chat or have a beer or a cup of coffee. "I bet James damn near lost his mind."

He stopped, rolled his eyes, and took a deep drink of his coffee. "Getting beat up gave me diarrhea of the mouth."

"I don't know. I think you're right, that it actually was good for you." Thomas laughed. "I've learned more about you waiting for bacon to arrive than in the last three weeks."

Speaking of bacon, huge plates of thick eggy, toasty bread landed in front of each of them, a giant plate of bacon, and refills for their coffee.

Sam moaned, the sound embarrassing, but this was just right. "Oh, damn. This looks fine. I'm gonna look like a gecko that swallowed a beetle bug when I'm done."

"There's something I'd like to see." Thomas took a huge bite, chewed for a second, and shoved it into one cheek. "So...sightseeing Saturday?"

"You want to? I mean..." He didn't want Thomas to give up a day because he was lonely. On the other hand, he wanted to see things, talk to someone. "I'd like to go, if you got no plans."

"Well, I suppose I could sit around in my living room, watch reruns of *Iron Chef* in my underwear, and feel sorry for myself—like I did last weekend. That was some real fun, I'll tell you."

"American or the original? I will judge you, so watch your answer." Fuck he was amusing himself.

"You're serious? It's not the same without Chairman Kaga biting into that bell pepper." Thomas winked at him and snagged a piece of bacon.

"Munch!" He started eating, digging in. Lord, this was

good shit. He loved the whole crunchy, sweet, orgasmic thing.

"Saturday, then. I've got a packed week at work, but text me if you'd like to visit the museum this week as well. Maybe we can manage a quick lunch." Thomas shrugged. "I'd appreciate the company."

"Me too." And that was that. He would too. "We cool about last night, then? All straight?"

"We're fine. I...I never thought it was about me, you know. You're a better man than that. I believe that."

"I try. I wouldn't be nasty to James's people for love or money. One day I'll tell you about the whip-crackers I met in Wyoming. Those boys were vicious in a fight."

Thomas laughed. "I look forward to that. I've tried it a few times. It requires a great deal more skill and precision than it seems."

"Yessir. I never tried, but I've seen the scars from the practice. Damn."

They ate and laughed, which was good, because their last meal no one had gotten to eat.

This promised already to be better.

Really, he should have got into a fight days ago.

12

*J*ust walking away, hm?
  Shut up, Clint.
      That had been the extent of his conversation with his friend and mentor. He'd told Clint he was taking Sam sightseeing and planned to bring the cowboy to the club for drinks after, and Clint had just given him that look.

He knew, though. He knew that embedded in those words, as always—along with taking the opportunity to bust his chops—was a commitment to support him when he needed it.

And he knew he would need it. Mother of God, would he need it.

He and Sam hadn't managed to get together for lunch because he'd been truly overrun with work commitments, but they'd been texting all week. He'd made a point of keeping it light and friendly, not mentioning James unless Sam did first. If this was going to work, if it was meant to work, they would have to develop a relationship that acknowledged their shared grief but that didn't invoke thoughts of James every time they saw each other.

It was working too. He was starting to think of the apartment as Sam's, and he'd been looking forward to seeing the man all week. Regardless of whether Sam ever was intrigued enough to walk the path Thomas wanted to share with him, he felt like he'd gained a friend.

He was lying to himself a little, he knew. You don't stress over an outfit to go sightseeing with a friend. He wanted to make an impression. That was part of the game he was playing.

He was meeting Sam at the Empire State Building at ten, which meant he'd better get going. He wasn't entirely sure what he'd be met with; he half expected Sam to show with a new black eye and one arm in a cast. He pulled on his jacket and grabbed his keys, impulsively lifting one of the hats James had given him off a hook by the door on his way out.

They'd look good together. It was about making an impression, after all.

When he wandered out toward the spot they were supposed to meet, he found Sam with two coffees, listening to God knew who talk to him. Sam looked good in what James called the redneck tuxedo. Jeans, chambray shirt starched to within an inch of its life, that huge silver buckle showing off a flat, ripped belly. The beard was neatly trimmed today, sunglasses visible under the brim of Sam's felt.

He felt a little underdressed. Ninety-nine percent of his casual wardrobe was black, but he'd worn his favorite blue jeans to go with his black Henley. At least it was nicely fitted, so he didn't look entirely out of shape next to Sam. And he knew he looked good in his hat—James used to love to see him in it.

"Hello. Is that coffee for me?" He smiled, walking up next to Sam.

"Yessir, it is." Sam grinned at him, looking him over, top to bottom. "Looking fine as frog hair. Morning. This is Mister Benny. He was telling me about Vietnam."

"Morning. And thank you. Hey, Benny. Thanks for keeping my friend company. You need a sandwich?" He pulled out his wallet and gave the guy a few dollars. "I have to borrow him now. You have a good day." He put a hand behind Sam's shoulder and steered him away.

Sam grinned at him. "Man, didn't he have some stories. How does life find you today, sir?"

"I was up early, spent an hour or so at the gym. It's a lovely sunny day, and I have been looking forward to this all week. Life's been kind today. Thank you for the coffee. You?"

"You're more than welcome. I worked some, talked to Momma on the phone, washed some clothes in the bathtub and got them to drying. Normal shit."

What? "Bathtub? There's a laundromat around the corner, you know."

"Yeah, I'm saving my pennies." Sam lifted his face to the sky, soaking in the sun. "That's nice, the sun."

Saving pennies? Was Sam that broke? Surely James had some money, managing to live without roommates. He'd never asked what James paid for rent or how much money his lover was making, but how much could a load of laundry cost?

He wouldn't know; he had a small stacked unit in his apartment.

"Come do it at my place. Your laundry."

"That's kind of you. I might come do jeans at some point, just to have both pairs clean at the same time."

Obviously, Sam needed work. His freelance earnings weren't going to cut it in New York. Sooner or later money would send him home, whether he'd accomplished what his family wanted him to or not. Thomas filed that away for thought, though he didn't know that there was anything he could actually do to help.

He knew better than to discuss it. That would just be one more blow to Sam's tenuous self-esteem. He'd start by picking up the tab more often—*that* he could do—and think about it.

"Sure. Anytime. I'm home by six most evenings, unless I'm—" *Home-home.* "At the club."

"Good deal. You get all that work off your desk?"

Sam paid attention—he liked that, the attention to detail, the care Sam took.

"I did. I have a free-and-clear weekend. Oh! And I found someone to sponsor that textile exhibit we want to bring in from DC. Can you believe it? Three weeks I've been looking. I got the call yesterday."

They headed into the lobby and straight for the ticketholder line. After the conversation he and Sam just had, he was glad he remembered it was easier to buy them ahead online.

"Not afraid of heights, I hope." He laughed, an adrenaline junkie like Sam? Not a chance.

"Not a bit. There's precious little I'm too scared to try."

"Yes. That was more or less a pointless question." He winked at Sam and handed him a ticket. "This is a great view," he said as they crowded into an elevator. They ended up packed together against a rear corner, and Thomas just shook his head. "Welcome to New York."

"Not much different than being in the chutes and prob'ly less dangerous."

God, Sam smelled good.

"Old Spice? I like it." Hm. He'd said that out loud, hadn't he? Interesting.

"Some things are eternal, I guess. Cowboys, Old Spice, horses." Sam got a distant expression that disappeared like smoke.

Too bad. It was lovely and peaceful, and he'd liked it.

He cleared his throat and tried to lean back a little, but there was no hope of putting space between them. All he managed to do was knock his hat down over his eyes. Smooth.

Sam tilted his head, looked at him over the sunglasses. "You okay?"

"Yeah. Someone has their elbow in my back," he lied. The elevator doors opened like magic at just that moment, and suddenly there was space. "This is such a great view." And there was more than the view. There was an exhibit about the building and some interactive things to do. It was a worthwhile trip.

They were exactly on time for their ticket window and were allowed right in. "Okay, I've seen all of this before, so this time I really am following your lead." He followed as Sam gravitated toward the windows, which was what he'd expected. It's what everyone did.

"I appreciate you touristing me. I'm sure it's old hat for you." Sam shook his head as he looked out, eyes searching, seeming to see everything. God, he wanted to know what was in that brain, what caused that hint of sorrow, why it dissolved into a smile, where that self-deprecating expression came from and what it meant.

"I never get tired of this view. Come around this side, you can see the park." They'd go outside in a bit, brave the wind to really feel like they were in the city and not stuck behind glass. For now, they made their way slowly around the floor, following the line of the windows.

There had to be a way to learn some of those answers

without having to meet for lunch after a fistfight. And for that matter, he needed to figure out what he could offer Sam that would make coming to him for that rush a more attractive option.

It fascinated him that Sam seemed fully aware of his needs, even more that Sam was unashamed of it, almost reveled in it openly, when his response to the club had been almost deadened.

Maybe it hadn't been the club. Maybe it had been timing. God knew he hadn't expected Sam to admit to being gay as if he'd assumed Thomas had known, as if it was a silly question.

"Hey, where are you?" Sam touched his shoulder. "Smoke's coming out of your ears."

"Hm?" *Oh, Earth to Thomas.* "Sorry. I got lost in the view." That was partly true. The rest was just what he did. When he was at work, he was working; he loved what he did. When he wasn't working, he was focused on his progress with...with his sub. He'd been taking care of one long enough now, it was habit. Sam wasn't there, might never be there, honestly, but the cowboy was the closest he had. Habit was comforting, right? Even Clint said as much.

"You want to get some air?" He grinned and pointed to the doors. "You'll want to hold on to your hat."

"Let's do it!" Little adrenaline junkie.

He laughed, looped an arm around Sam's waist and pulled him outside, slipping his own hat off his head and holding it against his chest as they stepped out into the wind.

He'd been up here on days that it was just breezy and days when the wind would literally blow him sideways. This one was somewhere in-between, the steady breeze very manageable, but the occasional gusts had him groping for a railing.

Sam, though, he moved with the wind like he wasn't even thinking about it, hips rolling to keep him steady.

Damn low center of gravity. Or something. Something that didn't want to make him watch those hips.

He'd brought quarters for the viewfinders, and as soon as one opened up, he coaxed Sam over and pumped a couple into the machine. "Have a look."

"Oh, dude! How fucking cool!"

He had to laugh because James had been so cool about the sights, so much the teacher, and Sam? Sam was drinking it in, the excitement buzzing from him.

There was insight there that Thomas filed away to think about later—the way that James took everything he knew and applied it to the world, and the way Sam opened his arms and let the world make its mark on him.

But he'd already been caught once thinking too hard, and Sam was more in the moment. He promised himself to be present for the remainder of their day.

"Can you see people? I always try, and I'm just never quite sure that's what I'm seeing."

"You have to just open your eyes wide and see the way we all move, man. Come on, try!" Sam offered him the viewfinder. "Wide-eyed. Don't try to see them and you will."

He looked at Sam. "Yeah? That easy, huh?" The viewfinder was warm where Sam had pressed his forehead against it; that was a plus. "Wide-eyed?"

"Yes, sir." One of Sam's hands landed on his lower back.

"Whoa. Wait." He wasn't seeing anything differently until that hand distracted him, made him shift his eyes a little, and suddenly all those little black lines were moving.

Weaving in and out of one another on the sidewalk. He could even make out people holding hands.

"Hey! I see them now!" He grinned; then the timer in the viewfinder made that ratcheting sound and the sight went black. "Shit."

Sam's smile was bright enough to rival the sun. "Rock on."

"They were moving around each other, going this way and that way, going in and out of storefronts. Very cool, Mister Wide Eyes."

A gust of wind got him from behind and lifted him off his heels. He reached for the viewfinder and missed it, stepping forward to catch himself. Sam grabbed him, caught him like he weighed nothing, and settled him back on his feet.

"I got you, honey. You're okay."

"Thanks." He rolled his eyes at himself and laughed at the irony. "I'm usually the one saying that."

"I worked safety a lot. I know how to make a catch."

"Of course you did. High risk, high adrenaline. I've got my eye on you now, Sam." He winked. "There's more fun to be had in this city. Should we finish our tour through here, then have it?"

"I'm at your disposal. Let's play."

He liked that thought, and he was hoping to keep Sam in that mind-set.

They spent a little more time touring the exhibit upstairs, before they took the far less crowded elevator down to the main lobby. He fished out his sunglasses as they left the building. "Okay. Pick a museum. The Guggenheim... or Ripley's."

"Ripley's. No question. I want to play with you. We'll go

be serious art historians another day." God, that was breathtakingly charming.

"Perfect. My friends are too stuck-up for Ripley's. I've never been." It was a silly tourist trap, but he was utterly fascinated by the concept. The one time he'd suggested it might be fun to his museum circle, everyone laughed and thought he was kidding. He wasn't, but he certainly never brought it up again. "It's a walk, but not a long one. Are you all right with that? Or we can take a cab."

"I'm completely able to walk. I am fueled by caffeine and adrenaline. Let's do this."

"Adrenaline? Please tell me you didn't get into another fight." He angled his head to look under the brim of Sam's hat as they walked. "I don't see a black eye."

"Not today. My ribs aren't ready for another go-round."

"Yet. Right?" He grinned and bumped into Sam's shoulder lightly. He had a suspicion he was just going to have to accept this part of Sam for a while.

Or keep accidentally poking him in his fractured rib. *Oops. Looks like you're out for at least another week. I'm so sorry.* He chuckled, possibly out loud.

"Yeah, yeah. I got invited back. They have a 'beat the fuck out of your friends' day. Like it's on a calendar. Rednecks are less about the plan and more about the moment."

He just shook his head. Maybe he should suggest that at the club. A "whip your friends" day? "Cuff and suck your friends off" day? "The planned aspect seems a bit artificial. Seems like a good fight should be more spontaneous. Not that I'd know. I don't hit with my fists."

"Right? Wait. Really? Never? Like not ever?" Sam looked honestly shocked.

"Not unless you count a bag at the gym, no. Flat, open

hand, certainly. Fists? No, I've never hit another person with my fist." Every single one of his brothers except William, who was nine years younger, had thrown punches at him. His older brothers, Terence and Peter, had knocked him out at least once each. He just hadn't ever hit back.

"Huh. That's different. Not bad. Kinda cool, in fact, because you can tell you're not scared to stand up for yourself. I can't remember my first, or how many times I've fought."

"You'd be surprised how much power there is in choosing not to fight. How many people are intimidated by confidence. I'm not judging, mind you. I just think we all have to find and use our strengths as we understand them."

The streets grew more and more crowded as they walked toward Midtown and Times Square. Corners were four and five people deep waiting to cross; here and there he and Sam had to walk single file.

Sam followed along. Every so often he thought he heard Sam humming to himself, but he wasn't sure.

They spent an hour or so staring at crazy exhibits, getting dizzy to the point of feeling sick in the black hole, and giggling like drunken frat boys. They left the circus that was Ripley's Believe it Or Not, and Thomas was laughing so hard his sides hurt, and they hadn't gotten half a block away before his stomach rumbled so loud it startled them both.

"Guess I'm hungry. Are you hungry?"

"Lord yes. I could eat a moose." Sam was pink-cheeked from laughter, happy relaxation written all over the man.

"Excellent." He took Sam's arm and led him across the street to a vendor cart and bought two foot-long hot dogs. "Do you want anything on it? There's sauerkraut, chili, cheese, onions, relish, ketchup, mustard...?" He got a little chili and some cheese on his.

"Mustard is good for me. Look at that monster. That's a mouthful."

"I can handle it." He grinned and put mustard on Sam's hot dog for him. "Come on, I know some great seats."

He led Sam across the street to Duffy Square. "They call these the red steps. I suppose because...they're red." He snorted.

"The logic works for me. I would have concerns if y'all called them the red steps and they were blue."

"You never know in New York." They climbed the steps as the sun was going down and Broadway was starting to light up as bright as the day and found a spot to sit near the top. "You haven't been to Times Square yet either? At night? Watch it light up."

"Nope." Sam was wide-eyed, all grins. "What a good day, huh? I've been having a blast."

"It has been good, hasn't it? Just goofing off and having fun? You're terrific company." It wasn't bullshit either. Sam threw himself into everything—silly, goofy, ridiculous, wild. It was refreshing as hell.

It reminded him that he hadn't been born with this rod up his ass.

"I was hoping after our hot dogs, and once you've had your fill of the lights, that you might...would you like to join me at the club? Saturday nights are their own sort of adventure."

"Really? I thought I'd...well, I thought I'd sorta fucked up bad, especially with you."

"You can't fuck up if you're being honest. Your reaction to those men was absolutely your truth." He looked at Sam. "I wouldn't ever ask more of you than that."

"Thanks. I'm trying to figure shit out. This is...new." Sam snorted, rolled his eyes dramatically. "And if that wasn't the understatement of the year, I don't know what was."

"Sam, you have a lot to sort through. I've been listening. I want to help. New is just another adventure, right?"

He wasn't sure what was more complicated, understanding Sam or knowing what the hell to do about him.

"Yeah. Yeah, I think we've figured a couple things about each other. You're a good man. A little weird, but good." Oh, look at that evil grin.

"I am. I'm a little weird. Are you good?" He dropped his voice low, grinning back. "Are you a very, very good boy?"

"Fuck, no. I'm a shithead; just ask me, I'll tell you." Sam hooted, but there was a flash of energy, a hum.

He laughed. God, he hadn't laughed so much in one day in...he honestly couldn't remember. He looked around. It was past dark now, though you'd hardly know it. "Would you like to head for the club?"

"Why not? I can't do worse than last time." Sheepish. That was the look.

He stood and offered Sam a hand up. "Well, let's see. You didn't tell anyone off, you didn't get drunk, and you didn't throw any punches. I think you did pretty damn well."

"Thanks. I like to think I can act like I was raised right, given the opportunity."

"I was impressed."

The club was walking distance from the square, and Thomas enjoyed the trip. He and Sam walked close together. Though whether that was because it had gotten cool out or more because they had grown comfortable with each other's presence, it was hard to tell. Whatever it was, he liked it.

"Looks like we made it." He reached for the door handle.

"Yeah. Come on. I'm sure not gonna get less nervous standing here like a moron."

"It won't change the way you're feeling in this moment, I know, but there's no need to be nervous." He took Sam firmly by the hand. "Does this make it better or worse?"

Sam's fingers wrapped around his, holding on. "Is it bad if I say better? No one ever touches anyone here."

He took a deep breath. That was it. Even if all Sam could manage was to walk into the club and walk out again, it wouldn't matter because he'd just earned his gift. He squared his shoulders, and he felt his chest expand a little. "It's very good, Sam. Really good. It doesn't matter what everyone else does, only what we do."

They went into the busy club together. The music was louder than it had been the other day, though not so loud you couldn't have a conversation over it. There were men dancing in club lighting, and the bar had a man on nearly every stool.

"Welcome, Sir!" Scotty called from behind the bar. "Hey, Sam! Good to see you again."

"Howdy. Pleased." Sam tipped his hat. "How goes it, Mister Scott?"

Thomas kept a firm hold of Sam's hand, partly for Sam, and he'd be lying if he didn't admit it was also partly for show. This part of the club was often about the show.

"Stellar, my friend. Are you drinking?"

Thomas spoke for both of them. "No, thank you. Just two bottles of water, please."

Scotty handed them both to Sam.

"What do I owe you, sir?" Sam asked.

"Nothing, Sam. Enjoy your night."

He let Sam figure out how to balance two bottles of water in one hand, and led him slowly along the bar. He'd reserved the room four days ago to make sure there would be something available for them. He knew it would be open and the key in it for him.

"Do you dance, Sam?"

"I can two-step and waltz, polish belt-buckles. Never with another guy. I mean, how do you work out who leads? Is it always the taller feller?" It fascinated him, how Sam's accent deepened when he was nervous. It was a lovely tell.

He reminded himself to ask, flat-out, why Sam was nervous. It seemed like the man sometimes did better with a straight-up question than a casual conversation.

"Not necessarily. It can be a negotiation." He grinned and kept moving, leading Sam toward the long private hall. "I love dancing. I'll take you out on the dance floor sometime. It'll be fun."

Inside he was chuckling, knowing that if they did head for the floor, there wouldn't be any negotiation about who was leading. He wondered, amused, how Sam would manage following.

"They have after-parties sometimes, after the big events. There's dancing then; the fans love it." Oh, Sam followed him like a dream, at least right now. "So where are we heading?"

He'd hoped not to have to answer that question directly, but their room was way down at the quiet end of the corridor and not answering would just make Sam more nervous. *Keep it simple and straightforward*, he reminded himself.

"I reserved a private room for us to use for a while. I know you're curious. I thought you might enjoy a very small taste of all of this."

Sam shot him a look but nodded and stayed with him,

still holding his hand. "I'm not sure I'm supposed to be, but I'd be lying if I said I wasn't, yeah."

He smiled outwardly this time; he couldn't help it. "You will learn over time that there are no expectations here beyond the ones we set for ourselves. There is no 'supposed to be.' There's no way to absorb it all at once. You just have to follow your natural inclinations, pay attention to your desires."

He stopped by the door and turned around, backed into the room and pulled Sam with him. "And most importantly, remember you're safe."

Sam's head tilted sharply, and he got a frown. "That's the sort of thing someone says before he knocks you out with a tire iron."

He laughed and let go of Sam's hand, leaving Sam in the doorway and walking farther into the room. "If you truly believe I have any intention of injuring you in any fashion whatsoever, I am not standing between you and the door, Sam."

"No. No, man. I just...you know how it is when someone tells you it won't hurt and you're going...wait." Sam snorted, visibly shaking off whatever demon he had before following him in, then handed him a water. "I trust you, man, as much as I trust anyone."

"Thank you. I thought so, but I am relieved to hear you say it expressly. What I have in mind is meant to be... enlightening. A new experience. Something to think about." He walked toward the door and turned the lock, making sure Sam saw him do it. "That's so we don't get interrupted, not so you can't get out. You understand?"

"Sure. I get it." Sam patted his front pocket, then shook his head. "I been quit for two years, and sometimes still I want a drag when I'm...I guess that's why they call it addiction."

"Anxious? Nervous?" The walls in the room were painted black. There was a single black chair in one corner and a small credenza along one wall. Otherwise the room was empty but for soft, indirect overhead lighting. He crossed slowly to the chair and sat down. "Is that right? What exactly is making you feel that way?"

"Who the fuck knows, honey?" That wall of bravado popped up like a switch had been thrown. Sam leaned against the wall, refusing to look away from him.

Well, he'd gotten as far as locking the door. "It doesn't bother you that you don't know? Or do you know, but you just don't want to share it with me?"

"You got this habit of asking questions I don't know the right answers to."

"Ah. And you have a tendency to assume that there is a right or wrong answer to the things that I ask you. I have no expectations when I ask you something, Sam. I don't like tests. I won't ever put one before you."

"Sometimes I think everything's a test. Don't you?" Sam took a deep breath, watching him from under the brim of his hat. "It's just fucked up, sorting through all this shit."

He'd had a slightly different plan, but Sam volunteered so little that he didn't want to stop the man talking. Not that Sam had actually said anything yet, other than answering questions with questions and diverting the conversation. Sam had impressive skills in that arena.

He could follow a runaway train. "Sorting through all what shit?"

Sam waved one hand, the motion dismissing—not him, he imagined, but Sam's own emotions. "I...I told you the day after I was here last. I don't do so good with working out all the worries in my head. I don't know that's a strange thing. It's part of being a guy."

Ah. Who knew? "Oh. Is it? I wasn't aware of that. I appreciate you filling me in." He leaned back in the chair and crossed one leg over the other. "In that cabinet in front of you are three objects. Open it up and pick the one that interests you the most. This isn't a test. I'm passing no judgment, nor am I drawing any conclusions from your decision."

Hopefully the staff had done as he'd asked. If Sam decided to open the doors, which Thomas wasn't counting on, he'd be choosing between a soft leather blindfold, a pair of sturdy fur-lined cuffs with a short chain between them, and a dense, stiff feather.

"First, it sure sounds like a test. Before I open anything, though, I got to say I don't appreciate your tone. I'm not making fun of you or how you are. You don't get to be snarky to me because you don't like something about me. No one made you ask me to come here with you."

How I am?

He wasn't offended. It took a great deal more than that to actually insult him, and he was, by training and instinct, a very good judge of intent.

But the use of judgmental language was insight into Sam's feelings about what and who he believed himself to be.

"I asked you to come here with me because I wanted to spend the evening with you. You're uncomfortable with talking, so I thought perhaps I would move past words and discussion. What you will see in that cabinet are three of my favorite tools. I don't care which one you pick—assuming you even decide to look, which is also your own decision—and if you are uncomfortable with choosing, I will happily choose for you."

Keeping his tone even and his voice low, he leaned forward in his chair.

"It's not a test. As I told you, I don't care for tests. They cause anxiety and feelings of inadequacy, when the goal is always confidence and a quiet heart. I don't know how you'd like me to prove my intentions except to remind you that you told me that you trust me."

"I bet your professors wanted to beat you sometimes. You know you come in here and you're different?" Sam pushed himself off the wall and walked over to the cupboard and opened it.

"I do." He had no intention of elaborating on that at the moment.

"Huh." Sam didn't so much as touch the feather, but the cuffs were picked up, explored, rejected; then the blindfold was carefully researched and brought over to him, placed in his hands. "Here you go."

Sam went to stand against the wall, and Thomas had to admit, the man could work that hat, hiding his face in shadow like a champion.

Okay. So the hat was a crutch now. Time for it to go.

Thomas flipped the blindfold over in his fingers like he was thinking hard about it, which he wasn't in the least. He knew precisely what his plans were. Finally he stood, removed his own hat, and hung it on a set of hooks on the wall.

"Might I respectfully request that you remove your..." *What did James always call it?* "Your cover? It will be difficult to work with the blindfold otherwise."

Sam's fingers clenched into fists, then relaxed. "I'm

putting a lot of faith in the belief you won't screw with me, man."

Oh for the love of Pete.

"I'm going to ask you to stand in the center of the room and instruct you that you need only say stop and I'll take it off. Also, you will understand that I have no intention of stopping you should you decide to remove it yourself. Then I'm going to put it over your eyes and ask you to stay still and quiet, or, if you prefer, you can tie it on yourself. We'll have to work through together whatever comes up after that. That's the plan. I care about you. I want you to succeed. I want you to have a good experience. I have no reason or desire to 'screw with you.'"

"Right." Sam carefully hung up his hat before moving to the center of the room and standing there, calm as a cloudless sky.

Maybe he should have shut his mouth and let Sam go on faith. He could try that next time. Sam's reaction might as well be a coin flip anyway.

"I want you to like it here, Sam. I want it to become your second home, as it is mine. I accept that might not be in your stars, but as long as you're curious and interested, I'm happy to have you here and teach you anything you like. Perhaps it will help you to know that I am not unaccountable. Members look out for each other, for the subs, the staff. Any one of those people will have your back if you walk out of this room and tell them I'm not to be trusted, regardless of my history here. You have that power."

He held out the blindfold. "Do you want to do this yourself?"

"I can't."

"What?"

One of Sam's eyebrows went up, his lips quirked; then he

lifted his arms—the left went up, the right got to shoulder height and stopped short. "Two rotator cuff surgeries in three months."

Oh. Damn. They were going to have to have a very serious conversation about physical limitations before they got into anything involving restraints. Good thing the St. Andrew's Cross wasn't high on his list of favorite apparatus. There were adaptive possibilities if it turned out to be something Sam needed, but...

Whoa, Tiger. Cart. Horse.

Blindfold.

"Allow me." He stayed in front of Sam and held it up just below eye level. "Sometimes we find the most unlikely things to be stressful. It's not a failure. It's never a failure. There's no right or wrong in truth."

Thomas reached around Sam and tied the narrow blindfold in place, then slid hands over Sam's shoulders, feeling the difference between the two, down his arms, and took hold of both of his hands.

Sam's nostrils flared, the look oddly like a fractious horse, and the urge to comfort Sam was huge, but he didn't pull away or move at all.

The exercise now was to stay quiet, make sure Sam knew he was there, and wait this out. Sam already told him still and quiet wasn't easy, and he understood why, given the barrage of thoughts and emotions the man was dealing with. He gave both hands a light squeeze but otherwise offered Sam little but the sound of his own breathing.

Sam's thumbs began to move, just the barest bit, and Thomas realized Sam had found the bass of the music, had latched on to that.

Okay. So that wasn't pushing a boundary, but maybe... Thomas pulled his hands away.

Sam swayed a bit but held his balance. One eyebrow went up, the question clear, before Sam rested his hands on his hips.

Thomas watched Sam carefully and started pacing a slow rhythm, making sure his steps were audible. He measured the rise and fall of Sam's chest, the set of Sam's shoulders, the tension in the man's fingers.

And he just kept pacing.

"What exactly do you want, man?" Sam's thumbs were pressing so hard into his waist that there were going to be deep bruises.

"Shhh." Thomas hushed him gently, as if soothing a fussing child. "Just quiet. I'm right here. I won't leave the room. You won't be alone at any point."

Sam pursed his lips, and the muscle in that angular jaw began to twitch.

He hadn't bothered to discuss safe words with Sam because he knew damn well Sam wouldn't use it if he had one. Not yet. Just as he knew that what Sam was enduring at this moment might seem to be about not disappointing him, but was likely more about Sam trying to prove something to himself.

Regardless, this was an exercise in trust, not in pushing beyond any real boundaries, so Thomas stepped up behind him and covered Sam's hands with his own. "I'm right here."

Sam leaned into Thomas, sighing softly as they connected, the sound unbearably satisfied.

The head rush was real. The ache in his chest so familiar. The pounding of his heart was a victory.

It was time to return the boy to him.

He spoke evenly and softly, just a couple of inches from Sam's ear.

"When I say you're safe, it's a promise. When I tell you

you're not alone, you can count on that. I will never lie to you. I have no expectations other than you be as truthful as you know how to be. There is no wrong."

Sam sucked in a deep breath. "I appreciate that. This ain't easy."

"No, it's not." He slid his hands together on Sam's lower back and let them glide up and over Sam's shoulders again. "Are you ready for me to remove this? Or do you need more time?"

"Let's take it off. I got to move."

"Of course. Keep your eyes closed; open them when they seem more used to the lighting." He untied the blindfold and tossed it on the cabinet, not wanting to break physical contact until Sam was ready. "Move whenever you like."

"You give damn good...hugs, I guess? But I'm hurting." Sam grunted as he stepped away. He dropped down into a low squat, hands on the floor, curling his upper body over his thighs. Thomas could hear the creak, the snaps of Sam's spine popping as he rocked on the toes of his boots.

He reached for their waters and handed one to Sam. He wasn't sure how much of that stiffness was from standing still and how much was from the clearly visible tension Sam had been contending with, but he made a note for next time to work in a conversation about it.

"You did extremely well, b...Sam."

"I never been praised for standing still, but thank you." Sam laughed, but it didn't sound raw, ugly. The chuckle was warm.

He let himself laugh along but rested a hand on Sam's shoulder. "You and I both know you were doing more than standing still. Thank you for your trust. Your homework is to think about what you experienced just now and how you feel now that we're finished." He grinned. "If there's enough room for one more thing to think about."

"You know me—there's nothing going on up here."

Right. Sam's brain was in fifth gear, constantly.

"Perfect. Then your answers should be clear." This was going to work; he was sure of it. Sam had responded on an instinctual level more than a conscious one, proving the boy was receptive. None of it would be easy, but the reward potential was high.

"How about a beer?"

"Sounds great." Sam stood up, nodded to him. "I could use one."

"Me too." He pulled their hats off the wall and handed Sam's over with a grin. "You're exhausting."

"I'm a cowboy. No one promised easy." Sam popped his hat on, hiding his face. "Come on, it's beer thirty."

13

"Have you done anything? You haven't sent home his things. You haven't..."

Sam closed his eyes and forced himself not to sigh. "I am in the detectives' pockets daily, Momma. I'm trying. Colletti's going to shoot me in the face if I don't stop calling."

"Then come home. You're not doing anything but spending money. We can use you here. Working."

He shook his head. No. No, he didn't want to.

God. Fuck. Did he just think that? Really?

"I'm going to cut you off, kiddo. I am not going to support you going to New York and just fucking off for months. I'm not Sally Fincher. I will not let you become some lazy shit that pretends to be depressed or some shit while—"

"Momma!" *Jesus.* "You sent me here!"

"And I'm calling you back. You have two weeks. Come home. Make yourself useful. I bet you can get a job teaching at the high school. Maybe the middle school."

"I'll talk to you later, Momma. I got another call. Love you. Bye."

He hung up and panted, standing still for a long minute before sinking his fist into the wall, the pain shooting up his arm. "Goddammit!"

What was wrong with him?

What the fuck was wrong with him? He was a cowboy. He belonged in Texas. His family needed him.

But...he wasn't ready to go.

What was he thinking?

Shit, he...he...

He tried to tug his hand out of the wall, and it was stuck tight. *Fuck.*

He assumed it was Momma calling back when his phone rang again and was about to toss the damn thing across the living room, when he got a quick look at the screen.

Not Momma. He didn't want to ignore Thomas's call, but what the hell was he going to say? *Hey, man. Hand's stuck in the wall. Any ideas?*

Okay. Okay, cowboy up.

"Hey, man." Jesus, he sounded like he was jacking off.

Who knew that stuck in a wall and pulling the pud had the same sound?

"Good morning. I hope I'm not interrupting anything."

Was that...did Thomas think he was...? Or was that just an overly polite hello? Who the hell could tell with this guy?

"No. Just dealing with...shit. How's it going?" He tugged, hissing as something tore at his skin, the bones shifting dangerously.

Motherfucker! God hated him. Seriously. God and James up there with his Granny Ellen laughing their ass off on their fluffy clouds.

"Are you okay? Did you get in another fight last night?"

"No! And no." He sighed, feeling like the worst kind of

dipshit. "I'm—"*in desperate need of a friend* "—stuck in a wall. No worries."

"I'm sorry, one more time? I think you broke up there for a second. It sounded like you said you were stuck in a wall." Thomas laughed.

"Did it? Damn. What are you up to today?" He pushed in deeper, trying dislodge more of the crap encasing his fist. When he came back in another life, he was going to be a temperless orphan without the ability to feel pain.

"I was calling to see if you felt like brunch, and maybe a quick trip to the ER—what the fuck is going on over there?"

"Brunch sounds amazing. French toast?" *Huh. Blood. Whoa.* He hoped that didn't draw bugs. Hell, he hoped it didn't make the walls stink. Thank God the cops had already squirted that glow-in-the-dark blood stuff in here, because damn.

"I'm putting you on speaker and ordering an Uber. How bad was it? Did they break anything? They didn't get your head, did they? Didn't we talk about this?"

"Thomas, honey. One, we didn't, no, and two, I didn't get into a fight. I swear to God. Nobody hit me. My fucking hand is stuck in the wall." He sighed and rolled his eyes. "Let me put the phone down a second, huh?"

He set the phone on the floor, put his free hand flat on the wall, and yanked, roaring as the world went sparkly and he hit his knees.

Dude. Okay. He was out.

Sam grabbed his phone, carefully not looking at his hand. "So, do I got time for a shower?"

"Call 9-1-1 first?"

"I got some peroxide in the bathroom, honey." He sat there and breathed. "I'm glad to hear from you."

"I'm looking forward to seeing you. In about twenty minutes. Try some duct tape while you're at it."

Thomas hung up the phone.

"No, dork. It's superglue. Duct tape just pulls the ripped skin off," he told the empty line.

Lord, how did the man survive on his own?

He got himself showered and glued up, dancing around like a howler monkey at the sting. "Fuck! Fuck me, that burns!"

God, he hoped the glue dried before he wrapped up his hand, because...yeah. *Fuck. Also, whoa. And ow.*

Sausage fingers and sticky bandages did not good bedfellows make.

He must have been at it longer than he thought, because suddenly Thomas was texting him. *I'm here. I remembered not to try the buzzer.*

Yeah, that thing was on the fritz. Also known as the floor.

I'm naked. Gimme 5.

La la la. Jeans. T-shirt because no buttons, and...

"Ah fuck."

Boots.

God hated him.

You do know it's forty degrees out here, right?

"Fuck." He hopped around, trying to get his boot on. He was going to freeze to death. He hadn't brought a coat, and he sure as shit couldn't buy one now. He dialed Thomas as he got boot two on. "Hey. It going to stress you out if I get one of James's coats? Be real with me."

He overbalanced and landed on the sofa. *Oof.*

"Oh." There was a bit of a pause, and Thomas cleared his throat. "No, that's fine."

Ah. Okay. Fair enough. He probably wouldn't be able to do it anyway. "On my way down."

He wasn't a delicate flower, after all. A little chilly wouldn't hurt anyone. He looked down at his wrist with a sheepish grin and shook his head. *Lord have mercy.*

He greeted Thomas with a smile. "Hey. How's your morning going?"

Thomas looked him over before answering, not saying anything about the coat, but pointing to his wrist. "Better than yours, it appears."

"Yeah. Not my smartest move ever." He rolled his eyes and sighed at himself. "Sometimes my temper is a thing."

"Would you like to talk about whatever set you off?" Thomas shrugged out of his jacket and handed it to him. "I've got a sweater."

His cheeks got fiery, but he accepted the jacket with a grateful nod. "Thanks, man. Seriously."

This cold was already making shit throb.

Thomas helped him get it on with his shoulder and his wrist and they started walking.

"My momma's...you know how it is. Your folks can make you so damn mad, but you can't be ugly, and it's like a pressure cooker in your head."

"I do. My mother asks me questions she doesn't want to know the answers to and gets upset when I answer them. Parents can be difficult. Do we need to pick up something to patch the drywall after brunch, or were you thinking about installing a laundry chute?"

Sam cracked up, just tickled shitless. "I'm opening up a vortex into the fuck-you're-an-idiot dimension."

"Oh, I've been there. The nachos are out of this world." Oh, Sam was proud of Thomas's straight face.

"Mmm...nachos..." He shook his head at Thomas and let

himself laugh, let the bullshit dissipate, the sudden lack of tension making him a little dizzy.

"We're getting quick with this walk." Thomas held the door to the café open for him. "Oh, yes. Coffee."

"Thank you, sir." He inhaled, filling his lungs with all the good smells. "Oh, hell yeah."

This time the hostess gave him a hug too when she seated them.

"Either you've been coming here without me, or it's that damn hat."

"Honey, I can work the hat." He dipped his head, tilted his chin, and winked.

"You like that hat. You use it well." Thomas looked at him...no, Thomas was watching him. Thomas didn't just look, not at anybody. The man went for details.

He shrugged but nodded. Everybody needed their armor. Even Thomas. "I can't remember not having a hat or a cap or something. It's part of me."

"It hides your eyes nicely, makes it hard to read your expression. What are you having? My treat."

"Really?"

Thomas didn't look stressed, just dipped his chin, and Sam took the kindness.

"I'll get the next one, then. I'm craving french toast. I keep saying I'll try something else, and I keep wanting what I want."

Thomas looked up from his menu, closing it. "I know exactly how you feel."

He nodded, leaning back into the booth, watching Thomas. It was the strangest thing—the Different Faces of Thomas. There was the laughing goofy man and the almost grumpy man of many words. There was the kind man who didn't make him ashamed of—*what he needed*—stuff.

Every so often he had to wonder if he was boring as hell. He didn't have faces. He had one face. Hidden-under-the-hat face.

Thomas ordered for them both, again, and they got their coffee. "So, did Colletti call you this morning?"

"Threatened to shoot me in the face if I didn't back off. Charming little guy. Seriously. I adore him."

"Mm. Yes, you've struck a nerve with his team for sure." Thomas took a sip of his coffee and set it down on the table, staring into it and tapping one finger on the rim. "They're moving into a...a new phase of the investigation."

A new phase. The part where they say the asshole couldn't be caught and they had other cases and other places to spend their energy. The part where James becomes a bunch of pictures and a bloody T-shirt in a box.

They must have called Momma. *Shit.* Momma and Thomas. Then he tells Momma he wants to stay and asks Thomas if it would bother him if he wore James's coat. *Rock on.*

He was batting a thousand and it wasn't noon yet.

God, he didn't know what to do, how to make anything better. Not true, because he could go home and help with Daddy and all. He didn't want to, though. *Christ.*

Sam closed his hand, letting the agony wash him clean for a single, raw second. *Answer Thomas, man. Engage.*

"Are they?"

"He said the department...he assured me that it was still active, but since there really hasn't been any movement in all this time, they have to devote fewer resources to James's case. They don't have anything solid to investigate. He also apologized that they've been unable to clear me completely because I don't have an alibi. That's amusing. I'm an active person of interest in a murder investigation. Never thought I'd say that."

"I'm way more likely to commit a murder than you are." Of course he'd never really considered that Thomas was James's killer. Was that stupid of him? Probably. But there hadn't been a whole lot he'd done that wasn't stupid, so he'd just stick with it. Thomas missed James like a lost tooth. He could see it. If he could give James back somehow, he'd do it, in a heartbeat, but...if frogs had wings, they wouldn't bust their slimy butts. "I'm sorry, man."

He was too. He didn't know how to find a killer. He didn't know how to make someone pay for this mess.

Thomas reached across the table and touched his arm. "I'm feeling all kinds of things right now. I can't say for sure that murderous isn't one of them." Thomas tried to smile for him. "Ravenous is definitely high on the list, though."

"Well, that part can get fixed up, easy as pie."

He tamped all the bubbles of acid down and promised himself that tonight he could go back to Mike's Tavern and vent his spleen on someone's face. Right now he was going to be here for James's lover, and if the thought *James's lover* stung like a bitch, well, that was idiot tax.

"Easy as french toast." That grin seemed a lot more like the man he knew. "If you don't have plans today, I'd love to take up your time."

How could he say no? Especially when he didn't want to. "I got nothing on my schedule that I know of."

Thomas exhaled like the man had been holding his breath all morning, shoulders relaxing a little. "Great. Thank you." Thomas nodded and picked up his coffee again. "Thanks."

"My pleasure." Lord love a duck, let this have been the hard part of the day. Let it get easier from here.

"Can we talk a little about your...well, about your body for a minute?" Thomas looked a little more serious than the question seemed to warrant.

"Um...okay?" That was a new one. "I mean, sure, I guess. What exactly do you want to know?"

"Well, I understand what's going on with your shoulder, and I know now that I shouldn't ask you to stand on your feet for very long without moving around. I'm curious about your other physical limitations."

"You mean my leg, huh?" He chuckled. "Lord, that was a stone-cold bitch. I wanted to die for a second when that mare landed on me. I've had a lot of injuries, but that one was the big wreck."

"The big wreck? Tell me what happened." Thomas was watching him again.

"Lord have mercy. I was riding J87, and I'd done my eight. Hank Waters was riding safety, and he reached for me, and the horses hit wrong. I went down, and she caught me —once in the back and on my left thigh. I went rolling and tangled under Hank's gelding, or so the story goes. I sure was scattered by then. They say I stood up to run and the whole thigh collapsed. I got a steel bar now and a hoof print above my kidney."

Thomas nodded slowly, looking thoughtful. "Okay."

"You can't tell through my jeans or nothing, and I covered all the scars with ink." He didn't think it was ugly. Hell, he was sorta proud of his scars. He'd earned every one, from his roper scar under his bottom lip to the burn mark above his nipple where him and James had been lighting cotton balls on fire with rubbing alcohol and throwing them at each other and he'd had one that decided to stick.

"Oh, scars don't bother me, even nasty ones. That won't

be a pro—" Thomas blinked at him, eyes suddenly focusing. "Sorry. I was working something out and...let me back up."

Thomas shifted in his chair. "That is an insane story. You're lucky to be alive. Can I take you to the club later so you can show me your ink?"

"Sure. It's fine work. Took days." Undertaker had been a fascinating dude too. Listened to Patsy Cline and Rob Zombie in equal amounts.

"I look forward to seeing it. I should have asked before I asked you to stand still for so long that first time. I apologize. I'll be more conscientious in the future. What else should I know? Balance issues? Chronic pain? Further injuries?"

"Balance I got, in spades. No stress, man. It ain't no thing." He grinned and shrugged. "Hurting's a part of rodeoing. I've broke so many bones, I can't tell you."

Thomas chuckled. "I'm no stranger to broken bones myself, and I have a few memorable scars, but I am quite sure that your scars and your stories are bigger and better than mine."

Their giant plates of french toast arrived along with a beautiful plate of bacon.

"Oh, this will improve my state of mind."

"Looks good, hmm?" He pondered whether his smart hand would hold a fork. He sorta doubted it. Really, he needed to learn to punch with his right hand.

Thomas cut everything on his own plate into bite-sized pieces, then without a word, traded plates with Sam. "Are you interested in seeing a movie this afternoon?"

"I haven't gone to a theater in about a million years. I'm all in." He offered Thomas a grateful smile, a dip of the head. The man was good to him, even when he was stupid.

He got a wink in return. "Perfect. I think we both could

use a distraction, don't you?" Thomas took a bite of his breakfast, obviously enjoying it. "Mmm."

"Totally." Because up 'til a few minutes ago, the day had sucked, and it wouldn't take a lot of thinking for it to start sucking again. He poured his syrup and started eating. *Hell, yeah.*

14

"I think in my next life, I want to come back as a stunt car driver." Thomas hustled Sam through the movie crowd, steering him out a side door.

"Yeah? You could just do it now. Do they have classes, do you think?" That might be fun. He could handle that.

Thomas laughed. "I'm too old for that now. I'd have to at least be badass first and care less about the speed limit."

"How old are you? James didn't tell me anything beyond 'hot boyfriend.' "

That earned him a real laugh. A big one. Enough that Thomas had to get out of people's way on the sidewalk. "He hadn't had a lot of them before he met me, clearly. I'm thirty-one."

"A few." More than him, for sure. "And that's not old. Bowie's older." Not by much, but older. "When's your birthday?"

"The twenty-third of April. You have the same birthday as James, and you're...twenty...eight? Seven? I forget what he told me."

"I'm twenty-six this January. James will...would have

been thirty. Bowie's gonna be thirty-three." He was the baby. Forever. James and him had talked about going to Vegas in January, staying in one of the huge casinos and causing trouble, stripping out of his teacher uniform and being one of them. For all that he'd left home, James's body was still built for Wranglers.

Sam had to wonder how Thomas would cowboy up. He'd looked right in the hat, after all. He could imagine him in Wranglers, a pair of chaps and all.

He stopped himself, because Jesus. This was James's man. Thomas was good to him, more than decent, but he had to remember, if he hadn't been James's kin, no one would have given him the time of day. *Do not be skeevy, Sam Houston O'Reilly. Do not perv on this man that's mourning your brother. That is a direct line to hell.*

"Young. I liked twenty-six. I was finishing grad school, I was making decisions for myself, I had a plan for my future. It was a good year, an optimistic year."

He didn't feel young. He hadn't felt young for a long time. Then again, he didn't have a plan, so...

They continued on their hike up to Midtown. They walked everywhere when they were together. Thomas liked the fresh air—they both did—and they were never in a hurry. And as long as they were moving, he wasn't that cold.

His hand throbbed idly, and he worked to keep anyone from bumping into it too terrible hard. It was like a weird game he played with himself as they wandered.

Thomas reached down and grabbed hold of his right hand at a crosswalk, tugging him across the street before the light changed, and didn't let go once they hit the sidewalk again.

It was the oddest feeling, to be holding another man's hand in public, like it was normal, okay.

"You know what I've been wanting to ask you? How are you feeling about the city these days? Still disoriented? Is it better? Do you feel like you're getting around well enough?"

"I do okay, I think. I don't feel scared to leave the apartment or anything." Hell, he knew how to find stores, find what he needed for the most part.

"Are you feeling less lonely? Are you starting to feel like you fit in at all?"

He wasn't sure how he wanted to answer that. He missed having people everywhere that knew him, but he was beginning to understand where he fit in, and he obviously didn't want to go home. He didn't want Thomas to think he was some tittybaby either, but he worried that the best friend he'd made might just be looking for a reason to leave. Then again, what if Thomas was? He wasn't a coward; he wasn't a shit. "There's some good folks, genuinely kind people."

"More than it seems at first, right? The longer you stay, the more you'll get to know people who are on your same routine, you know? The guy at your corner bagel place, the neighbor you run into on the way out the door every morning, someone who sits in the same section of your favorite coffee place. It's weird. People are looking for connections."

"We are, all of us. We need each other." He looked down at the sidewalk as they walked. "My mom is trying to call me home, now that things are cooling off with the police." He took a hard breath. He wasn't going.

He didn't want to.

God, he was a selfish motherfucker.

"Oh?"

What did that mean? Oh, it's about time? Oh, are you really going? What kind of answer was "Oh?"

He grinned at himself. It was an answer he'd give.

"I feel bad, but I'm not going back. I don't want to." He firmed his jaw. He knew he was a bad son, but...

Thomas glanced at him. "No? Why not?"

He shook his head. He had a thousand reasons, and all of them were selfish and awful sounding. "I don't know what to say that makes good sense."

Thomas snorted. "I didn't ask you to make sense. I just asked for your reasons. Someday you'll believe me when I say I'm not judging you. I feel like a broken record."

"*I'm* judging me, man." He wanted to be a better man than he was.

"You do that a lot. Would it help to know that I am glad you're staying? I think you should. I want you to stay." Thomas gave his hand a squeeze.

"Yeah. It does. Thank you." He took a deep, shaky breath. "She's really pissed. I hate hurting her." But not enough not to do it.

"She's probably more sad than pissed. Give her some time. I bet she thought you'd never leave home." They took the corner and headed toward the club, about halfway up the block.

"Yeah. No one did." He wasn't supposed to. He was supposed to stay in Emory and have babies and run the ranch and die there.

"Look forward, not back."

At this point, Thomas didn't even ask—they just went into the club hand-in-hand as usual.

He had a few folks he nodded to, especially Scotty. The man had a decent way about him.

"Room seven is ready for you. Your things are in it, key is on the bench, Sir."

"Thanks, Scotty." Thomas gave Scotty a nod and looked

at Sam. "Would you like to sit for a bit and relax before we head back, or are you ready to show me your ink?"

"I'm easy. Like, for real." He wasn't scared of showing his ink. It was beautiful—this secret that he held on his skin. But he could have a Coke and a visit if Thomas wanted.

"I'm ready to get a look at you."

He knew Thomas was ready by the change in his tone. So strange how the man did that. He still hadn't figured out why.

"Let's do it." He had one request from the powers that be —*Please, God. Please don't let me get hard in front of Thomas. Please.*

"Room seven. Excellent." Thomas led the way down the long hall. "That will do very nicely." Thomas stopped outside the door and gestured for him to go in first. That was new; the last couple of times Thomas had gone in before him.

"Thanks." He went in and put his hat on the hook. It was too porn movie to drop trou with your hat on.

This room was nice. It looked like a super comfy lounge or something, only with a long padded platform in the center about table height. All the seating was covered in a lush red fabric, and the walls were black with—oh. The walls and the ceiling were covered in U-bolts at various heights and distances from each other.

"I'm locking the door." He heard the lock click; then Thomas headed for a trunk at the far end of the room. "On the table, please. There's a step stool at the far end."

"Do you want me to lose the jeans? You can't see my ink otherwise." Did he just ask that? Out loud? That was what they were doing here, though, right?

Sam stroked his hand over the table, smiling at how it felt like a million threads touching him back.

"I was going to help you with that once you were on the table, but thank you for thinking to save me the effort, Sam. Go right ahead."

Thomas pulled two lengths of rope out of the chest, one black and one bright white, and set them on the platform.

Sam reached out, curious to see if they were soft or rough. They felt silky on his swollen index fingers. "These aren't tie-down ropes, for sure."

"Surely not."

He worked his belt open, one-handed, then looked to Thomas. "Can I ask a favor, please, sir?"

"Anything, Sam." Thomas looked up from where he was working with a couple of shorter lengths of rope. "Oh. Of course. A little help?"

"My boots. Please?" He could do it, but it would hurt and be frustrating as all get-out, and for the first time, he felt like he vaguely understood what he was doing. He was eager to show off his ink.

Thomas looked at him for a moment, then down at his boots and back. "Certainly, sweetheart. That can't be easy for you, can it?" Thomas knelt and wrapped a hand around the heel of his left boot.

Sweetheart? Was that a tease? Was that meant to be ugly? Sam gave it a thought, but Thomas hadn't been ugly to him, hadn't given him reason to believe he'd start now, so he'd let it be something fond and kind.

"You should have seen me trying to get them on. It involved a lot of tipping over like a drunken stork." He tugged, his boot sliding off.

"It might be time to consider an alternate pair of shoes for such occasions." Thomas chuckled and helped get his other boot off. "I'll just set these by the door. Would you like me to get some ice for that hand? That swelling is starting to look rather ugly. Are you sure you haven't broken anything?"

"I might could use some ice in a bit, yeah." He was about ninety percent sure broken-something was a thing, if he was honest. He clenched it, feeling the bones creak and the torn skin pull, and his belly yanked in tight and sudden enough that his jeans hit the floor from the weight of his buckle.

Thomas pressed a button and a chime went off in the room, sounding kind of like the bells that go off in fancy elevators. "I'll get those." Thomas bent and picked up his jeans as he stepped out of them, folded them neatly, and set them on a low bench.

There was a knock at the door, and Thomas opened it just the tiniest bit to speak softly with whoever was there. "Ice is on the way." Thomas closed the door. "That's a very nice view, cowboy."

"Didn't he do amazing work?" Sam turned before he got up on the table, lifting his T-shirt to show off the ink that covered him from knee to the hoof print on his back. The main lines were barbed wire with torn feathers and nails, wildflowers and braided horsehair caught in the hooks. The wire was weighted at his knee with a horseshoe, caught at the top near his kidney with a knotted rope.

"Lovely." Thomas stepped closer and lifted his shirt higher; then warm fingers were on his spine, tracing the actual scar beneath the ink. "This is brilliant. Just gorgeous."

His eyes went wide as his brain tried to process the whole "almost numb, tingling, burning, near invisible, Jesus Christ someone's touching" thing. "Thank you, sir. It was worth every penny."

Thomas helped him up on the platform just as someone knocked on the door again. "How long did it take?" There was an exchange at the door, and the lock clicked into place.

"Four eight-hour sessions." He'd been flying by the end of each one of them too.

"So you sat still for eight hours on four separate occasions. You. For that long? Endorphin high?" Thomas placed a pillow at one end of the platform. "Lie back, sweetheart."

"We took smoke breaks, but yeah. It was...I can't explain it." He eased himself into the pillow, trying not to let awkwardness creep in. "My skin was puckered and raw, and this made it better."

Thomas placed another pillow by his left hip and a large bag of ice on top of that. "Just rest your hand here. I'll get it packed in some ice. It's not elevated, exactly, but hopefully it's comfortable."

Sam eased his hand down, and Thomas began to pack it. Sweat popped out on his chest, and he panted, the shock of the cold making the world spin. He flailed with his free arm, needing to hold on to something so he didn't fall.

Thomas twisted and caught his arm. "Easy. I've got you."

"Whoa. Sorry. That was a little intense." Sam felt his tight muscles begin to relax, and he closed his eyes for a second.

"The cold was a little shocking, hm? Sorry. There's really no subtle with ice." Thomas let him rest that hand on a broad bicep and finished working the ice around his hand. "I am going to let that bring down a little of the swelling, and I'm taking off that haphazard-looking bandage you have on it to see what's going on."

"Haphazard? Man, you ever tried to doctor your smart hand with your dumb one? This is a work of art."

"No, I have not. You do recall that I was standing downstairs and could have come up to assist you with it? Is it really that difficult for you to ask for help?"

Wait. Wait, what? Thomas hadn't even been there when he was bleeding. He'd texted after Sam'd got himself bandaged up. And he had asked for help with his boots.

Christ.

He was never going to not feel like he was wandering around like an idiot.

He was beginning to think that he needed to stop talking altogether and just let Thomas say what all he needed to.

"Sorry, man. I was teasing."

"I know." Thomas patted his shoulder. "Let's get this back on track, shall we? I really just want to see this ink, up close. I can't even imagine sustaining this sort of injury. Was the surgery long? How long were you off your feet?"

Thomas started touching again, curious fingers drawing the length and the outline of the scar on his thigh.

"Twelve hours from recovery to walking on it, believe it or not. Once they got the rod in, the pain was bearable. Before that, I seriously begged God to take me." He pushed Thomas's fingers with his own, letting him feel the hard ridge of muscles over the steel rod. "My balls swelled up like baseballs; everything turned black-and-blue down there."

Thomas looked up at him, over his hip and the length of his torso. "That's...terrifying. My God. But getting up that fast? That's incredible. This is just beautiful work." Thomas's touch grew lighter as those long fingers started tracing over the pattern of barbed wire. "Is your riding career over?"

"It didn't have to be, but I had to think about the pressure on my hip and my knee with each go-round. I've broken my pelvis, had the shoulder surgeries. At some point, your body can't get hit by a car over and over." He could either walk for sixty more years or ride for five.

"I can't say I'd have done half as well with a single one of those things, let alone compounding injuries." Thomas straightened up. "You have numerous other scars to tell me about, no doubt, and I'm interested in all of those stories. But I'm going to have to look at that hand. Or should I just assume you need urgent care?"

"I can't afford a doctor. I got the skin glued up as best I could, but there's no way I can swing X-rays and all." He wasn't being a bitch or a drama queen. It was what it was. Thomas asked for honest, right?

"Hm." Thomas leaned a hip against the platform and looked at him. For a long time.

Without saying a word.

Finally the man shifted onto his feet. "Will you be all right if I leave the room for a few minutes? I'm not leaving the club. I just need to talk to someone."

"I'll just hang here." He was comfortable, his hand numb, and he was swinging from feeling like he was stupid to feeling almost confident.

"I'll be back in a few minutes. Just relax." Thomas patted his shoulder again, and he heard the door open, the sound of club music filling the room for one second until the door closed again.

Then it was quiet. Unnaturally quiet.

Sam let his eyes close. Why on earth could he rest like this, trust that he was safe here? Strange, but wonderful.

God, he was really going to stay here.

There was a soft knock at the door, and he blinked, wondering how long it had been. It seemed like Thomas had only just left. Had he dozed off?

"Sam? I'm back." Thomas came in, rested a hand on his shoulder. "Are you all right? Sorry I was gone a bit longer than I thought, but we've found some help. He should be here shortly."

"Help? Did I miss something?" He felt a little dazed. "Do I need to get dressed?"

"He's a doctor...well, a combat medic of some variety. Retired Army. I'm fairly confident he's seen legs before." Thomas smiled at him.

"I'm sorry, man. Seriously. I was so fucking mad this morning, and I just...popped."

"We're friends, Sam, aren't we? I'm not asking you to change who you are. You know that if I can help I will. You don't have to apologize to me."

There was a knock at the door, and Thomas let a burly-looking guy in. "Evening, Thomas! Been a long time since I made a house call to this place."

"Hello, Angel. Thanks for coming. I'm glad to hear that."

"Who's this?" Angel—*was that a name or a nickname?*—grinned down at him from what seemed like a hundred feet away. The guy had on a well-worn baseball cap, a gray hooded sweat shirt, and had a silver beard that stopped four or five inches below the chin. "Looks like your shaking hand is good. I'm Gabriel. Gabe, Angel. Whatever."

"Pleased to meet you, sir. How goes?" There was something familiar in this man—he imagined in his carriage. He recognized it from his daddy, from Bowie.

"I never have a bad day, my friend. Thomas, can you clear all that ice, please? Really don't want too much ice on a break until after it's set."

"Oh. Of course." Thomas got to work.

Angel pushed Thomas's ropes off the bench and put a big black backpack on it. "So tell me what happened."

"I got into a scuffle with a wall. The wall won."

"I do understand that. I've been there. Hit between the studs."

"Yessir. No shit on that."

Angel unwrapped him, and Thomas made a soft sound. He didn't look. He'd seen it already. "Superglue, hmm? You did a decent job of it."

"Yeah. I patched it up best I could."

"It'll do. I'll just clean it up a little. Ring finger's fucked up and maybe the little finger too, but not from the hit. You know how to throw a punch, at least. What did you do, yank it out of the wall? You gotta watch that in the city. There's a lot of plaster in those older buildings."

"Yep. I got stuck and couldn't get it out." Maybe he'd panicked a bit.

He rolled his toes, clenching and unclenching. Vince Nedders had taught him that on his first bad fall from a bull while he was waiting for someone to pop his arm back in. *Roll your toes and it'll help, son.*

Angel fucked with his skin, then grabbed his fingers. "This isn't going to feel good."

"I'm cool." Icy, even. Like a snow cone.

"You know what my favorite joke is, man?" Angel asked, and he shook his head. "What did the sadist say when the masochist begged, 'Beat me'?"

"I got no idea."

Angel winked at him. "No."

Then he pulled, and the world went white-hot for a screaming second, and it took all his willpower to be still and silent and cowboy up.

Roll your fucking toes, son.

"Jesus."

"Whoops, hang on." Angel disappeared from his blurry vision for a second. There was a solid *thunk*; then the big guy laughed. Hard. "You okay, Tommy?"

"Fine. Fuck you. Get to work."

Angel laughed again, and he was back. "You did better

than your Master did. I give you permission to bust his chops when you can sit up again."

"This ain't my first rodeo. Feels better." It always did, when they were in place.

"Yeah." Angel wrapped his hand loosely in gauze, put on a soft splint that covered his last three fingers, held them still. "Don't make it too tight, huh? You've got to give the swelling room. Watch for infection. If pieces of plaster work out, just clean it real well."

"Fair enough." He'd made sure the blood ran clear before he glued it shut. "Is he okay?"

"I'm fine."

Angel laughed and gave him a wink, then started cleaning up. "Big badass Dom."

"Thank you, Angel. I very much appreciate the emergency assist."

"That's my cue." Angel gave his hand one more look. "Good thing we understand each other. I know I'll be seeing you again."

"Yes, sir." He was a bit of an accident waiting to happen, and he knew it. "I owe you."

"No, Tommy here does, but the thought is kind."

Tommy. That just didn't suit.

When Thomas appeared alongside the platform, he looked totally fine, and walked Angel over to the door. "Really, thank you. Let me know how you want to settle up."

"I'll think of something. If he needs anything, give him a couple Tylenol. It should throb, but it's going to feel a shit-ton better already." Angel grinned. "He's a tough little stud. Lucky man. See ya."

"Take care. Have a beer on me on your way out."

"Sounds good."

The door closed, the lock turned, and Thomas was back, smiling at him. "Better?"

"Yeah. Yeah. I mean, I don't want to repeat the experiment right now, but yes. Thank you for the help."

"I'd prefer that as well." Thomas rested a hand on his chest. "I'd had a slightly different plan for the evening, but it will keep."

He could feel every single one of Thomas's fingers; he could feel Thomas's heartbeat. "I'm sorry. I seem to fuck up your plans pretty regular."

"Nothing to worry about. My most important plan is you." Thomas's fingers traveled under the hem of his T-shirt and settled on his belly.

His abs rippled like they had a mind of their own, responding to Thomas's touch instinctively.

Thomas was quiet and looked thoughtful for a bit, those warm fingers spreading wide across his belly. "The other day when I took your hand, you told me no one touches in this city. Is that right? Am I remembering that correctly?"

"Yeah." At home, there was constant contact—hugs and slaps on the back, rubbing elbows, high-fiving, handshakes, playful punches. He ached for it sometimes. Stupid, but true.

"And since you've been in the city, you've had a hug or two from me and...a fistfight? Is that all?"

"The hostess this morning. The teachers at James's school hugged me when I went to see his classroom." He remembered every one.

The temptation to lift his head and see Thomas's hand on his belly was huge, but he didn't, because it might make Thomas stop.

Thomas smiled. "You remember them all. Touches are

important to you? They are to me too. Is this okay? Would you be comfortable removing your shirt? If not, that's fine."

"I want to." God, that was—he was— *Breathe. Breathe.* He was going to hell one way or the other, right? He huffed out a shaky breath. "Hell, I just want you to stay here with me."

Yeah. Totally burning in hell for eternity. Brimstone. Pitchforks. Demons tap-dancing on his eyeballs.

Worth it.

"I'll stay here. We'll stay as long as you like." Thomas pushed up his shirt, then patiently helped him work the left sleeve over his hand and the other side around his bum shoulder. "Okay?"

"Yessir." He rolled up a little to help Thomas slip the shirt off, grateful for his three hundred crunches a day.

He was not going to think about how he was mostly naked with a man who made him willing to— *Nope. No thinking. Breathing. In and out.*

He watched Thomas neatly fold his T-shirt and put it aside. "What kind of touch makes you the most happy?"

He made himself answer, testing Thomas's promise of no judgment. "There are at least a hundred answers to that question, and my answer right now would be...yours."

Oh. That smile. Thomas seemed...well, touched. Happy. He could see it in the set of the man's shoulders and the light in those clear brown eyes. "Thank you, sweetheart."

Grateful, like he'd given the man a gift.

Thomas's hands started to move over his skin, the touch warm and light in some places, firmer and more purposeful in others. The expression on Thomas's face was intense, eyes following along like they were looking for something.

No, not looking...learning.

"Such a treasure."

He didn't have an answer in words, so he just stroked Thomas's arm in thanks.

His cock was heavy, but not embarrassing, so he focused on Thomas's hands. The man knew he liked guys, had to know he thought Thomas was fine, so they were just going to have to ignore it together.

Thomas spent some time on his shoulder, working his fingers around the joint, across to the base of his neck, down into his armpit, and around to his back, lifting him slightly off the platform and setting him down.

"I understand what caused this one. But I want to know about this scar." Thomas rubbed the little bare spot above his nipple.

"Oh, God." He started laughing at the memory of running around banging at his chest and screaming like a howler monkey. "You know how you can stick your hand in rubbing alcohol and set it on fire without hurting yourself? We used to do that behind the barn where Momma couldn't see. When I was a kid—I think the summer before I was ten —James and I decided to soak cotton balls in alcohol, set them on fire, and throw them at each other. That one stuck."

Thomas shook his head, grinning. "That sounds exactly like something my twin brothers would've done. I, on the other hand, had no idea you could do that. I must have been reading a book or hiding in the warehouse when they taught that lesson in How to be a Real Boy School."

"We had Bowie. He paid James a dollar to set his dick on fire in the bathroom once."

"Jesus." Thomas snorted, then grinned. "Well, there didn't seem to be any lasting damage."

"Yeah, I was little then. Three or four." He smiled, the memories fond. "I got lots of scars. I never get out of anything without a mark."

"I see that. You're also in exceptional shape." Thomas's fingers were still moving. They found the hollow of his throat and slid lightly down it to his sternum, then traced the curve of his lowest ribs around to his side. "You seem very content right now, Sam. This is the most relaxed you've been as long as I've known you. This might be the longest you've been still as well. How do you feel?"

Sam sorted through answers—relaxed, present, happy, settled, welcome, warm, buzzed—and he settled on "Real good."

"I'm glad. I have to tell you again how relieved I was to hear you want to stay in New York. I would have missed you. I think you belong here. I believe you can find friends, and I am hopeful that you and I can keep working together, as it seems to be benefiting us both."

Those hands seemed to grow hot against his abs as Thomas spoke, searing into skin and muscle.

He sucked in a breath and curled up, shoulders leaving the couch.

"Shhh." Thomas pressed him gently back down. "Too sensitive? Do you want me to stop?"

"No!" He blinked at himself. *Okay, stop that.*

Thomas arched an eyebrow, but he was smiling. "All right. Perhaps another spot, then." Those hot hands landed on his thigh, the one that didn't get stomped on, Thomas's fingers working into the muscle. "Are you able to kneel at all?"

"Yessir." He thought. How often did that come up in life? Kneeling? "I mean, I clean the bathtub and all. I never think of the leg unless I'm cold and it throbs. The frozen shoulder is way more of a bitch."

"Wonderful. Not about your shoulder, but that you'll be

able to kneel for me." Thomas bent his knee up and worked fingers into his calf. "Are you ticklish?"

He had been when he was a kid, but he had learned to clamp that shit down. Being tickled until you pissed yourself was a torture no one needed. "I am not."

"Also good. That can be a painful surprise if I'm not expecting it. It's much easier not to have to worry about it. Do you have any food allergies? Allergies to medications? Latex? Anything like that?"

"Feathers. They make my eyes swell up like whoa. It's gross. Also, scorpions and me? We're not friends."

"Feathers?" Thomas laughed. "Oh, that was a poor choice the other day, then, wasn't it? I apologize. Is it all feathers? Synthetic feathers are okay, or not?"

"There's synthetic feathers? No shit? Why would anyone have those?" Maybe for...uh...dreamcatchers? Costumes? Art projects in schools?

"Well, so..." Thomas squinted at him, then headed for a cabinet that hung on the wall. "Roll over. Let me know if you need my assistance."

"Okay..." *Huh. Weird.* He sat up easily before he turned over, trying to figure out what to do with his arms. He ended up with his elbows bent, hands at his shoulders like he was in a push-up.

"Hm. Are you able to just put your arms down at your sides? Will your shoulder do that?"

He rolled from one side to the other, extricating his hands. Oh. Better. "Yeah. Yeah, this is cool."

"Good, I want you to be comfortable." His head was turned the other way, but he heard Thomas come back over. "So synthetic feathers come in several different textures. This one tends to be a popular one."

He felt a light touch at the base of his spine that made its way slowly up to between his shoulder blades and fanned out across one, then the other. Thomas repeated the same motion slowly.

"It's not really about the initial touch. That's not typically very exciting, but it sensitizes the skin when you repeat the same thing, again and again."

"Like Chinese water torture, but not bad?"

"Exactly. Pleasurable torture. So well put, sweetheart." Thomas continued fanning the feather across his shoulder blades. "So what you might find after a while is that this feels nice, maybe relaxing, maybe gets boring. Everyone is different. But after a while when I switch to something else, it might have a surprising effect. Maybe not, not everything works on everyone's skin. These might be too subtle for you with your various scars back here, especially that hoof print."

Thomas took that feather away and blew cool air across the skin where the feather had been.

His toes curled, and goose bumps popped up all over his back, his nipples going rock hard. Oh. Fuck, that was weird. Like walking into air-conditioning after working in the sun all day.

"Mmm. Pretty. Maybe subtle isn't such a bad idea after all. You've had a great deal of...harsh attention. How do you like this one? It's a tiny little tickler, so simple." Thomas barely touched the very same expanse of skin.

"Is that weird?" He wiggled, the touch more like the promise of an itch or dust blowing against him.

"Does it matter? Do you like it?"

"I don't know if it matters. Sometimes that matters." Sometimes it was good to be like everyone else because being different was fucking lonely. He thought that people that said it was better to march to your own drummer were just trying to make themselves feel better. Hell, he was a gay rodeo cowboy with a master's in art history who just decided to stay in New York City because he was fascinated with his murdered brother's boyfriend.

"Here it is literally you, me, and four walls that don't talk. The only thing that matters is what we want, what we need, and what we like." Thomas blew across his skin again.

"That's..." He'd never felt that before in his whole life. Never. He could hear his heartbeat in his ears.

"Good? It's okay, Sam. You don't need words. I'm listening. You'll tell me you want more, less, or to stop if you're not into it. All right? That's all you need for now."

He nodded and squeezed his eyes closed. Big. It was big. How was something so little so big?

"I'm going back to the big feather. It's rougher, and your skin is more sensitive now; you'll have to let me know how intense it is and whether you want me to stop."

Thomas gently fanned the feather across one shoulder blade as he had before, only this time it felt like a million little tiny pinpricks, like being stung by a hundred tiny wasps all at once.

He jerked away, his eyes flying open. It was like getting ink, but so much more immediate—less a line of fire than a wash of burn.

"Shhh." Thomas moved around to where Sam could see him and held up the feather. "That was this. Just a synthetic feather. Too much? I'll stop."

"No fucking way. That burned like fire. Jesus. Weird." He met Thomas's eyes. "That is messed up."

Thomas grinned at him. "It is a bit, isn't it? You wouldn't have believed me if I'd explained it to you. You needed to experience it. Right? A lot of what happens here is about learning yourself, your true needs, your deepest desires, and how liberating that understanding is. Big concept, one very small example."

Thomas started cleaning up the room, putting the feathers on top of the credenza, tidying up the ropes he hadn't used.

"You want some help, man?" He wasn't broke. Well, a little, but he had one hand and two free fingers and a thumb.

"Sit up and prove to me you're not light-headed first." Thomas winked at him.

He swung himself up, the world spinning like he'd been on a good ride. Oh, he fucking loved that little rush.

Thomas watched him. "You should see your pupils. You'd think the room was dark. You just sit there a second, please, and let the blood make it back down to your toes. Oh, and be careful when you put your T-shirt back on. It might sting."

"Yeah. It feels like you cut me a little."

"I promise I did not. But every little nerve ending is firing off at once. The nice thing is it will fade very quickly, in just a few minutes really, and it doesn't leave any kind of mark or raw spots. But you get all that sensation. It can really help you find the right headspace."

Thomas lifted his clothes and set them on the platform beside him. "So typically after spending time together, working, playing, a scene, whatever we're doing, I like to give my subs time to reorder their thinking. It's loud out there. This room is soundproofed. The lighting and the crowd, it can be a lot. So I'll give you a second to breathe, get dressed, and when you're ready, you bring me the key to the room and meet me at the bar. Sound good?"

"You got it."

As soon as Thomas left, he sighed, grinned at himself. *A second to breathe. Right.*

It was going to take him half an hour to fasten his buckle. He might get his boots on by tomorrow morning.

He started laughing at himself and this insane fucking day. God help him.

15

"Ally. Ally, there's a typo in the flyer for that new Russian doll exhibit. They spelled the sponsor's foundation wrong."

Thomas flung the brochure on his assistant's desk.

"Oh...is that...? I'm sure I had it right."

"You did. It's not you, Al. It's media. Just get them to fix it." Thomas sighed. "Please. And thank you. And have I told you how much I appreciate you today? I need more coffee."

Ally laughed. "On it. Not the coffee, you can get that for yourself."

Thomas snorted. He adored her.

That opening was scheduled for Friday. Four thousand full-color brochures in three days? Good luck. He was glad he wasn't in that department. He breathed a sigh of relief to discover he was alone in the break room. He wasn't up for water cooler nonsense right now.

He set up the Keurig and waited for his mediocre but still caffeinated cup of coffee to brew, and checked the weather on his phone. It was getting colder and colder as winter set in for real.

There was a text waiting for him too. From Sam.

Thomas hadn't known Sam could send unsolicited texts.

Hey. Can I call when ur not busy?

Thomas read the text twice, dissecting it a million different ways. "When ur not busy" could be code for "I need to talk to you right this very second but I would never admit that." Or it could mean Sam had bad news. For example, he could have decided he was going back to Texas after all, and "when you're not busy" could mean "I'm already at the airport."

"I got my head stuck in the medicine cabinet" also came to mind, as did "I'm in jail." He grabbed his coffee and hurried back to his office.

Just please don't be bleeding to death somewhere.

That wasn't actually funny.

He dialed as soon as he stepped over the threshold, closing his office door behind him.

Sam picked up on the first ring. "Hey."

Calm. Don't ask him if his arm is stuck in the garbage disposal. Breathe. "Hey there, it's nice to hear from you."

I hope.

"Thanks for calling. I just...I wanted to...I mean, I wanted to hear your voice and stuff."

And stuff.

All right. Something was up. Something Sam wasn't able to articulate at the moment but thought he could help with. Right? He'd try that route. "Take a deep breath, sweetheart. I'm listening. Tell me what's going on."

"I'm looking at the view from the bedroom here." Sam's voice was husky, raw. "I didn't want to bother you, but...I was hoping you had a second."

He's upset. He's upset and he reached out to me.

He'd gotten through, and Sam trusted him. He

swallowed back the pride and focused on his sub. "I do, as a matter of fact. I was just getting some coffee. It's a great view, isn't it? Of the square? Is today the first time you've seen it?"

"Yeah." There was a wealth of emotion in that single syllable, all these feelings that Sam seemed to be unable to verbalize. Thomas was beginning to understand that had nothing to do with him, that Sam was willing to share if he asked the right questions.

"I can only imagine how difficult being in that room has got to be for you. What have you done so far?"

"Not a whole hell of a lot, but I made it in. Can...do you have plans later?"

He set his coffee cup down on his desk before he dropped it. "Do you have plans later?" could mean Sam had gotten into a fight with his landlord and the guy was tied up in the closet.

Or it could just mean, "Do you have plans later?"

"I don't." He didn't want to ask a leading question, so he phrased his reply very carefully. "What did you have in mind?"

"I could meet you somewhere, take you to supper or to have a beer?" Sam sighed softly. "This is fucking hard, man. It smells like him in here, and I'm fixin' to lose my mind."

Thomas's stomach twisted. It did smell like James. The bedding, the books, all of it. "I know just what you mean. Dinner, a beer sounds great. I can meet you anywhere—" He knew already Sam didn't care where they went. The man just wanted out of that apartment. "Let's try that Italian place in my neighborhood again. We'll see if I can be more polite this time."

That was a good place. It was quiet, the food was good, it didn't say James everywhere they looked.

"Perfect. When? I'll be there."

"I can be there by...let's say six? Will you be all right until then? Tell me the truth."

"I'm going to go buy a carton of cigarettes, pretend to smoke them all, and meet you, huh?" Sam laughed, the sound raw. "I got this. I'll see you at six. Thank you, huh? For calling."

Oh, that voice. He just wanted to...make it better. He wanted to...God, talking to Sam made his fingers itch. It made his spine tingle. "Thank you for reaching out to me. It...means a lot. I'm looking forward to seeing you."

"I needed to hear your voice. See you after a while." The line went silent.

"Bye."

He took a deep breath. Every step forward with Sam was as heartbreaking as it was exhilarating. He looked forward to the time when they weren't...what? Weren't grieving? God, what a selfish thought. Weren't dealing with demons? That day, if it ever arrived, could be a very long way off.

He would just look forward to dinner.

There was a knock at his door. "Come in?"

"Off the phone? They need you in the marketing meeting."

He looked at his watch. "Oh, shit. I'm late." He jumped out of his chair and let Ally lead him down the hall.

16

Thomas nodded to his doorman as he left home and pulled his collar up higher against the chilly air. Thanksgiving was less than two weeks away, and it was already this cold in the city? This did not bode well for February.

He walked quickly, motivated not just by the cold air but by his stomach, which had been growling at him for the last hour. And he was motivated by seeing Sam.

He wondered if he was allowing himself to take too much pride in Sam's small victories—not blinking an eye at pet names, making no comment when someone referred to him as Sam's Master, initiating contact when needed. These were all things he would expect of a sub, but honestly, for Sam, who despite all appearances didn't officially have that moniker yet, these things weren't that small. They were the very early manifestations of a hard-won and still tentative trust.

And God help him, every single new victory made him want. Ache. Need.

He knew that was natural with any new sub. He got a little turned-on by pride and winning, of course he did. He'd accepted that truth as one of the reasons he'd chosen this lifestyle. But when he thought about it, he really couldn't separate his love for James as a man and his love for James as his sub. He couldn't even say for sure which had come first. And he honestly couldn't compartmentalize his feelings about Sam at this point either.

It was clear he needed to get a handle on what he was ready for and what he wasn't. His slow progress with Sam at the club was perfect because it let him use his hands, let him work, let him engage that piece of his mind that didn't know how to take a back seat to anything. But it had awakened a desire he couldn't bear to look at head on, and his control over it was quickly slipping through his fingers.

He didn't want to dishonor James, but he couldn't lie either.

Dinner. Didn't he decide he was just going to focus on dinner? His stomach growled again as he opened the door to the restaurant.

For a single agonizing second he knew, without a shadow of a doubt, that James was standing at the hostess's station, that ridiculous sheepskin coat that he wore with the strange defect on the shoulder familiar as breathing. Then he heard Sam's laughter, darker and heartier than James's. He could see how the coat hung on Sam, the damned thing at least two sizes too big. He could smell Old Spice and Irish Spring, not Grey Flannel and Ivory.

He didn't speak right away. He wasn't sure what sound was going to come out. He needed to see a different face to dispel the rest of the illusion, so instead, he took a breath and rested a hand on Sam's shoulder. He managed a smile, hoping it didn't look too forced.

"Hey, stranger." Sam looked over at him, the circles under his eyes brutally dark, but the way Sam smiled was honest and totally unique. It was the scar, he thought, pulling the corner of Sam's mouth the slightest bit.

"Hey there." That was much better, even with the dark circles. He glanced at the hostess and back at Sam. "Making friends?"

"You know me, I can talk to trees."

Uh-huh. Mr. Grunts and Clicks was positively chatty.

The hostess gave them a smile and waved them over to a table.

"Well, you talked us into a table anyway. Nice work." He wanted to help Sam with his coat. He should. But he couldn't touch it. He knew what it would smell like close up. He knew how familiar it would be in his fingers. He just couldn't do it.

Sam managed just fine, slipping it off his shoulders and setting it in the chair beside him. That hat brim stayed down to hide his face, the barometer of Sam's mood unerring. "Thanks for agreeing to have supper with me."

"I'm glad you called. And I've been looking forward to this since we spoke, so perhaps I should thank you for the lovely invitation." His smile was genuine this time, easy to find for Sam.

That didn't stop him from wanting wine, though. "Are you strictly a beer man, or would you like to share a bottle of wine with me?"

"I love a velvety red. One that sticks to your tongue." There was a distant, warm smile on Sam's face, a fondness. Both the words and the expression surprised him.

He picked up the wine list and handed it to Sam. "Sounds wonderful. You pick." That was a nice change.

James didn't care for wine, so he'd always ordered by the glass.

"Surely." Sam read over the list, lips pursed for a second, and nodded. "You drink Chianti? I like this one here. I had it in Austin."

"We're in the right place for it, right? Sounds good to me." Sam could order wine. What a lovely surprise. He watched Sam wave someone over and order a bottle, letting his impression of Sam evolve yet again. There were worse things in the world than having to pay attention.

He grinned, trying to find a natural way to ask the questions he wanted to. "How was the carton of cigarettes?"

There was a pack in the breast pocket of Sam's shirt, along with a lighter. Sam patted it like it was a comfort. "Only a pack and I haven't opened it yet."

"Don't." The temptation to hold out his hand and take it away from Sam was huge, but he didn't.

"Yeah. I quit because I spent six weeks blowing up balloons."

He shook his head. "If you don't trust yourself, leave it on the table and I'll take it with me later." That was enough harping on that. Sam knew what he needed to do. "When you're ready, whenever that is, we should make some plans to go through that room together. There's no reason to do it alone. And you...*we* don't have to pretend like it's okay. Just have company."

"That seems real mean, to ask that of you. Is there stuff you want? I'd let you have whatever before I mail things back to Texas." Sam's hat brim dipped deeper. "I only wore the coat because I don't have one here, and...well, I just don't have one, and it's awful cold."

Sam needed a new coat for Christmas. He was on it.

Possibly before, he wasn't sure he could look at that one for a month. He made no comment about the coat. What was he going to say? It looks nice? It didn't, really. Sam swam in it.

"I don't know what I'd want, but that's not the point. You didn't ask; I'm offering as a friend. If you'd prefer to do it alone, just tell me so."

Dammit. He hadn't meant to take that tone at all.

Sam exhaled, and Thomas saw the muscle in his jaw jump, but he didn't answer, just thanked the waitress in a husky voice as she poured the wine.

"Are you ready to order?"

"Give us a couple-three if you would, please, ma'am."

"I am so sorry." Thomas picked up his glass and took a sip. "I ask for an awful lot of honesty from you, and I'm not reciprocating very well. So, the truth. I walked through that door and James was standing at that hostess station waiting for me. I'm just a little...I don't have my balance back yet. I shouldn't have asked a hard question in my present state of mind."

"I would bring him back if I could." Sam patted his hand, the touch gentle, incredibly so, like Thomas might shatter. "I'm sorry. I should have known better. I wasn't thinking."

"You were thinking you didn't want to freeze your ass off, and you have every right to wear whatever you want. James would tell you you'd be a complete fool not to wear a perfectly good coat, and he'd be right. I just..." *I wasn't ready for it.*

He caught Sam's hand in his. "I want to help you with James's room. I thought James and I were...I felt like we..." What was the matter with him? They were just words. But it felt like if he said them out loud, he was closing the door on the rest of his life. "I don't like to think of someone else going through his things without me. Even you. Will you let me help?"

"Of course." Just as simple as that. Of course.

He exhaled, breathing out the tension. "Thank you. I'm sorry I snapped at you." He gave Sam's hand a squeeze and let it go, picking up his wine again. "You have excellent taste in wine."

I really am sorry, and it's so good to see you.

"Thank you, sir, and no worries. You got any idea what you want to eat?"

"The mushroom ravioli. It was the first thing that came to mind after how nice it would be to see you." Possibly he ought to have put his honesty back in his pocket after "I'm sorry" so he didn't also make a fool of himself. Well, maybe that would help Sam believe he meant it. He sipped his wine since he didn't have a hat to hide under.

Sam chuckled and picked up his wineglass, toasting him. "Thanks for coming. I appreciate it. Mushroom raviolis, huh? I think I'm going to have noodles and red sauce."

"Sounds great. So how is the freelance work going?"

"It's going. You know how it is. Feast or famine. I got a job offer at a bar that I'll probably take for the short-term. We'll see."

Oh, good. Getting a job was a wise move. "That works. The rent can't be cheap where you are." He didn't say James's rent; it was Sam's place now. But one thing worried him. "Can you keep your weekends open if you take a bar job?"

"I don't know yet. It's real amorphous. I got to talk to the owner's wife and get her nod. If I can't, I'd just have to work late nights, so maybe you'd want to still see each other during the day."

"Of course." Losing Saturday nights, though...that would be very disappointing. He couldn't send Sam off to his night job floating. They'd figure it out. Sam obviously needed the work if he couldn't buy himself a coat. That was an unfortunate truth. Sam hadn't even asked to use his laundry facilities.

"Yeah."

They ordered. They sat there, both of them totally inside their own heads.

Finally Sam broke the silence. "You go to your folks for Thanksgiving?"

He snorted. "I don't. Are you flying home?"

"No, sir."

He heard the complicated subtext behind those two words as clearly as if Sam had actually found words to explain. He was getting better at this. He felt badly for Sam but possibly better for himself.

"I'm sorry, I'm sure that was a hard decision. If you're not working, would you like to be my guest at the club?"

"Please." Sam's scarred, callused hands shook for a second, then disappeared under the table.

Oh. And a layer he'd missed. "Were you not invited home, Sam?"

"Apparently I ain't welcome."

He quickly and firmly suppressed the flash of indignant anger in his initial reaction, but honestly? What was so wrong with this beautiful, brilliant young man sitting across the table from him? Welcome or not, Sam would still throw himself in front of a train for any one of them. How could they possibly not understand that?

"Can you tell me what happened?" Did he want to know?

"Long story short, I said no and no one likes it. It's got nothing to do with me, not really." Sam shrugged one shoulder, the motion practiced, like it was meant to protect Sam's chest.

"You're probably right about that. I remember the first year I didn't go home for the holidays. Any of them. It was hard. I'd like to tell you there's a way to make it easy, but it's an opportunity to start a new tradition for yourself. I'm very happy you'll be joining me."

"I appreciate the offer. Really." Sam chuckled for him. "And don't we both sound all nice and shit for two assholes that are mourning the same man and trying to figure out what we're doing?"

He laughed. "Don't we? You'd think I was trying very hard to be respectful and mind my own business without letting on how much I'd *really* like to throw my first ever punch at a member of your family. I don't care which one, just pick your favorite."

"Oh, Bowie. Totally. That would amuse the fuck out of me." Sam's eyes rolled like dice. "I swear to God, I'm trying hard to stand tall, but some days it's harder than others."

"I've got your back. I know sometimes it seems like I have a rod up my ass and I'm choking on a silver spoon, but I'm resourceful and I think on my feet pretty well." He grinned and sipped his wine. If he knew anything, it was the difference between who he was and who he'd decided to be.

"You do just fine, honey." And that was high praise, wasn't it? He'd take it.

"You think?" That was flirty. Like the first time he'd met Sam. Just out of the blue.

"Yes, sir." And that full eye contact, serious, dead-on look was so hot it threatened to burn him.

He held Sam's eyes, feeling so torn. Drowning in that ache again. This time he let Sam see it. He didn't want to work through this confusion by himself anymore.

"It's okay, honey. I got you, no worries."

He was about to say something—like how was that even remotely possible and what did Sam think he understood—when their food arrived, interrupting his train of thought and their stare.

"Hey, this looks good."

"Smells good too. I do love me some noodles."

"It's so much easier to think when you're not hungry, right? Things make more sense."

"Uh-huh. Eat your supper, mister."

He chuckled at himself. "Yes." He took a couple of bites—the warm, savory mushrooms and the rich cream sauce melting together in his mouth. "Oh. You should try this. Have you had these before? Would you like a bite?"

"Surely. It smells rich and good. I'd love to try."

"It is." He cut a ravioli in half so Sam could get a good taste and held out his fork.

"Thanks." Sam took the fork, humming softly as he ate the bite. "Oh, that's nice."

He nodded. "It's one of my favorites here. Earthy and creamy. It's like comfort food." He took his fork back and had another bite. "Oh. Thanksgiving is potluck. What should we bring? I usually bring a pie. I'm a horrible cook, but we should bring something else too."

"Sure. I can bring whatever folks need—rolls or paper plates, Cokes, whatever. I live on peanut butter and cereal, as a rule. I haven't turned the stove on since I got here."

"You really need that job. Have you thought about...

about moving?" He wouldn't mind. It was getting easier, but he wasn't sure he would ever be able to stand on the front stoop comfortably again.

"I'm gonna have to, and I know it. I don't know how James did it. He must have had a buttload of savings. Right now, I just freeze at the idea of it. I've never—" Sam's lips snapped shut, and Thomas got, "I bet I'll figure it out after I get through the holidays."

"Mhm." He nodded. "After the holidays." This season was going to be really hard on Sam. They'd be hard enough on him, but he'd made his peace with his family years ago. Dealing with all of that loss at once seemed so...cruel.

"Yeah. I'll figure it. I'm a smart dog."

He put his fork down and took his last sip of wine. "I am stuffed. That was delicious."

"It was. Thank you for coming. I was in need of good company."

"Me too." He pulled out his wallet and waved the server over to hand her his credit card. "Thank you."

"Wait. No, I invited you. It's my treat. That's only fair." Sam handed over a card of his own. "Tell the nice man he'll have to save his pennies, huh?"

Sam should have just let him get it. The man couldn't buy a coat, but he wanted to pay for dinner and wine?

"We won't drag you into an argument." Thomas pulled his card away so as not to embarrass Sam, but he shot Sam a meaningful look.

"Thank you, ma'am." Sam's upper lip quirked. "Don't look at me like that. I invited you, and I wouldn't have if I couldn't buy yours. I got a buddy that sold a bunch of my stuff for me back home, so I got a little bump coming. No worries." Sam touched his wrist. "I needed to see you, huh? I was in a bad way."

Thomas nodded and took Sam's hand. "This will get... better." Somehow he couldn't promise easier. The server brought the check for Sam to sign and he stretched before standing up. He decided to help Sam with the coat. He could be looking at the damn thing until Christmas. He'd better get the hell over it.

17

Terrance and Rocket had both vouched for him, and Daddy Mike had interviewed him, and Darla had done everything but count his teeth and check him for an enlarged prostate.

So, barring his final interview, which Rocket had slipped up and called his initiation, he had a job at Mike's, the tavern that he'd gone to fight at that first night. He'd been coming by a couple times a week, looking at his phone for want ads, having a single beer. They were good folks, rough, but familiar and welcoming. They saw one of their own, he reckoned.

Another blue-collar dipshit that had "no shit there I was" stories, ink and scars, and would wade in without a thought if a guy hit a lady.

God help them if they hit one of the bikini-clad bartenders in his sight. That shit pissed him off.

Barbacking seven to midnight. Bouncing midnight to four. One meal a night. Sundays off. Cash under the table. Free Wi-Fi after his shift if he agreed to stay with Darla while she did the deposit.

Like Darla needed protection. *Shit.* Call it what it was. He sat near the door so he took the first bullet and gave Darla time to hit the alarm.

It would be tough as shit, but it would pay bills.

He had to deal with shit. He had to get out of James's apartment, find a way for Thomas to understand he wasn't James.

He was his own man.

Thomas wasn't ready to hear that, he didn't think. Thomas was still hurting for James, maybe always would be. Sam didn't know. Maybe he was the biggest fool that ever lived for hoping.

Nah.

He was the biggest fool that ever lived for sitting at the bar knowing he was fixin' to have to stand still and get beat on to get a minimum wage job at a bar so he could stay in New York City and be close to the man that was in love with a ghost.

"Pour out a shot of Jager for little Sammy, Dave!" Terrance pulled out the stool next to him and slid it to the side but didn't sit.

"Little painkiller, huh?" He took the shot without flinching. "Lay off the face, huh? I ain't got money for dental work."

"Fair enough. No head shots. We don't want to kill you."

"Y'all won't kill me." Hurt him, sure, but he'd been hurt before. He held out one hand to shake with Terrance.

Terrance's eyes went wide. "Dude! What happened?"

He looked at his hand, rolled his eyes at the slash there. "Some dickhead thinks putting razors on doorknobs is so fucking funny. When I catch him, I'm going to feed him his own arm."

Terrance grinned at him. "Call us. We'll help you out.

See you on the flip side. Rocket?" They shook hands; then Rocket knocked his knees out from under him, and he was grateful that he wasn't wearing one of his two best shirts. He was fixin' to eat pavement.

———

"Jesus, did you stomp on him?"

Sam heard the voices from a distance. He didn't wince, but he would admit to praying that they thought he was out.

If they asked him to walk home now, he wouldn't make it half a block before the vultures fell on him.

"Nah, Gabe. Just making sure he could take it. He took more than any of these assholes ever did. He can sleep it off here. Darla will bring him coffee in the morning."

He felt hands on him, very lightly testing out the line of his ribs. "I'll leave him something stronger to take with the coffee. When's the last time one of you jokers heard him speak?"

"He never said a fucking word. Not one."

He looked over, met Angel's eyes. Okay. Well, this was probably good.

"Well, well. Good morning, sunshine. I knew I was going to be seeing you again. How many fingers?"

He saw six. "Three. How goes?"

"I never have a bad day." Angel shook his head. "They were nice to you. Your face is still pretty. Deep breath."

"Ask me for something easier, like moving the earth." He sucked in a breath through his teeth, telling himself not to make a sound.

"Okay, let it out slow. Better?" Angel's hands were all over his torso, moving quickly and gently, searching. "Good, good. Just want to look at your back. Can I roll you?"

"Yeah."

He went over, and Angel grunted. "You took it, didn't you? Damn. You have a core of steel. This needs aftercare, kiddo, not a night on a bar floor."

But a night on a bar floor was what he was fixin' to get, so why bitch? What was anyone going to do?

Angel sat up. "Clear everyone out, huh? Go. Out. Give us some privacy, please. That's it. Thank you."

He heard mumbling and boots scuffing on the floor, then quiet.

"I have to call him, you know."

"He'll understand." Thomas got him, knew how bad he needed this job.

"Okay. Next dilemma. I can send him here to get you, you can leave with me, or you can try to haul your own ass out of here. But you're not staying here. You need a little work, and I assume you'd rather this crew not see that."

"I can walk. I can. Just give me a hand up." If he didn't die or throw up, he'd be fine.

Angel got him to his feet, and it was a close thing—both death and vomit—but he managed. "Good deal. Tell him I'll call him later, huh? When he wakes up?"

The whole world was soft, fuzzy on all the edges.

"Work on Monday, little Sammy. See you at seven."

"Yessir. Work on Monday."

He was pretty sure Angel ran a little interference for him on the way out. The man was, like, three feet wider and six feet taller or something. Huge. Really big. You could hide three of him behind the man's back.

When they got outside, Angel apologized, pointing to his Harley. "I'll get you home, but you're gonna have to hold on." Angel stuck his pack in one of the saddle bags and got on. "Come on, cowboy."

"Hey! Wait!" Darla came running out into the cold in her bikini and someone's humongous leather jacket, carrying his hat. "Can't forget this, little Sammy."

"Thank you, ma'am." He crawled onto the bike, his body screaming at him. For a wild second, he swore he saw James, out there on the street, and his whimper was hidden by the sound of Angel's bike.

Angel looked over his shoulder. "You hang on like your momma's life depends on it."

They took off, not giving him a chance to reply.

He closed his eyes and rested his head on Angel's broad back. Thomas trusted him. Daddy Mike trusted him. Sam would trust him.

———

"He's still out. I fixed him up, tucked him in....What?...Oh no, all his shit was on the couch, so I figured...yeah. No, he's beat to hell and bruised but nothing dangerous. He's good. He said to tell you he'd call you in the morning....Would I say he was good if he wasn't good, Tommy?" Angel laughed, the sound huge in James's apartment. "I'm going to give him a couple pain pills. He'll piss blood for a few days, probably. I have his back packed in ice now. He's a fucking stud."

The last thing he remembered was a red light somewhere on...somewhere. He heard Angel digging through his pack and the rattle of a medicine bottle.

"Well, I wouldn't leave him alone long. He won't be getting up or back down without help. And if you can convince him to use the bed, he'll do better....Yeah, I get it. So what are you doing for Thanksgiving?" Angel's voice drifted off in the direction of the kitchen.

Look at you, bubba. You look like hammered shit.

"Shut up, asshole. I need a job."

I know. I know. Damn. You're after Thomas.

He didn't answer that, because James was dead; he wasn't real. He was hallucinating from all the pain. It happened. Sometimes you had to accept that.

Love you, you little idiot. Next time, fight back.

"That wasn't the job interview."

"What?...No, not you, your boy here is talking. I'm gonna hop. Don't panic if you don't hear from him until tomorrow afternoon. I'm giving him the good shit....Yep....Yeah. Night."

Angel cleared his throat. "You passed the interview, Sam. You're home now."

"Good deal. Thanks. That's a long walk."

Angel snorted. "You were on my bike, man. So, I talked to your Master. He's going to keep an eye on you, I bet. What's the deal with the razor blades on your counter?"

"Dunno."

"Huh. Okay, take these. I'll leave you four more—ten a.m. and four p.m. Repeat it."

"Ten and four. Dr Pepper."

"*Water,* pills, bottle if you need to pee. Bucket. Phone. If you need the bucket, the next thing you do is call 9-1-1. Clear? Stay put until Tommy comes over. He'll bring more ice. I'm going to give him your key, okay?"

"I hear you. He had one before. Turn the stereo on? Please?" He needed noise.

"You got it, little Sammy. Music for the cowboy."

"Thanks." He should have asked James when he was here if he called Thomas "Tommy."

Sam just couldn't.

18

Thomas was going to be stepping around invisible police tape outside Sam's apartment building for the rest of his life. It wasn't even about James really anymore; it was just habit. Come up the sidewalk, grab the handrail, and climb the first two steps on the far left side. It was like walking under a ladder or putting shoes on the bed. He just didn't walk over there. Superstition.

In recent years, Thanksgiving Day had become his favorite holiday. Good food, chosen family, some good music and conversation. No expectations, no gifts to shop for, no Thanksgiving "eve" to draw the holiday out longer than it needed to be. There were people he'd miss today, James at the top of that list, but many things to be grateful for as well.

He'd hoped to be grateful for the NYPD today, but that seemed to be at a standstill.

He pulled his key ring out of his pocket, careful not to drop his apple pie, and let himself in without a second thought. That was a new habit, actually using the key he'd been given, one of what he hoped would be a handful of things that made this Sam's place. He'd rearranged his thinking. He was trying.

He rapped twice on the door and turned the deadbolt with his key but hesitated before reaching for the doorknob. Some practical joker in the building thought it was cute to leave razor blades out for unsuspecting tenants. Well, he'd made sure Sam contacted the landlord.

All clear today, so he let himself in.

"Hey, it's me." Sam really needed to get his buzzer fixed.

Sam was sitting with his legs up the wall doing crunches, one after another, like a machine.

For a moment, Thomas was captivated, and he froze in the doorway, halfway in and half out, watching Sam's abdominal muscles work overtime. "You're something else, O'Reilly." Something else being code for ripped. Or scorching hot. *Damn.*

He came in and let the door close behind him, then set his pie down on the counter.

"I totally am. Happy turkey day, sir. How goes?"

There were two things he'd learned he could count on from Sam every time they saw each other. The first was a valiant attempt at a smile no matter what was actually going on in the boy's life at the moment, and the other was "How goes?"

"Well, I've been to the gym and I made my pie, so I'd say I'm fairly well prepared for the day. You?" *Other than the fact that you're not in Texas and you're doing crunches despite being black-and-blue everywhere.*

"I'm..." Sam kept crunching, the oddest look on his face. "I'm excited."

It was hard to believe he was looking at the same man who had alternated between sleeping, hallucinating, and swearing colorfully just last Saturday. They'd spoken on the phone on Tuesday, and sure enough, Sam had hauled that bruised body uptown and started work Monday night. Thomas was caught somewhere between awe, respect, and utter disbelief. "Excited? Ready for a party?"

"I am ready to just enjoy you. This. Us." Sam was sweating, those abs rock-hard. "Twenty left. I bought three big bags of rolls."

"Just twenty?" He dumped his jacket on a chair, sat on the floor against the wall next to Sam's legs, and grinned at him. "Do ten extra, for me. I'm enjoying the view."

"No problem." Sam pumped them out, slowing down for the final ten, letting him watch.

"Very nice, thank you. You didn't enjoy that at all I'm sure. Being watched?" One more thing to be grateful for.

"I work hard on my core. It doesn't hurt my feelings that you see it."

"I was being sarcastic. I noticed you slowed down for me." Thomas stood and offered Sam a hand up.

"Oh. I thought you were paying me a compliment." Sam snorted and hauled himself up. "Let me towel off. You want a coffee?"

"Sure. I got it. You want me to make you one while I'm at it?" He headed for the kitchen, but not before he got one more look at those abs.

"Please." Sam took about two seconds to return, wearing a worn flannel that was huge.

"Where did you come up with that?"

"Daddy Mike gave me some winter shit he wasn't using anymore. Mostly sweats and all."

"Looks comfortable." Thomas made an effort not to sound like an asshole. Sam was scrambling, but he was making headway, and he hadn't asked for help. For the moment his head was above water, and it wasn't Thomas's place to step in. Not yet.

Daddy Mike. Thomas had spoken with Angel at length about this bar where Sam was working. Angel knew it well and spoke fairly highly of this Daddy Mike fellow and the bar's staff. He'd be the first to admit he was nosy, probably more than Sam would have liked, and asked Angel a handful of specific questions.

But he hadn't heard much from Sam himself, other than this horrific beating he'd received was the final component to what was essentially...what? Orientation? On the job training? And he was absolutely torn in half about it.

He handed Sam the first cup of coffee. "How are you feeling?"

"Good. Tired. It's new, being on my feet so long, but I'm learning the ropes."

The part of him that was a friend to Sam, that tried to be supportive and understanding, was glad to hear that things were starting off well, even if the establishment itself was a bit dubious. What he was struggling with was the part of him that was far more protective, even possessive, the piece that wanted to stand between Sam and anyone who had thrown a punch that night.

It took more discipline than he'd expected to keep the Dominant in him at bay. "It's not easy being new, right?"

"No, sir, but I am at peace with that. Easy isn't my thing." Sam settled on the sofa, curling in the corner. "It's a job. I've been in a situation to get my ass kicked a lot, but that was... anyway they trust me, and I can do my freelance work at the office. I'll just make a plan now—bills, moving, more work."

More work?

Thomas knew he was light years ahead of Sam in terms

of his hopes for their relationship. He was a Dom. He wanted a sub. He was forcing himself to slow down, to wait for the appropriate cues from Sam before he would even consider demanding Sam's weekends. At the moment, Sam worked evenings and nights in nine-hour shifts plus freelance jobs and only had Sundays off. Thomas was essentially nine-to-five. That contrast in schedule would become unsustainable for them should Sam show earnest interest in working with him as a sub. Up to this point anything that had happened at the club had been at his initiative, his request, not Sam's.

So for now Thomas's plan was to keep Sam distracted during the holidays by giving him something—and someone—else to think about other than family and Texas. He would keep bringing Sam to the club for short, intense visits on Sundays, keep him curious, unsatisfied, make him hungry.

Dangle the kind of carrot Sam couldn't resist reaching for.

Maybe it would work; maybe it wouldn't. That was up to Sam.

He took his coffee into the living room and joined Sam on the couch. "More work? Aren't you already six days a week?"

"I mean real work. Research. I am not going to be a bouncer until the end of time. This is rent until I can figure out how to make my freelance work enough." The sudden flash of pride and passion burned the air.

Burned the air and burned in his own chest. Sam's pride had become as important to him as his own. "I have confidence you can do that. I can see it in those complex hazel eyes of yours. Let me know if I can help. I do know some people in the field."

"Yeah. Yeah, I'm going to pick your brain. This is harder

than back home because fewer people need cowboy art specialists, but ninety-five percent of my jobs are electronic, so...I will make this work somehow, dammit. I'm not stupid, and I know how to put my nose to the grindstone." Sam blinked, touched the tip of his nose. "That saying always makes me think *ow*."

"Ow." He chuckled. "Yes, I was going to suggest that it shouldn't matter where you work. You can serve the same clients." Sam just needed an office. One with fewer distractions than the back office at the bar. For instance, one in Thomas's condo. He filed that thought and barely hid a grin. "You just need a good setup."

"Yeah. I can do this. I swear to you." The line of Sam's jaw was sharp enough to shave with. Shave...

"You shaved your beard!"

Sam cackled happily. "I was wondering if anyone would notice."

"You know when you know something is different about someone, but you just can't quite put your finger on it? You look great. I prefer it. I can see your smile better. What made you decide to take it off?"

"The girls at the bar keep tugging on it. That seems real...personal to me. I didn't like it."

From what he understood from Angel, much of the staff had a reputation for getting personal. "That's to be expected in a bar like that, especially if you're the new adorable barback." He winked and tried for a grin, but found himself wrestling again, this time with what he thought might be jealousy. It had to be.

Well. *That's a new one.*

"Yeah, yeah. Adorable, that's me." Sam flexed playfully. "Small but mighty and able to fell drunk assholes with a single bound."

Sam started laughing, the sound filling the air, just ringing out.

He started to laugh as well, because joy was rare these days and Sam's was contagious. He wasn't sure he'd ever heard Sam really laugh. Not like this. "You need a cape, 'little Sammy.' Oh...don't look at me like that. Angel told me."

"Yeah. I'm never going to get away from that. Good thing I don't have short-man syndrome." Sam actually kept a straight face for fifteen seconds or so; then they were howling with laughter again.

"Don't let it get around the club. It's been nearly ten years, and I still can't live down *Tommy*. Ugh." He lifted his coffee to take another sip but spilled it in another attack of the giggles. Right down the front of his shirt. "Oh, shit."

He stood up, still chuckling, and set the cup down on the coffee table. "Damn. I'll get something for the couch. Just let me..." He reached back and tugged his shirt off over his head. "Let me just deal with this before it stains."

"Here, I'll rinse you out." Sam stood and reached for the shirt, missing altogether, hand landing on his belly.

Reflexively he covered Sam's hand with his own and blinked. "Your hands are warm, cowboy." Sam's eyes were wide, and he could see every fleck of gold and brown in the green. Oh. This was a little close. Just...a little too close. "Not quite the washboard you've got."

"You don't know, do you? How fucking fine you are?" Sam shook his head a little, that scarred corner of his lips quirking up in a half smile. "I guess none of us know how we are in someone else's eyes."

He cupped a hand to Sam's cheek, eyes narrowing thoughtfully. "Well, they can tell you, but that doesn't mean you believe it." He drew his thumb along Sam's bottom lip.

"How long should you hold on to a moment when you know your next move changes everything?"

"You cain't. You got to nod your head and open the gate and ride."

Open the gate. Thomas took a deep breath, gave Sam a nod, and kissed him gently, just a taste, as if they might both shatter if he moved too quickly.

Sam's hand trembled on his belly, but only the barest bit, and Sam never looked away from him, didn't hide from the connection, from the kiss. Hell, from him.

He needed that and let it guide him like a lighthouse in a storm. He never gave a thought to anything but Sam, but he knew what was brewing in him, and he knew eventually the wind would blow and the waves would crash over him and he'd need Sam to tell him this was okay.

He hooked an arm around Sam's back, pulled him closer, and tangled his fingers into Sam's hair. Sam responded by sliding those warm hands around his back and steadying them.

"I ain't scared, honey." The words brushed against his lips.

It's your first rodeo, cowboy. You don't know any better.

"I'm...terrified." He kissed Sam again. "And hopeful. I know what I want. I just don't know if I'm allowed to have it."

"Don't think I haven't prayed on this, because I have. I'm not dishonoring anyone's memory." Sam kissed the corner of his mouth. "I wouldn't hurt you for love or money, though."

If he were a praying man, this might be a lot easier. He only had himself to answer to. "I don't think being happy is a dishonor to anyone. I just need someone to tell me that's the truth. There's no...definitive text on this. You're not hurting me. It just...hurts. And it doesn't. It's confusing."

Sam nodded and kissed him once again, the caress gentle enough that it made him ache. "I got your back, honey. I got all the time in the world."

He shook his head. "You don't, though. The only thing we know we have is today." He'd learned that lesson, right? He wasn't going to rush, but he wasn't going to hesitate either. "So far today is making me happy."

"I can handle happy."

He chuckled. "Me too. Can you handle coffee stains, though? Do you mind stopping by my place on the way to the club so I can change? I might even have something you can borrow to show off your washboard."

Somehow Sam had found just the right thing to say. He didn't feel like he was going to fall apart at all, and if he did, he wasn't worried. It was the strangest feeling, knowing he'd be okay. Sam had his back.

"I'd love to see your place. I got stain stuff, though, just to save the shirt. I'm like the laundry king." Sam took his shirt and headed to the bathroom.

Something about Sam taking care of his shirt for him brought that itch into his fingers and made him grin.

Then he realized he was freezing. He snagged Sam's blanket off the back of the couch and tucked it around his shoulders. Did the thermostat really say forty degrees? Surely Sam knew how to turn the heat up. Surely. But how do you ask that question without being insulting? Maybe it was down to finances again. "You know your heat is set at forty, right?"

"Yessir. That'll keep shit from freezing in the house, and I'm never here anymore except to sleep. Hold up." There was a rustle, and Sam appeared with a gigantic sweater with a moose fucking a unicorn on the front. "It's ugly, but it's warm."

"If you tell one single living, breathing soul, I will have your balls in a vise. I'll show it to you at the club tonight if you require proof." He'd rather stay wrapped up in the blanket, though. It smelled like Sam.

"Shit, I sleep in it. The damn thing goes down to my knees. Your secret is safe with me."

The only thing weirder about pulling on that sweater was that someone named "Daddy Mike" actually wore it first. "It is pretty warm, you're right, but...*Jesus*. How big is this guy? Look at the sleeves on this thing!"

"Daddy Mike? He's a monster. I swear to God, man. Four hundred pounds, six-six—he's like a slab of meat. He smacks me on the shoulder every night and I think I'm fixin' to fly out the door, and he's not being an ass! He's just saying 'Hi, let me remind you I could kill you with one hand.'"

Mother of God. "Tell me again about that plan to get more research work?"

"No shit, huh? Worse? Darla's the mean one. She's fierce. She's the one that lets me work in the office in exchange for sitting near the door while she's doing the money. She's been messed up a couple times, and it's my job to get in the way of that mess for internet access." Sam held up his shirt, staring at it, then nodding. "I looked into getting a carry permit, but *damn*."

"Yeah, New York isn't Texas. Besides, it sounds to me like she's the type to have one of her own."

And there was his opening.

"Why don't you use my home office? You could use it while I'm at work, or I'm up at five to go to the gym."

"Oh...that would be...would I be imposing? Because I don't want to be a bother, but—" Sam stopped himself, rolled his eyes, and breathed. "I think we might could talk about that, yeah."

He curled his fingers into Sam's shirt and tugged him into another kiss, laughing against Sam's lips. "I think we should. You won't be imposing. Think of yourself as a guard dog."

"Woof. Be good or I'll take a picture of you in my nightgown." Sam's eyes were lit up, joyous, bright and so clear.

"Balls. In. A. Vise. It has teeth, did I mention? And a lock." He let Sam go but stayed close, soaking in that sunshine.

"You're shitting me. Teeth and balls are not intended to be in the same sentence, much less vise."

"Rather like unicorns and Thomas don't go together either." He stepped away and started folding up the blanket. "Can you hang that up for me? I'll come get it later. We should probably move along since we're headed to my place first. Oh! You can see the office and tell me what you think. I'll call an Uber. I'm not getting on the subway again with that pie." *Or in this ridiculous sweater.*

Whoa. Diarrhea of the mouth. How very odd.

———

"THOMAS, are you sure this is okay?"

They were almost at the club, and they had the pie and the rolls and some hummus and crackers because somebody had texted Thomas.

Sam had decided he was going to have fun, dammit. No drama, no psycho family shit. Just a bunch of folks giving thanks.

This shirt, though.

Jesus.

Thomas had offered it to him—a fitted black sweater that left nothing to the imagination, up to and including where his nipples were and every single ridge of his six-pack.

"It's perfect. You're walking in on my arm, aren't you? You think I'd let you look like a fool?" Thomas grinned at him, gave his knee a squeeze.

He looked at that hand on his leg, sitting there like it belonged.

Something inside him had...not broken, but shifted, slid the night of his initiation to the club. He'd paid James in flesh. He'd paid for deciding to stay. He'd let himself be taken down until he couldn't stand back up. He'd given what all he was fixin' to in penance, and he was done now. He was here, and he was going to keep on staying on.

"This is us," Thomas told the driver, then got out of the car and held the door. "You're going to love this, such good company."

"I'm ready." A little nervous but nothing more than facing anything new warranted.

Thomas actually did offer his arm. "Hey, breathe a little. Everyone is well aware that James is missing from the table. We'll be well looked after. Maybe too well, you know what I mean?" He winked.

Personally he didn't think James would be missing this year. Sam had missed his brothers at the Thanksgiving table for a long time. This year in this place, though, Sam had no doubt James would be present, even more present than he was. He could live with it. He didn't think Thomas cared to hear any of that, but it eased him. "I reckon, yessir."

They made their way inside. Men were milling around, talking and laughing. There was music, but it sounded like cocktail-party fare, not the usual thump-thump. There was no club lighting, no bartender, no host. Most remarkably, though, no one that he could see was in leather, and almost no one was kneeling.

"Thomas!" A red-haired man in jeans and a gray sweater greeted them almost immediately, someone Sam hadn't seen before.

"Bill. Good to see you. Happy Thanksgiving."

Bill hugged Thomas and smiled at Sam. "How are you? Are you okay?"

"I'm okay. Bill, this is Sam O'Reilly."

"Sam...O'Reilly. It's good to meet you." Bill offered his hand and a slightly confused but genuine smile.

"Thank you, sir. Pleased to meet you." He dipped his chin, acknowledging the weird. "I'm James's little brother."

It was ironic—at home he was always trying to make up for the fact that the others weren't there, and he was going to play that role here, he bet. Hell, right now that was what he was for Thomas, and he was just going to have to work until he was more than a stand-in for someone everyone really wished was there.

"Should have known. It's in the eyes. So sorry. But I'm sure you've heard plenty of that. You guys want to put your food down?"

"That would be great."

"So the dinner stuff can go right on the buffet table, the munchies on the bar."

"Got it. Thanks, Bill."

"I'll let you two get settled. Welcome to the club, Sam."

"Thank you, sir. I appreciate it." He set the rolls down where it looked like the rest of the bread went before dropping off hummus—which seriously, what the actual fuck was that? Bean mayonnaise? Who ate bean mayonnaise?—and the crackers.

The smaller tables had been pushed together to seat eight or ten and spread out around the room and over the dance floor. Along the far wall was an enormously long table with a space in the center that had to be for turkey, and covered dishes of all kinds spread out on either side.

Thomas leaned close to his ear. "I'm going to go set this pie down and hang up my coat. Can I take yours?"

"Surely." He was kinda hiding in it, though. "I'll come with you."

Thomas led him along the table. "Ah. There. That looks like a bunch of sweet stuff." The pie sat nicely among what looked like lemon bars, a couple of pumpkin pies, and a huge tray of cookies.

"Lots of new faces, right? They're harder to recognize without the leather and the leashes." Thomas grinned at him and took his hand. "The first year I did this, Clint had me try to guess which of them were the Doms and which the subs. It was impossible."

"Yeah? It's easy to tell what rodeo people do, but that's a sport, huh? You know who the running back is versus the tackle in football. This is more a game than a sport?" He handed over his jacket and his hat, feeling pretty near naked, but you couldn't wear cover at the Thanksgiving table.

"It's not a game. It's important." Thomas's tone wasn't stern or defensive, but Sam knew the man was serious.

"That's not what I meant. It is, but—I meant chess doesn't rest on whether you're built a certain way. Or poker. Heavy guys don't ride bulls. Tiny guys don't bulldog. A certain kind of mind plays chess. I don't have the lingo for what I mean, but I wasn't being glib." This part was getting easier—they seemed to be learning each other's language.

"Oh, I see. Yes. It doesn't seem to matter how you're built. Needs and desires aren't governed by size and shape, gender, any of those conventions that are characteristic of a sport."

Thomas led him over to a taller set of tables that had bottles of wine on them and coolers of beer and bottled soft drinks underneath.

"I guess that's why we call it a lifestyle. But actually, you're partly right when you call it a game. It does have rules. There are certain traditions and rituals."

He nodded. Exactly. "That I understand—that's a huge amount of Western culture, especially when you start getting into tribal artwork, because it's still very much a living thing. Cowboy art looks backward, there's a longing for before, but..." Sam stopped. "Sorry. I get going and I can bore the world."

"Why do you assume you're boring me? I know very little about cowboy culture and practically nothing about cowboy art. I majored in art history as an undergrad before I got my MBA. Western just wasn't on my radar. We have this art-geek thing in common, right? I'm interested. You're interesting." Thomas smiled at him. "Wine, beer?"

"I think I'll go with a beer today." He grinned, warm in the pit of his belly.

"I can't begin to guess, so go ahead and hunt around." Thomas stepped out of the way so he could get to the coolers, and picked out an already open bottle of wine.

"Hey! Is that the same boy that tried to pass out on my bike last weekend?"

"Hello, Angel. Wine?"

Angel looked at Thomas. "Get serious. What are you drinking, cowboy? Grab me one."

"Yessir." He found two bottles of Dos Equis and stood, then popped the top of Angel's and handed it over before opening his own. "And I didn't fall off, did I? I owe you a drink or five, next time you come into Mike's."

He didn't know what he would have done that night without Angel. Not gotten home, that was for sure.

"You did not fall off. Not only that, but you hauled your own ass up the stairs to your apartment even though you couldn't tell me your name, or mine. Cheers to you, little Sammy." Angel held up his beer.

Thomas snorted. "That might have been more detail than I necessarily needed."

"I'll be there this weekend, kid. There's something on the schedule they want me on hand for Saturday night."

"They put events they need an EMT for on the schedule?" Thomas looked at him. "Are you working Saturday night?"

"Yessir. I'm working the fight crowd apparently. I'm not fighting in the ring."

"Nope. You're not ready. I get to make that call, kid."

Sam snorted. He got to make that call, and the fact was? He wasn't ready. Nowhere near.

"Sam tells me he is only there temporarily, that he's planning on making his freelance research work more lucrative." He saw the look that passed between Thomas and Angel, and he knew what Thomas was asking.

"That's the plan and the prayer. I just need to make it work." He went for comforting. "I got this. I can hold my own. I have been hit by a two-thousand-pound bull, and this time I can hit back."

"So what did you two bring?" Angel looked over Thomas's shoulder, changing the subject like a champ.

"Apple pie and rolls. And Mark called and asked for hummus."

"Hummus? Was that on the table at the first Thanksgiving?"

"I don't know. You were there—you tell me."

"Bean mayonnaise," he muttered, loving the banter between the two men. Playing seemed tough for Thomas, like he didn't use that muscle often.

Angel laughed and clapped Sam on the back. "Right? All right, I got my beer. I'm going to go surf the food bar. I'll be sure to try your hummus."

"Funny. We'll catch up. Thanks, Angel." Thomas took a sip of his wine. "Mmm. A good one. So you tell me, Sam, jump in and meet some people? Stuff our faces with starters?" Thomas took his hand again.

"Let's meet folks. I'm looking forward to meeting your family."

"Perfect. I'd love to show you off a little and let people get to know you. Make sure they're not just thinking about you as James's little brother, you know? I'm hoping they'll eventually become your family too." Thomas gave him a tug.

He followed along, meeting one man after another. Most everyone paid their respects. He heard lots of stories about James and got a couple three shocked looks. All in all, it felt pretty damn good to be here and to be able to breathe.

"Is Master Thomas dressing you now?" A guy popped up at his elbow, and it took him a second to recognize Mark in a sweater and without the leather harness. "That shirt is totally hot on you."

He glanced over to where Thomas had just been beside him, but someone was dragging the man toward the bar.

"He gave it to me, yeah. It's a little different, that's for sure." Master Thomas, huh? He was going to have to think about that. Later. In the dark. Not now.

"How are you two getting along together? It's nice to see Master Thomas happy again. You're a newbie, right? You must be a very good boy. And a quick learner. What's your thing?" Mark winked at him.

"Western art." He knew what Mark was asking, but he didn't have an answer, so playing dumb was easier. He didn't have any answers. He sure as shit wasn't sure he'd learned much—other than the fact that he'd take a beating to be able to stay near Thomas. "And yeah, I hate to see him sad."

"It's okay. You don't need to tell me. I get it. But whatever it is, you're doing something right. Master Thomas sure seems to like it. I get that you're private, but if you ever want to ask a question or go compare notes, I'm totally up for that."

"Sam!" Thomas was waving him over from the bar.

"Oops. You better go. Really, really like that top."

"Thank you. I'd like that. We could have coffee." He found Mark a smile but took his leave, because he wasn't ready to admit that he was more confused now than he'd been at the beginning.

"Sounds good! Master Thomas can get you my digits."

"Hey." Thomas slipped an arm around him as soon as he was in reach, pulled him in, and kissed his temple. "Look! Queso." He got a grin and a wink. "I might just stay right here for a while."

He had to laugh. James had been obsessed with queso. Loved it. Of course, what was not to love? Cheese, Rotel—magic on a chip. "I'm in."

"It'll be dinner soon. I'm usually seated at Clint's table. Are you getting hungry?"

He nodded. "Looks like a great spread. Smells like Thanksgiving."

His phone vibrated in his pocket, and he checked it. Bowie.

Happy Tday baby brother.

You too. Love you.

Ditto

"Everything okay?" Thomas rubbed his back between his shoulder blades.

"Just Bowie happy Thanksgiving-ing me. He's off saving the world."

"Well, I can be thankful for that. I couldn't do it. The twins are deployed someplace right now too. No idea where, but Katie texted me. My baby sister. She went home Wednesday."

"It's like a minefield, isn't it? Family." He couldn't think too terrible hard on that, because there was a shit-ton of hurt he could only bear to look at when he was locked away alone.

Thomas nodded, looking thoughtful; then he smiled at Sam. "That one is. This one isn't. Should we go figure out where we're sitting?"

"Surely. Just don't put me where I'll bump elbows."

Thomas snorted. "Sure thing, southpaw."

They found their seats, set their drinks down, and got in the line that was forming at the buffet.

"Hey, Thomas! Good to see you back. Doing okay?"

"Fine. Hungry, Butch. You?"

"I could eat. New boy?"

Thomas didn't directly answer that question, and Sam couldn't tell if Thomas just didn't want to go there or if not answering meant yes. "This is Sam. Sam, Butch."

"Pleased to meet you, sir." He held out one hand to

shake. Lord have mercy, there were a ton of men here that didn't have kin that they could be with.

"And you." Butch shook, then looked back at Thomas. "Are you making plans to bring him to New Years?"

"Oh, I doubt it. I think it's a little early for that yet."

"Why not?"

"Butch."

"He's adorable. You should bring him."

Thomas turned to Butch. "Enough." Thomas was a good six inches shorter and half as wide, but that didn't seem to faze him, and his posture wasn't allowing for an argument. "Let's enjoy our turkey."

"You got it." Butch didn't flinch but didn't say anything else either.

Thomas turned around again and took a step closer to him, practically bumping hips. "You won't make fun of me if I have a plate full of potatoes, will you?"

"I won't. It's turkey day. No judgment." It was the fun part —eating what you wanted. He was mostly hoping for a deviled egg. He loved those.

And he'd be working New Years, no question. Busting his hump bringing up kegs and breaking up fights.

"That's my philosophy." They loaded up their plates, and Thomas grabbed a bottle of wine and brought him a fresh beer.

"Hey, what does your work schedule look like this weekend?" He noticed that Thomas took a bite of the potatoes first.

"I'm off 'til seven tomorrow. Then I work a full shift, then the fight on Saturday, off on Sunday."

Thomas frowned. "And that will be your normal weekend schedule? Or close to it?"

"Yeah." He sighed softly. He was going to miss his

Saturdays with Thomas. Sometimes they were the only good parts. He needed to just push harder. He could take his laptop to a coffee shop and put in a few more hours. If he got to the apartment by noon, he could get a solid five hours sleep...

"All right." Thomas put a hand on his thigh. "We'll make it work. What time do you get off shift Sunday morning? And when do you need to be back on Monday?"

"The bar closes at four. There's no deposit on Saturday night. I'm back at seven Monday night."

"And you have to get some rest. You need to do your freelance work." Thomas cleared his throat. "Well. Could I ask for a couple of hours of your time on Sunday evening? Here?"

"Please. I'm doing this so I can be here with you, for chrissake. It's going to suck if I never get to see you." Wait. Wait, did he say that out loud?

"Oh." Thomas put his fork down and gave him a sidelong look and a smile. "If you'd have told me that sooner, it would have saved me a great deal of anxiety."

"I'm sorry, honey. It ain't easy for me sometimes, telling."

"I know. But you try, and you're honest. I can't ask anything more of you than that." The hand on his thigh shifted up over his hip as Thomas leaned closer, and the fingers tucked into his back pocket. "It wasn't my place to tell you not to go, but I was considering selling my soul to get you to stay."

"Your soul's safe." God, he sounded like a crow, but Thomas's hand in his pocket was the most erotic thing on earth, and his entire body felt alive in the best way.

"So is yours." Thomas's eyes were clear and looked right into him like the man would know. He got a kiss so hard and quick it left him blinking; then Thomas went back to his supper.

God, he missed having his hat right now.

Of course, if he had it with him, it would be in his lap, covering the bulge in his jeans.

The conversation over supper was friendly and light, with lots of laughter and good stories. People made him feel welcome, drawing him into the mix, asking questions, filling him in when he needed it, just as if he belonged there.

There was so much food at dinner it was a wonder anyone had room for dessert, but everything on that table was pretty well demolished by the time the nightcaps went around. Little shot glasses of something strong and sweet that Thomas knocked back with a shiver. "Whoa."

"That's a concoction." His lips tingled.

"I don't drink stuff like this except...well, ever really. Feels good going down, though. Warm."

"I'll buy you shots at the bar one night. Gina and Darla have some neat ones they've come up with."

"You might have to send me home in a car or kick me under a table and let me sleep it off." Thomas laughed. "I'm good for one. If you expect me to continue after that, I can't take responsibility for my behavior."

"Me too. I drink water in my longneck after one at work." At Thomas's surprised look, Sam shrugged. "I'm over the legal limit at two. I got no padding, and I'm not a big guy."

"Years ago, Clint wouldn't let me use a flogger until I gained ten pounds. I have to go to the gym and do the protein powder thing or I look like a string bean. I'll show you some pictures next time you're at my place—you'll laugh."

"I'd like that." He was solid as a rock, and he knew it. It

was one thing that him and Bowie had in common. James had been the skinny one. He was as built as his big brother, just half the size. Same rank, different weight class.

"Would you like to dance?" Thomas pointed toward the ceiling. "Music."

"Why not?" Today had been his day for firsts. It seemed the thing to do.

"Why not, indeed." Thomas stood up and held the back of his chair, the gesture sincere, not campy. "My lead, though. My invitation. And don't worry, I expect to get stepped on."

"Right." He chuckled, tickled shitless that Thomas remembered their conversation. "I'm not bad at moving. I'll figure it."

They headed for the open area where the buffet used to be and had somehow disappeared during the nightcaps, and Thomas led him right into the middle of the crowd. Whatever Thomas was up to started off on the wrong foot and too slow, but Sam caught on without scuffing anyone's toes.

They didn't need whatever lighting had been put on to make the dance floor glow. Thomas's smile could have lit up the floor by itself.

He had his hand on Thomas's waist, and he stayed close, letting himself have a ride, trusting in Thomas and his own body to get them through. Thomas telegraphed just fine, so he didn't have to think, just feel the way they created a heat between them.

"Why am I not surprised that you're having no trouble with this? I love how you just...do things. Try things."

"I was made to ride, yeah?"

Thomas lost his lead for a second, and they went all off-meter. "Whoops. Sorry. I...thinking. Shouldn't think and dance."

"No worries. You cool?" *You bored? Tired? Too much wine?*

"Far from it." Thomas had the lead back, though, that hand strong at his back. "I mean, look at you. Am I supposed to be?"

Oh, now that made him blush. "Listen to you."

Thomas grinned at him. "I will say that sweater looks fantastic on you, but I know it's not your style."

"This is tight. You can see my heartbeat, I bet. I like how it slides, though. I can see why you'd wear it. It wears like being loved on."

Thomas laughed and shook his head. "If you say so. It must feel good. You wear it like you know you look good in it."

"Thank you, sir. I appreciate it." He did look good. He worked for it, even if his six-pack was kind of purple and green right now.

They danced a little while longer, before they helped clean the place up, clearing trash out to the dumpsters and pushing tables back where they belonged, and everyone pretty much said good night at once. The longest line of cabs he'd ever seen was waiting outside the club as men left and one by one drove away. Thomas hustled him into one and closed the door behind them, then told the driver to take them to Union Square. His place.

"Thank you for today. It's been something else." Something good. Something that he'd remember when he was old and gray, like his first short-go or when his thesis advisor called him gifted or how big the water looked from the Galveston seawall.

"It was a day to be grateful for, wasn't it? Thank you for

sharing it with me." Thomas gave him a tug and settled an arm over his shoulders.

There was a little part of him that couldn't believe this was real, but it was happening, real or not.

They made it back to his apartment in record time, the streets quieter than usual. It was cold when they climbed out of the cab, and Thomas stayed close, keeping the wind off him.

"You think it's going to snow? It's sure chilly."

"That would be unusual for Thanksgiving, but not unheard of."

"You want to come upstairs and have a cup of coffee, honey?"

Thomas moved in close. Closer than really seemed ought to be allowed on the street. "No, sweetheart. Sam. Sorry. No, I think I shouldn't. You'll forgive me, won't you?"

"Surely." He could go upstairs and curl up and jack off, take a nap before he found a place that was open for Black Friday that had Wi-Fi. "Thank you for today again. It was fine."

Thomas tipped his chin up and kissed him. It started out like earlier, just slow and sweet, but then it became...more. But it seemed like just as he was about to hit on what was different, Thomas ended it and took a step back.

"I better...you were wonderful tonight. I'm just...tired. You know? Thank you." He got a self-conscious smile, and Thomas started down the stairs. "Good night, Sam."

"Good night, honey." He smiled and watched Thomas go, just in case that last shot was really too much, but he made the stairs just fine.

He headed inside, whistling softly under his breath. He climbed the stairs, smelling the remnants of turkey dinners.

Sam reached to unlock his door when a shadow

appeared behind him, and he spun, caught short by a hand on his coat. "What the fuck?"

A sharp blow cracked him, right under the ear, and he let himself drop, fist shooting out, catching whoever the fuck it was with a hard damn blow. "Back off, asshole!"

The hallway swam, and he was scattered, but he wasn't down, and he wasn't helpless.

It would help if he could see clear, but all he needed to do was get his back against the door and...

He hit out again, connecting once more, and he heard a deep curse ring out; then the guy ran with James's coat.

"Motherfucker!"

He slumped down against the apartment door, trying not to—*what? Cry? Run outside and try to find Thomas? Hurl? All of the above? Shit.*

"Dude. Dude, what happened? Dude, it's me. Skip. You remember? Next door? What happened?"

"Someone stole my coat."

"You got your wallet? Your keys? He follow you in? Who was it?"

"Skip. Man. You're killing my head."

"Sure, Tex. Sure."

"Skip Smith! You get away from there."

"I didn't do it!"

"I know. He took off down the stairs. It doesn't look like you're helping, though."

Uh. Woman's voice. Young. Not the old lady in 4B...this was the blonde from one floor up.

"Someone took his coat, Haley."

"Hey." Haley got down on his level. "Are you okay?"

"Yeah. Yeah, he knocked my noggin. Good thing I'm hardheaded." And no one stole his phone or his wallet. "Happy Thanksgiving, y'all."

"Skip, maybe you should call the cops. That could have been any of us."

"Haley, I am not calling cops."

"Why? Was it one of your friends, Skip?"

Skip disappeared back into his apartment and slammed the door.

"It's...Sam, right?"

"Yes, ma'am. You okay? Nobody hurt you?"

"No, I'm fine. I saw the guy's back, but I don't think that will be very helpful. Just dark, you know? Hair, clothes, just dark, like that guy that...I think it might be time for me to move."

"Yeah." Him too, except, what if it had been James's killer. What if he'd had James's murderer close enough to punch and he lost him? *Oh God.*

The hallway lights began to swing wildly for a second, and he had to fight his urge to scream. Instead he stood up. "Let me walk you up. I'll stay at the stairs. I just worry."

"No, that's okay. Thanks. You look like you'd fall down them anyway. You should get inside and call the police. I'm calling my boyfriend. You and James are brothers, right? You have the same bad luck. Maybe it's you that should move."

"Maybe." He offered Haley a nod before he unlocked the door. "Night."

He closed the door behind him, locked it, then stood there for a long minute before he reached for the pack of cigarettes on the table with a half grin.

If today wasn't the day to start smoking again, he sure as shit didn't know what was.

Lord help him.

19

Thomas got back from the gym later than he'd intended, but then his whole morning had been a little off because he hadn't slept all that well.

When he'd gotten home from the Thanksgiving party, he was high on his day and a little high on that last shot too. But mostly, he was high on Sam, on Sam's candor and kisses.

He'd taken a shower and managed to get just a little higher on Sam before he dove into bed.

But at some point, he'd had that dream, the one where James was sitting there, then just wasn't. Sometimes it was in a coffee shop, sometimes on the subway. Last night they were together in James's bedroom, in James's bed, and this time when James disappeared and he woke up in his own bed...well. He'd lost it. It wasn't anything he'd have wanted anyone to see.

But routine was his shelter, and the gym got him back on track, and now that he'd showered and had coffee, it seemed like it was a polite enough hour to try Sam and get on with the rest of his plan for the day.

Good morning. Do you have plans today? I'm off—I thought you might like to come use the office.

Sam could use his office, and he could read and maybe take Sam out for lunch. Something to make up for the fact that he was too anxious last night and hadn't trusted himself not to do something he'd regret if he'd gone in for coffee.

Sam began to answer him almost immediately, but it took forever for the text to drop.

I would, but I can't. I got mugged. I lost James's coat. I smoked a lot and puked and the neighbor said I was bad luck. I can't do it today. I'm broke dick and low and I can't do no more.

What? He hit Call, his stomach tightening.

It didn't even ring. " 'M sorry."

"Don't. Can I come over? I'm coming over."

"I can't cowboy up right now. You got to know that."

"I get it. I just want to be there. Will you...do you want to stay on the phone? I'll take a cab."

"Yeah. I'm...Jesus, I'm fixin' to lose my shit, swear to God."

He rushed around the living room finding shoes, getting his coat, his wallet. Trying not to panic. "Keys. Where are... oh. Coat pocket. Why didn't you call me sooner?"

"I started to, over and over, but it's your day off, and I hit him. What if it had been him, man? What if it was him and he was right there and I let him go?" Sam sounded shattered. Totally.

His day off? His fucking day off? He wanted to scream into the phone, but he forced himself to take a deep breath before he said anything at all, and reminded himself that Sam could have just said no, would have just said no without any explanation at all not even two weeks ago.

Breathe. He's in pieces; you can't be.

"It's okay, Sam. You've got me now, right? Your door is

locked? You're safe right now, and I'm on my way." He got in the first cab he could find, not caring that it was headed uptown and he needed to go down. "Make a U-turn."

The guy glanced at him in the rearview mirror, and he tossed a twenty into the front seat. "And step on it."

"Am I ever not going to be fucked up again? I swear to God, I feel like I'm on the circuit again, somehow." Sam sounded hollow, like his boy was speaking down a well.

It did seem like every time Sam started to get his feet, someone pulled the rug out again. Sam's voice was painful to hear. It sounded hoarse and washed out, nothing like the laughter he'd enjoyed at the party yesterday. It hurt, made his chest ache. He leaned into the little window between the front seat and the back. "Move it. Please."

Thomas turned his attention back to his phone. "Sam, you're all right. I know it feels overwhelming, but we'll sort it through. When I get there, you'll tell me what happened?"

"Yeah. Yeah, I'll tell you everything."

"Make some coffee. Turn the heat up a little, okay? You need to be able to think." He was almost there. He sat back in the seat and closed his eyes, breathing, trying to find center. Sam had been mugged, hadn't slept; the boy would be green from overdoing it with the cigarettes. He refused to be shocked by any of it.

He opened his eyes just in time to see Sam's building go by the window. "Here. Stop. Let me out here." He paid the driver and pulled out his keys.

He didn't worry about the stoop, about anything but getting to his Sam.

"I'm here. I'm coming up." He shut his phone off and took the steps two at a time, then took a breath and reined it in before he keyed into the apartment.

Calm. Solid and calm.

He opened the door, finding Sam on the sofa, eyes red, wrapped in his blanket, teeth chattering. "Hey. You came."

"Yes, Sam." He closed the door behind him and locked it. Taking in Sam's sunken, slightly wild eyes as he took off his coat, he stopped by the thermostat and turned it up to sixty-five without asking. He'd pay the goddamn bill. "I'm going to come sit with you, all right?" It seemed worth asking permission, because Sam looked like he was either going to shiver to bits or take off like a rocket any second.

"Please." Sam pushed himself into the corner of the sofa, giving him room, opening the blanket to let him in. "He took James's coat."

"It's just a coat." He didn't need room; he needed to get his arms around Sam. He slid under the blanket, though; it was still so damn cold. "Come here. Come lean on me." He held his arms open and waited.

Sam didn't hesitate. Thomas's arms were filled with shaking, shattering man. Sam had found that final straw.

It was raw and painful, and it worried him more than a bit if he were honest, but Sam was finally offering him the level of trust he'd asked for, that he needed. He knew what he had in his hands, and he had to step up now and keep his promises.

But fuck, Sam was so cold.

"I've got you. You're not just free-falling, Sam. I'm here." He'd get to questions in a minute.

Sam took one breath, another; then he began to relax and warm, which made the tremors worse. That he understood, the shock, how muscles had to remember how to relax.

He rubbed his hands over Sam's arm and back, but mostly he just stayed there, as present and attentive as he could manage through his own veil of worry and the queasy feeling in his stomach. "That's good. Breathe. I'm yours all day. I wouldn't want to be anywhere else. Take your time and breathe."

"I'm sorry. I can't figure out how to get my feet under me." Sam closed his eyes. "I can't stop thinking."

Jesus Christ. Sam would apologize to the sun for making it rise. "All right. Tell me what's on your mind. Think out loud—get it out."

"I hit him. I hit him twice, Thomas. What if it was the same guy? He has James's coat. I had him, and he got away." He could feel the tension ratcheting up. "Jesus fucking Christ—what if I had him right there, after all? No one's ever going to forgive me for letting him go."

There was no reason to believe it was the same guy, was there? "You were mugged, Sam. What did he take besides the coat? Did he get your wallet? Where were you? Did you go back out after I left?"

"I was here. At the door. Thinking about you. And I saw a shadow. He grabbed the coat, and I turned and started punching. He hit me in the head, and things got a little fuzzy. He only took the coat." Sam shook his head. "The girl said he was just a guy in dark clothes."

Right. Just a guy in dark clothes that got spooked when Sam fought back, that was all. The guy didn't have time to get anything else. Simplest explanation was the best. "The girl?"

"The neighbor girl. She said we're unlucky, that I should move." Sam made a soft, odd sound. "I came in and locked the door, and the world fell out from under me."

Why had he gone home? If he'd come in, it was possible things could have gotten complicated, but not this kind of complicated.

"I should have come in with you," he muttered.

"What if he'd hit you? Hurt you?" Sam rested one hand over his heart. "Jesus, I'm so fucking tired in my soul."

If he'd hit me first, you'd have had him.

"I know." Thomas threaded his fingers into Sam's. "But you're not alone. Just let it rest with me." The heat was kicking in. It wasn't warm yet, but he could smell it.

"Okay." Sam hugged him hard, the action sudden and surprising and incredibly dear—Sam accepting the comfort he offered without question.

"Oh. All right. All right." Thomas wrapped his arms tighter and held him close, holding back the emotion stinging the corners of his eyes by sheer stubborn will. He hadn't the slightest understanding of what it meant, and he didn't have the luxury to indulge it right now. He was here for Sam. He was fine.

"I was afraid you'd be so disappointed." The whisper was barely audible.

"About a coat?" The question was out of his mouth before he thought better of it. This wasn't about a coat. Even James's coat.

"The coat. The whole thing. My whole thing."

"I haven't imposed any expectations on you, Sam. You can't disappoint me. I've grown fond of your...whole thing." Words were so important, weren't they? Even he didn't know what "grown fond of" was supposed to mean. The words were just peeking out of a fog.

"We all have expectations, don't we? Christ, some days I don't feel like I can stand up from them weighing on me. I can't be the only one like that." Sam chuckled. "I'm rambling. Also, I'm fond of your whole thing too."

"Well." He snorted. "I'm glad we're clear on that at least." He shifted a little, giving Sam more room to breathe. "You make a fair point. There are things we expect of ourselves and things we expect of other people. There are also things we expect of people, but only in certain situations. So, yes. We live under the weight of a lot of scrutiny. I think you need to sort through who is really putting your feet to the fire. It's not me. You can't disappoint me when the only thing I expect is truth. That you live what's in your heart."

"I don't lie to you. Sometimes I don't know the truth, but I don't lie." Sam was melted against him, boneless, soaking up their contact.

"No, you don't. I know. You're a master of leaving out details, but you don't lie." He grinned and kissed the top of Sam's head to soften his words.

Sam's cheek rubbed against his chest. "I vote no one else hits me in the head. Body shots are way more fair."

"Oh, God. Your head. What am I thinking? Let me look at it."

"Looks like a head." Sam winked at him but tilted his head, the bruise under his ear dark blue and angry. "I didn't go down, but it scattered my chickens."

"It's not pretty, but you'll live. Alternatively, I could amputate at the neck."

"Promises, promises. Good thing you're not expecting pretty."

That made him laugh. "You're plenty pretty. Sort of... punching bag chic. I'm not sure I'd recognize you without all the green and purple."

"Shut up, you. Punching bag chic...good lord and butter." Sam looked up, met his eyes. "Thank you. I was lost."

He held Sam's gaze and breathed a sigh of relief, recognizing them again, seeing the Sam he knew in there. "You're welcome. Don't hesitate next time, just call. Any hour, about anything. Okay?"

Sam nodded once. "I needed a hand up."

"I'm glad I—" There was a flash of familiar confidence in Sam's eyes with those words, just enough to distract him, and he leaned down to take a kiss. Sam met him halfway, the connection like a key in a lock.

He tightened his fingers around the back of Sam's neck and pulled him in, a sudden heat building in his belly and exploding out in all directions. His head swam with it, and he reached out with his tongue to explore Sam's lips, begging to be let in.

Sam groaned for him and opened, lips parting like butter for a hot knife, no hesitation, no fear. Just an answering desire.

Oh God. Sam was an irresistible cocktail of freshly showered skin, toothpaste, and raw heat. Everything about the cowboy felt new and clean; even their kiss was curious. Wild.

He took his time, exploring with his tongue, answering Sam's groan with one of his own.

Sam touched his jaw, fingers sliding down his neck as they luxuriated in each other. Their lips parted, they stole a breath, and dove back in.

He wanted to see Sam, to feel him, and right now the man was swimming in fabric. He tugged on the blanket and shoved it to the floor, then started gathering the enormous sweat shirt that had tangled and wrapped itself around Sam's body, shoulders to knees. "Skin. I want to feel you."

"God, yes." Sam stripped the mass of fabric off and slid over to straddle his thighs, pulling on his shirt before he even got a chance to explore. "You too?"

"Me too." He helped Sam pull his sweater up and off, before he went right after Sam's collarbones, tasting his way from one shoulder to the other while his fingers read those washboard abs like braille.

Sam mapped his body, stopping to explore when he shivered, when his breath hiccupped, and he had to admire Sam's focus, because there was no hiding Sam's responses. The strong muscles jerked and rolled, nipples hard as rocks, strangled sounds on the air.

Fuck, the man was glowing like a pint-sized Adonis.

He went after a nipple, rolling the stiff bud between his tongue and teeth. "You taste so good."

"Oh, fuck..." Sam curled over him, the motion fluid, abs catching his fingers. That tiny, tight ass rocked on his thighs.

Sam was right—this body was made to ride.

"Good, right?" He turned his head and caught Sam's mouth again, tongue invading, and shifted his hands to Sam's back, fingers sneaking under the waistband of another pair of Daddy Mike's gigantic sweats. If Sam had tensed, had pulled away, Thomas would have stopped, but no, Sam arched for him like a huge cat, welcoming his touch.

"Fuck, Sam." Habit and deeply ingrained principle had him listening for that voice that would tell him to slow things down, to consider circumstances and timing, but if it was there, Sam's heat, Sam's need was drowning it out. That was his calling, wasn't it? His whole purpose? Seeing to Sam's needs was what he was made for.

Sam nodded, cupped his face, and kissed him again, trapping their shared moan between them. Sam was hard as diamonds, rubbing against him restlessly, the entire beautiful body begging him for more.

That put Sam light-years ahead of him, and perhaps that was for the best. Thomas hadn't rushed anything in his life, and he wasn't interested in rushing this. Not wanting what he wanted. Not with everything he knew was at stake.

He took Sam by the shoulders and turned them, dumping Sam on his back on the couch. He caught Sam's eyes and held them as he slid the sweats over Sam's hips. They'd barely been holding on anyway, even with the waistband cinched tight.

Sam never flinched away from him, staring right into him, waiting for his reaction. Brave. Sam gave himself over, knowing that it could be a fucking disaster.

It wouldn't be, though. He'd just get Sam feeling good, take the edge off for him; then he'd think about his next move.

He glanced down and grinned. Big things really did come in small packages. Wait, was it good things? Well, it worked either way. "Lovely." He gently curled his fingers around Sam, careful not to set the boy off. "Heavy." Solid. Like the rest of the cowboy.

"You make me ache, honey, deep. Ain't never been naked and hard with a man at the same time before."

He wasn't the least bit surprised. He'd assumed as much, but they weren't seventeen and fucking around in the back of a car. They were grown men, and the moment had more weight. "I almost envy you right now." He smiled. "Firsts are memorable."

He bent his head to Sam's cock, his fingers still gliding gently, balls to tip over hot, silky skin, and touched his tongue to the head, flicking it experimentally, gauging Sam's reaction.

Sam's shoulders left the couch cushions, body rolling right up, curling over his head.

Jesus, that was the fucking hottest, most genuine reflex ever. Sam didn't even know enough to know most people were self-conscious during sex. His balls drew up tight, and he had to squeeze his eyes closed. That honesty was more than a turn-on; if his middle name wasn't "control," he might very well have lost it right then.

Thomas wanted to make this mind-blowing for Sam, send him flying. They had time for real intimacy when Sam didn't have a shift hanging over his head. He took Sam into his mouth and scrubbed his tongue over the shaft, ready in case the boy went wild.

"Jesus, Thomas. *Please*." Sam reached for him, hands hot as fire on his bare skin.

Goddammit! That "please" was enough to settle a heat like he'd never known at the base of his spine. He forced himself to concentrate and not listen, to keep his focus on Sam. In compensation, he swore to himself he'd have this boy on his knees to him by Sunday if it was the last thing he ever did.

He swallowed Sam deep, throat working, and lightly pinched the sensitive skin behind Sam's balls.

That was all Sam could take, Sam's cry ringing out, clear as a bell, salt pouring into his mouth.

It was a rush, to know he was the first, to know no one had ever tasted Sam like this before.

He lingered, licking and nuzzling, letting Sam's scent settle on him. Then he lifted his head and tried to memorize the stunning look on Sam's face, feeling a little giddy, and curious to see how long it would take for Sam to come back from whatever planet he was on.

"You...damn." Sam began to breathe, hands moving over his shoulders, his scalp, keeping them connected, even as Sam's abs began to tremor, trying to let go.

He knew his jeans would burn against Sam's hips in all the wrong ways, and there was no hiding the neglected bulge behind the denim anyway. So instead he settled himself back on the couch and pulled Sam into him, letting Sam have all the contact he wanted. He pulled the blanket over them so Sam didn't catch a chill.

"That's it, just breathe, stud." He grinned, combing his fingers through Sam's hair.

Sam leaned in close, one hand flat on his belly. "Breathing. You want me? I ain't a selfish man."

He laughed gently. "Yes. I do want you. But you only have a couple of hours before your shift, and I don't want to rush. I want to enjoy you all night."

"All night sounds amazing. Like a gift."

"That's what it is. Like a shared gift. And believe me, it's better when the clock isn't involved. Especially the first time." Or so he understood. His first time was definitely rushed, and although it wasn't horrible, it wasn't particularly good either. Sam would be his first...well, his *first* first, and he had this strange sense of responsibility and pride about that, since he was able to make plans and not be impulsive. Maybe Sunday night, at his place. Not here. Definitely not here.

Sam kissed the corner of his lips, his jaw. "I have a thousand thoughts, but they're not so loud. Thank you."

"You're welcome. Now, don't start thinking you're going to get a blowjob every time you call me."

Sam began to laugh, the chuckles starting low and becoming warm and full, honestly happy.

He had to laugh too. Possibly because Sam probably would, but also because when that wonderful joy Sam had in him got out, it just couldn't be ignored.

"Okay, stud. You should close your eyes for a while so you're not a complete disaster at work. And before you even ask, I am staying with you until you leave, and I'm walking you out." And he was giving Sam his coat too, but he wasn't even opening that to discussion right now.

Sam searched his eyes; then he just snuggled in like he was used to not sleeping alone. "I will take it. I'm going to be on pins and needles until I get this place behind me."

Sam kissed him again, almost asleep.

He whispered good night, but he was fairly certain it fell on sleeping ears. Even now, in the quiet of his late lover's apartment, James wasn't on his mind. At the edges, maybe, but it was Sam that had been his priority every second since he'd left his condo.

He'd sincerely, earnestly loved James. But he was captivated by Sam, enamored by everything raw and honest about the man, and utterly beset by needs of an entirely different nature.

20

Sunday was cold and clear, and Sam thought it would never ever not amuse the hell out of him to see his breath.

He had his coffee, Thomas's coat, his gimme cap on, and hope.

He'd done his job the last couple of nights, controlled the crowd, didn't get his ass kicked—he was pretty fucking proud of himself. It wasn't his dream job, but he would be lying if the adrenaline hadn't been going ninety to nothing.

It had been something else to walk out and see Angel and his Harley there, waiting to make sure he got home.

Embarrassing as fuck, but also...

Yeah. He hadn't put up too much of a fight, had he?

Sam went into the club, tucking his cap in his back pocket and searching the quiet bar for the man he needed to see.

Scotty raised an eyebrow at him, looking him over, then half pointed down the bar, hands full of bar towels. Thomas had a glass of ice water and was watching football on the big TV behind the bar. The rest of him was a study in black and hard to make out in the shadowy bar lighting.

"Thanks." He nodded to Scotty and headed to Thomas. "Who's winning?" Hell, who was playing? He felt like he didn't know anything without any TV.

Thomas turned to face him and looked him over frankly, head to toe. "I am." One more sip of water and Thomas was on his feet and holding up a key. "Room six, boy. Take the key."

It made him a little dry mouthed, the way Thomas became so different in here. He didn't know that he was ever different. But maybe. Maybe. Little Sammy wasn't a guy they'd recognize at home. Maybe Bowie.

He nodded and took the key. "Yes, sir. Room six ahoy."

He wasn't going to pretend not to be in a fine mood, or that he wasn't tickled shitless to have a day to spend with Thomas.

Thomas sighed behind him, and the man's boots echoed against the tile in the quiet hallway. When he keyed into the room, Thomas stepped around him. "Hang the key on the hook on the doorjamb and come to me."

Thomas's orders were stern, but not overly loud or angry.

He did as he'd been asked, the key dangling and making a sound oddly like wind chimes.

Thomas smiled once Sam had stopped moving and kissed him. "Hello, sweetheart. It's good to see you."

"You are a sight for sore eyes, I swear to God." He couldn't hide his grin.

"I have a wonderful day planned for us, but it will be new and strange to you. You may not understand it all, and at times I may decide not to explain. So I need something from you before we begin."

Thomas paced away, leaving him standing there. "Do you know what a safe word is?"

"I think so. I know what it is, but not how you decide about the why of it. Nothing I've read makes sense on that front." He got the whole "yes, yes, no" concept, but how did you use it? Why not use it whenever shit was worrisome? Did that piss someone like Thomas off? What if you just totally fucking forgot it? This was not real clear.

Thomas chuckled. "All right. What you've read probably indicates that you would use a safe word to end an activity when words like 'no' are an expected part of a scene. That's true and fine, but that barely scratches the surface. Your understanding of the depth and power of a safe word will grow as you start to understand yourself better, your own needs and limits, and mine."

Thomas took something from a small box on the credenza and walked back to him slowly.

"For now, think of it as a word that will get my attention. We won't be doing anything today for which a simple 'stop' or 'no' won't have true weight. I expect you to speak freely. So think of your word as a step beyond that. It's not just 'Stop,' it's 'Stop and I need something.' It's 'Stop and there's something wrong.' Because sometimes it's hard to articulate what it is you need. You just know, for example, that simply removing a blindfold isn't enough. You might need reassurance, but if you're overwhelmed, saying that in the moment isn't possible. Does that make sense?"

"I think so." If not, he'd figure it out. The thing he appreciated out of all those words was "hard to articulate." That was him. He didn't understand how Thomas could do it, unpack all the mess inside and make it something worth forcing out of your mouth.

Thomas handed him a piece of chalk. "Write it on the wall in big letters."

He tilted his head, confused for a second. Write it on the wall? People don't write on walls. Write what? Had he missed something? All those thoughts zoomed through before he could blink, but then he figured it out.

Right. Or write. On the wall. The word.

He'd thought about this part, because he'd reckoned Thomas would ask. It seemed like a deal.

Revolver.

Part of his studies and his favorite Beatles album.

He stepped back after carefully drawing the letters on, chuckling as they tilted dangerously to the left: Revolver.

Thomas nodded and took the chalk away. "Okay, now just humor me and say it for me?"

"*Revolver*?" That was a little weird but easy enough.

Thomas laughed. "Are you unsure? Say it again, please. With a bit more conviction." It was weird, but Thomas did seem to be listening.

"Sorry." He had to chuckle too, just because. This was one of the weirder things he'd done, and he'd been to the snake museum in Waco. "*Revolver*. Better?"

" '*Revolver.*' Better. Yes. Give me your shirt, please." Thomas stood in front of him, waiting with his hand out, and trying out his safe word a few more times. "*Revolver. Revolver.* Seems like a lot of syllables, but we'll see how it works for us, shall we?"

"Is that a deal?" He started unbuttoning—cuffs first, then the front. "The syllable thing, I mean."

"Well, in the heat of the moment, you don't want to be trying to shout out 'megalomaniac' or something, when 'cheese' would get the job done faster and with less brain work." Thomas gave him a big grin.

"Fair enough. Supercalifragilisticexpialidocious would be...a tongue twister." Okay, now he was tickled. He handed Thomas his button-down, then pulled off his undershirt.

"Mmm." Thomas took the shirts and drew a line from his collarbone to his waistband with a warm finger. "Sorry, did you say something?" He got a wink, and Thomas went to hang his shirts over the back of a chair.

He hooked his thumbs in his waistband, watching Thomas move. The man moved like a bullfighter somehow, steady, like he knew what he was doing but was ready to jump if he had to. Sam could watch that for a while and be happy.

Thomas turned to look at him and rolled up the sleeves on a crisp black dress shirt. The leather pants the man was wearing were tight enough to pull, leaving absolutely nothing—like, *nothing*—to the imagination. He came over, carrying a red-and-black thing all made up of a handle and straps in one hand, stepped close, and dropped a thick pad at his feet.

"On your knees."

His immediate and damn near undeniable reaction was *Fuck you*, but the simple fact was that if he could let a bunch of bar-fly badass wannabes beat him into the ground for a job? He could give this to Thomas. The man had earned his trust, had earned this. Hell, he'd cried in front of Thomas. Had been out of his mind with guilt and hurting. At least today he was in a good mood and he'd slept.

Didn't mean he didn't want to snap. It just meant that he knelt down and trusted that Thomas had his back.

Thomas put a hand on his head and sighed, the sound long and maybe...relieved? Neither of them moved for a bit except for Thomas's fingers, stroking through his hair. He thought he might have felt them trembling.

Finally, Thomas hooked a hand under his chin and bent to kiss him. "Thank you, sweetheart."

"I trust you." And if Thomas needed this from him, it was something he'd give.

"You're a wonder, Sam." Thomas kissed him again and pressed the leather thing into his hands and took a few steps away. "Just look that over. Have you seen one of those before?"

"No, sir. It's heavier than it looks, isn't it?" He looked up at Thomas, curious. What was this about? He knew what it was for, but what did Thomas want from it? He'd proved he could take a beating, so that couldn't be the endgame.

"It is. It's called a flogger, which is fairly self-explanatory, I'm sure. They come in lots of different configurations, but that particular one is fairly advanced. The falls aren't very wide or very long; the handle has a decent weight. That one has a bite when I want it to."

"So that leads to a shit-ton of questions..." Why advanced? What was simple? Why did the handle matter?

What scenario involved "bite when I want it to"?

"You get three." Thomas didn't take it from him, just left it in his hands.

"The big one is why? The little ones are just...details." The little questions weren't near as important.

"That is the big one, isn't it? Why what, exactly? You're leaving that to me?" Thomas paced past him, and the next time he heard the man's voice, it was almost directly behind him. "Why did I give you the flogger? I like that one. The answer is because it's probably the most often-used instrument in the scene, the most well-known outside it, and the one that best illustrates what I do."

"What do you do?" Or more specifically, why? What is

the deal? He almost laughed at himself. That question never had an answer. A thousand answers, sure, but not one.

"Today? I answer questions." Thomas laughed. "Back to the flogger, then. While that is immediately recognizable to everyone in the scene, there isn't just one type. I told you that one is advanced. That one hurts. It can hurt a lot if I want it to. But you can find them with longer falls or wider falls, lighter handles, longer handles. They can be all different types of leather. Some of them have weights or balls on the ends. Some of the falls are cut on an angle for a deeper sting. The combination you pick is important. So the lesson is probably obvious by now, hm? That everyone has different goals and a different combination that works for them. That goes for Dominants and submissives alike."

Jesus, who knew? There must be a market for shit to beat people with. He couldn't wait to inform Bowie. The son of a bitch would have a new life's calling.

"All right. So why am I telling you that? Think about this. Why are you on your knees right now? And try to go deeper than because I told you to be. Really. Try to think about what it has to do with you."

That was something he didn't know the answer to—even though he'd learned not to say that to Thomas, it didn't change the truth of it. He was down there because Thomas wanted it, because obviously he was trying to figure something out, something he was pretty sure he didn't want to figure out, maybe. It was easier to not be a part of the whole equation because he wasn't sure, and the bad whys were more than he could face right now and he knew it. He'd been about as fucked up—both high and low—in the last few months as any man he knew.

Sam looked up, met Thomas's gaze, and hoped to hell

somehow Thomas understood that he just had no way to answer.

Thomas nodded and took the flogger from his fingers. "You have shown me such trust. I know it has to be awkward for you to be on your knees and not understand why. I am so grateful for that gift. Stand up, sweetheart."

Sam felt the ratcheting tension dissolve with a pop, the mounting rush of thoughts ease back to a buzz. *Okay.*

Okay.

He hadn't fucked that up.

He took a deep breath and hopped up, trying to figure out the right thing to respond with. He went with "Thank you" because that was what he meant.

"I don't want you to kneel again until you want to. I'll ask. I may even ask often. No matter what else is going on, I'm telling you to say no if you don't feel you fully understand the nature of the gift you're giving me, and how that is reflected upon you. You won't disappoint me if you say no. It won't upset me if you say no. It's important to me that kneeling be done in the proper spirit, or it's simply about control. I don't want that. Understood?"

Not even a little. He didn't understand altogether why he did something for Thomas that he flat-out wouldn't for anyone else. Why he did a bunch of things that he wouldn't for anyone else. He'd done it, though, because Thomas asked him and that was important to him. "I fucked up, didn't I? I'm not trying to, I swear to God." He chuckled softly at himself. "Do you regret showing me James's book sometimes?"

Did it make Thomas regret that he didn't have James here to do things right?

"I don't have any regrets about you. Not a single one. You didn't fuck up. There's no way to fuck this up, sweetheart. I meant that if the only reason you're doing any of this is because it's what I..."

Thomas's eyebrows dipped into a deep frown for a second; then his whole expression changed and he smiled. "You're doing everything right. You've done everything I've asked and even offered some things I haven't specifically asked for. You haven't fucked up at all."

"Good deal." He answered Thomas's smile, feeling like he was on one hell of a bucker, just trying to keep his free arm up. Thing was, he suspected Thomas was on a ride of his own and trying not to face-plant. "You know, there's this saying that if you get off on your feet, you weren't riding hard enough. I think this is like that."

"I think you might be right." He'd seen Thomas in leather, in a cowboy hat, and in a sweat shirt with a goddamn pink unicorn on it, but he wasn't sure he liked any of those looks as much as this one. It was the same look Thomas had when he was standing with that twenty-foot cross-eyed gorilla at Ripley's. Relaxed, light. Young. And he figured it wasn't one Thomas gave himself permission to wear very often. "You want to get a beer?"

"Sure. Let me get dressed, honey. Two shakes." He unfastened his belt as he headed over to the chair with his shirts.

"Hang on." Thomas snagged his arm, pulled them together. "It has to be the right combination. If this is something you want, we'll figure it out. If it's not, it doesn't change this." Thomas's kiss was strong but sweet. Heated but patient. "They're separate things."

Sam cupped Thomas's jaw, confused as hell but willing to go with it. He loved Thomas, right? Right or wrong, it was what it was, and he was going to deal. "We'll reckon it, honey. No worries."

"No worries? I'm talking to the king of worries." Thomas let him go, but he felt those eyes on him. "Come home with me. Stay the night. We can start figuring it out."

"I'm all in." He grabbed his undershirt and tugged it on, then started working on his shirt. "Let's go."

21

S am stared out the window of Thomas's apartment, watching the sun set. They'd shared a couple of beers, and they'd managed canned soup and grilled cheese sandwiches without killing each other or burning anything important off.

He thought they were dancing around each other a little bit, but that was the deal. Negotiations.

Can I kiss you? Would you kiss me? Are we going to get naked? I would like to get naked. With you. What happened earlier? Am I ever going to get it? Does it matter? Can I touch you? Love on you?

Okay. Right. Negotiations.

He found a George Strait song on his phone and walked over to Thomas, who was sitting on the sofa. "Wanna dance?"

"I would love to." Thomas stood up, grinning. "I suppose you want to lead too?"

Negotiations.

"Shut up and dance." He eased into Thomas's arms, tucking himself against Thomas's shoulder and sliding one hand in Thomas's back pocket. Thomas could lead all he wanted; he was picking the songs.

"The dancing part I got. The shut up is more challenging." Thomas hung both arms around his hips and sighed. He wouldn't call that a lead. They kind of found the rhythm together. He hummed, happy as a cricket, a long-held fantasy come true. Dancing to King George. *Damn.*

"I used to watch the couples dancing, and it liked to kill me with wanting. Not the dancing, per se, but...the way they held on." Like it was breathing.

Thomas's hands shifted, one arm wrapping around his back and the other sliding into the hair at the nape of his neck. "Better, cowboy?"

"Yes, sir." His heart set to pounding, and he melted into Thomas's arms.

"George Strait has what, a hundred love songs? At least?" Thomas held him tight, and he felt a heart beating as hard as his own.

"At least. And I got them all on my phone."

"That might be enough. Maybe put it on shuffle in case we run long." Thomas leaned away just enough to get the buttons open and shrug out of that black dress shirt.

"Oh..." He bit his bottom lip, the scent of Thomas flooding him. Leather and soap and man—he inhaled until he was dizzy, filling his lungs with Thomas.

Thomas took another second and untucked his shirts, working on the button-down first with steady fingers, then lifting his T-shirt off over his head. Then those arms were around him again, just like before only...even better.

Oh. He could die a happy man right here. Sam closed his eyes, singing along under his breath and floating about a foot above the floor.

They swayed together for maybe a couple more songs,

two, maybe three, he wasn't keeping track. Thomas's hands had started to roam, into his hair, over his shoulder, down his chest. At the moment, Thomas's thumb was making lazy circles around one of his nipples, and when he lifted his face, he was rewarded with a kiss.

"This is perfect. You feel so good."

"Yes. I don't have the words, but...there's nowhere I'd rather be." No one he'd rather be with. No one he would share this with, if he had all the choices in the world.

Thomas got hold of a belt loop and pulled him in tighter, tight enough he could feel the hard ridge under Thomas's leather rubbing against his belly as they rocked together.

Oh, sweet Jesus. He leaned hard, needing to feel Thomas more than he needed his next breath.

"Sam." Thomas said his name on the same breath as a low moan and rocked again, angling a thigh between his legs.

"Yes." He spread a bit and went up on tiptoe at that delicious ache. He lifted his face, taking another kiss. The glide of his belly against Thomas's drew a raw sound from him, one that got trapped between them.

Their tongues slid against each other, and the kiss got heavy and hungry. Thomas gripped Sam's biceps and forced him back a step without breaking the kiss, hands diving for his belt buckle. He sucked in, giving Thomas room to work. His hands were filled with Thomas's hips, the leather soft as butter.

Buckle, belt, button and fly, then Thomas's hands slid into his jeans and around to his ass.

He started exploring. The line of Thomas's throat fascinated him, the tendons, the hollow at the base of the neck. Thomas exhaled and tilted his head back, giving him more room to explore and stretching the skin tight. "Collarbone. Like it there."

"Mmm...yes, sir. So fine." He nibbled, licked, moaning and lingering whenever Thomas shivered. He dropped his hands to Thomas's waistband. "Can I?"

Thomas's sharp inhale almost sounded desperate. "Yes. I'm...yes." Sam had to grin when Thomas looked down to watch his fingers.

He understood. He wanted to see, wanted to know— everything. He focused on the task at hand, unfastening, baring Thomas, making sure to touch—the fuzz at the base of Thomas's belly, the long curve of Thomas's cock—with every step.

"Fuck. Want to see you too." Thomas moved his hands around, worked his jeans low on his hips, let his prick fall free, then gave it a light rub. "There you are, so pretty."

"Can we get naked, honey? One of us—probably me—is going to go ass over teakettle." He was shivering with anticipation. He supposed he ought to be nervous, but he wanted to know. Everything. Everything Thomas could show him and whatever they might could figure out together.

Thomas laughed. "I was just getting to that, impatient young man." The leather pants were gone in a blink, tossed onto the couch, and Thomas dropped to one knee, tugged his jeans down, and rubbed a cheek against him. "Fuck, you smell good."

He followed Thomas down, sliding along his body until they were pressed tight together, bare as the day they were born. Thomas made his eyes cross.

"Come to bed?" Thomas rocked back on his heels and stood, holding a hand out to Sam. "We can stretch out, get to know each other better."

"There's nothing I'd like more." He took Thomas's hand with a laugh, letting the man draw him in for another hard kiss that liked to burn him to the ground.

Thomas had a giant platform bed, more than enough room for the two of them to roll around and never find the edges. The bedding was black and tan, the pillows neat, and there were just enough of them to be functional, not decorative.

Thomas tugged the duvet down and crowded him against the edge. "Do you know what you're doing to me? Do you know how bad I want you?"

"I'm yours." The back of the bed hit his knees and he sat, coming face-to-face with Thomas's erection. He leaned forward, feeling as daring as he ever had in his whole life, and kissed the tip.

Thomas hissed and caught the back of his head, smiling at him. "Have you ever?"

"No. Couple of hand jobs in the dark. I had to be careful not to get, well, handed my teeth." Sam looked up along Thomas's body. "Wasn't for lack of interest, though."

"I'm game." Thomas winked at him. "If you want to."

"It would be my pleasure." He leaned down and inhaled deep, then dragged his cheek along the shaft. Fuck, Thomas's skin was hot, so silky.

Thomas kept that hand on his head, but just light contact, affectionate. "I'm hoping it's actually mine. Take your time. I'll try to keep it together." That was followed by a low laugh.

He'd try to make sure Thomas enjoyed it. He started at the head, exploring with the tip of his tongue, tracing the ridge, testing the spongy flesh. There was a tease, a hint of Thomas's flavor, and he groaned, searching for more.

He felt Thomas's eyes on him and the fingers

tightening in his hair. Thomas's prick stretched and hardened to steel in his fingers, making Thomas moan. "That's...yes. Sam."

Yeah. Pleasure built up in him, and he took Thomas in, his fingers wrapped around the base. He sucked, listening for his clues—harder or focus there or ease up.

Thomas made it easy. He didn't know enough yet to know if the man was always that way, but Thomas told him what was good, would shift away or lean in, and he knew. He knew when he was getting it right.

Thomas was patient, let him push, let him experiment, and finally started losing control.

"Fuck, I'm...can I? Jesus..." Thomas groaned, and his head rolled on his shoulders.

Sam was sure it made him all kinds of a slut, but he wanted to know. Hell, he needed to know how Thomas tasted. He knew how Thomas had made the top of his head pop off. He wanted to give that back, make Thomas feel like he could fly.

He answered by sucking harder, forcing himself to relax, to let Thomas in.

"Fuck!" Thomas gripped the back of his head and held it still as those hips rocked forward. Two thrusts and Thomas eased up and groaned as he came. Sam swallowed hard, trying his best not to choke, the bitter and the salt strong on his tongue.

He'd never not know this again.

He backed off and let Thomas pop free as he rested his forehead on Thomas's belly, trying to remember how to breathe.

They stayed there a minute, both of them just breathing, but when Thomas dropped to his knees and kissed him, he knew the man was just as stunned as he was. "Fuck, Sam."

Thomas grinned at him, eyes bright; then he was being herded over onto the bed.

Every single place they touched burned, and Sam pushed into it, willing to catch fire. Thomas climbed over him, eyes locked on his, and pressed a hip down, giving him something to feel, something to move against. He groaned, caught as any fish on a hook. It was easy to arch, take the friction, the strength Thomas offered and ride it.

"Yeah. You're feeling good, right, stud? You want that." Thomas went after his shoulder with hungry teeth.

"Yessir." Jesus, yes. He felt like he might bust, like he was fixin' to just crack down the center; then Thomas bit or shifted or touched and it got bigger.

Thomas worked down to one nipple and stayed there, licking and biting and licking again, making him arch, making it hard to keep still. "Beautiful," Thomas whispered and moved lower, hot lips landing on his abs.

He ached, his hands opening and closing. "Please," he whispered. He didn't know what he was asking for, but he knew Thomas could give it to him.

"Right here, Sam." Thomas coaxed him to bend one knee, licked the inside of his thigh and pinched the skin between his teeth. But it was the fingers easing under his balls and across the smooth skin there that got his attention.

A sound slid from him, just as rough as a cob. Thomas's touch was everywhere, and Sam spread wider to get more.

"This will feel chilly for a second. It'll warm up quickly." Thomas's fingers touched him again, cool and slippery as they moved over him, circled over skin no one else had ever touched.

His abs drew up, sudden and hard, stealing his breath for a long second. He stared up at nothing and forced himself to inhale so he could be here. Right here. "My skin feels all tight."

As if in answer, Thomas shifted to one hip and leaned over him, running a wet tongue up the length of his erection and around the head, which disappeared into a hungry mouth.

"Thomas!" Sam's hips rolled, up and back, and the touch against his hole pressed harder. He stared down, needing to see, to know this was happening.

He watched as Thomas took his cock in farther, feeling that tongue working over his shaft, distracted until the pressure eased up and one slippery finger pushed inside him.

His eyes rolled, and he sat up halfway, curling up. Thomas used his free hand to ease him back, settling him on the sheets again, and released him just enough to talk.

"You're all right?" Thomas's words were low and soothing, the tone only a half question.

"More than all right." His voice didn't even sound like his own. He sounded husky, needy, almost raw.

"Yeah. It'll be good. You're on fire. One more." He felt a stretch; then Thomas's fingers were moving, adding pressure, twisting inside him.

Sam couldn't have stayed still for love or money. His body demanded that he shift, take more. He was fucking flying.

Thomas groaned this time, a hot, needy sound. Those fingers worked him over and over, sinking inside him, twisting, stretching him, until he thought he might lose his mind. Until he wanted more. Needed more.

"Christ, Sam. I'm so ready for you. Tell me you want me. Tell me I can have you."

"Please." Sam caught Thomas's gaze, held it. "I'm yours, huh?"

Thomas's eyes flashed. "Mine."

The sudden empty feeling as those fingers slipped away made him gasp, but Thomas kept his focus, tearing open a foil wrapper with savage teeth and rolling on the rubber.

Thomas climbed over him, pushing his legs open wider, and began to stroke him off. "My own." Then that pressure was back, only...hotter. Heavier. Stretching him so, so slow.

"Yours. Yours, please." Oh, sweet Christ, that was Thomas. Inside him. Spreading him open.

"Fuck. Fuck, Sam." Thomas sank into him gently, so careful, and in the middle of gasps and moans, he saw a change in Thomas's brown eyes. Behind the heat was something else. Something bigger, deeper, warming him in a different way.

He reached up and cupped Thomas's jaw, and that shifted Thomas inside him. Lightning slid up his spine, and he bore down, a cry escaping him.

"Sam!" Thomas ducked his head as his hips shifted into a different gear. He started to move, pulling out slow and diving in harder, breathing in thick pants, rocking them.

Fucking him.

It took him a minute to figure the rhythm, to meet the thrusts and add his strength, his hunger. The burn was so deep, the ache so fucking right that he wanted to beller.

Thomas was a stunning mix of control and need. Part of him so deliberate and thoughtful and part just wild need. But those brown eyes were steady, the whole world reduced to that connection. Sam held on, stuck between *Never let it end* and *Let me come* and *God yes, please*.

"Want it, stud? You ready?" Thomas's eyes narrowed.

"Yes." Whatever Thomas was offering, he could take it.

"Me too." Thomas chuckled softly and kissed him; then Thomas's hips rolled just so and that lightning flew right up his spine again.

He bit out Thomas's name, grabbing for Thomas's shoulders and holding on tight. He needed more, needed that touch over and over. "Help me. Please. Please, I need..."

Thomas nodded. "Yes, Sam. Got you." Thomas's muscles worked under his fingers. The man's jaw was set tight, and rough grunts filled his ears. "Fuck, yes!"

The world went white-hot, and when Thomas's thumb pressed against the slit of his cock, he shot so hard his fucking bones rattled.

"Jesus!" Thomas pressed their foreheads together and blew hot air across his face, hips madly flying for a second, then sinking deep. "Sam." Thomas's voice was tight and barely above a whisper as he trembled, and Sam felt him jerk and pulse inside him.

Sam blinked, trying to focus, but he couldn't. He was fucking melted. All the way. Damn, it felt good.

Thomas must have been pretty bleary-eyed too, because the man was dropping kisses on his forehead, eyes, cheekbones, pretty much anywhere but his lips. He snorted and turned his head and Thomas finally made contact, laughing against his lips. "There you are."

"Right here." He stroked Thomas's cheek, his shoulder, his side. "Damn."

"Yeah. Fuck, that was...you are incredible. Beautiful. Fuck, so hot." Thomas's skin was slick, and he was still catching his breath. He rolled and landed on his side next to Sam. "Damn."

Sam wasn't sure what was supposed to happen next, but Thomas would let him know. Right now, he'd breathe, let the world be a soft place for a second.

"Did we run out of King George?" Thomas grinned and kissed his shoulder. "I was going for it."

"I bet my phone's still playing in the front room."

"Let it play. I'll get it later." Thomas reached for him. "Can I hold you? Come here."

He moved in without a second of hesitation, pressing into Thomas's arms with a happy little sigh.

Thomas tucked him close and kissed his head. "You're okay? That was...I mean, you're going to be sore tomorrow, but you're okay?"

Sam began to chuckle, because damn, he was happy. "I got to admit, I been sore after a lot of rides, but this one was damn fine and more than worth it."

"Mmm. Tested my patience a bit, I'll tell you, but also more than worth it." Thomas sighed. "I'll be honest, Sam. You surprise me at every turn."

"Is that bad?" Surprises kept a person young, right? Kept you on your toes?

"No. Not at all. I tend to live in a neat and orderly world, and you are neither. I sort of love it. It's reminding me...I don't know. That I'm still young, I guess."

"You are. Young and about the hottest man I ever saw."

Thomas snorted. "You're sweet. You sure make me feel that way, anyway."

"I'm not sweet. You said honest. I'm telling you the truth." Thomas made him ache.

"I did." Thomas lifted his face, looked into his eyes. "Thank you."

"You're welcome." He'd remember that, that Thomas didn't know how fine he was. Sam could tell him, anytime.

He got one of those kisses, the slow, gentle ones. The ones that made him feel like Thomas was taking care of him. Then Thomas settled into the pillows. "I wonder how many guys can say they got their lover off twice on their first try?"

Sam's cheeks burned, but he wouldn't forget. He'd done that—made Thomas come. He intended to goddamn do it again too. Over and over. It was good to have a plan.

22

The ride to Midtown from the Met was very straightforward. Get in the cab, head straight downtown. It was probably the easiest thing he was going to do all night.

Thomas went to work this morning in a fantastic mood. He'd left Sam sleeping in his bed along with a note and King George playing on the kitchen counter.

Before Clint called him around morning coffee-break time, he'd been debriefing himself on his night with Sam and hadn't gotten a damn thing done except to think about how perfect it had all been. From Sam's lovely first move with the dancing, to a gem of a first-timer blowjob, to Sam telling him he was hot. So, when the call came in, that's what he told Clint, with a big fat smile on his face.

But Clint hadn't called about that. Clint asked him how his afternoon had gone at the club. He started to put up a little smoke screen and talked about how Sam had knelt for him, but being evasive with Clint had proved to be a bad call more often than he cared to admit, and he had to confess that it hadn't been one of his better moments. That their afternoon had ended with Sam essentially calling him out for being human. He'd gotten the rodeo cowboy version of "better luck next time."

After a long pause on the phone, Clint had sternly reminded him that Doms weren't supposed to look human or be called out for anything, and had given him a dinner invitation he couldn't refuse. Even if he wanted to. Clint wasn't just any Dom; he was Master at the club. A personal invitation wasn't so much of an invitation as a summons.

But he'd so much rather have kept his mind on Sam's body, and he promised himself he could, later, assuming he survived dinner.

His phone buzzed, a text from Angel showing up. The picture was Sam from behind, muscles tight under his button-down as he carried a keg.

Yep. That was all his. Mother of God. He spread his legs a little wider in the back of the cab, forgetting for a second where he was headed. *You are a true friend, Angel. Keep your damn hands to yourself.*

I'll do my best, Tommy & you're welcome.

Thomas chuckled, shaking his head at himself. He couldn't help it—Sam made him young. Other parts of him were feeling young too, so he took a couple of breaths and told his body to cool it.

He climbed out of his cab and walked toward the club, wishing he'd had something less suit and tie and more leather and ink to wear to this meeting, but it was what it was. At least he looked good in a suit.

Scotty gave him a smile and a nod and pointed across the room to where Clint was seated at a table, presumably waiting for him.

All the way across the room. Of course.

He made his way over, noting the irony of feeling underdressed in a business suit.

Clint nodded to him, then to the chair across from him.

All right. He popped open the button on his jacket and took a seat. "Good evening."

"Good evening, Tommy." Clint looked him over. "You do pull off a well-cut suit better than most, I'll admit."

"Thank you." *And you manage to keep me off guard better than most.* "Can I...are you interested in something from the bar?" Clint didn't drink, so that was probably the worst possible way to try to break the ice.

One of those dark eyebrows rose into Clint's hairline. "Okay, boy. Close your eyes and take a few breaths. Find your way here."

Boy. He sighed, trying to let Clint's tone ground him.

"I'd really just like a glass of wine." But he did exactly as Clint told him to and closed his eyes, breathing in the calm energy coming from across the table, letting it blanket his anxiety, and breathing out all the chaos that made up every reason he needed to be here right now. "Sorry."

"Don't be." Clint held up his finger, ordering a glass of Pinot Noir and a cup of coffee before turning back to him. "I haven't seen you this ramped up in years."

He had to acknowledge that he hadn't felt this off in a long time. "I know. I'm...there's all this..." He looked at Clint, trying to find an anchor, and after another breath, he did. "I'm not grounded. I need to work."

Clint dipped his chin, once. "Talk to me. Why aren't you able to work? What do you need to do it? Basic information, remember?"

If Thomas had a dime for every time he heard, "talk to me" or "basic information," he'd have a lot of dimes.

The trouble with basic was that it was difficult to

dismantle this puzzle. It started with not understanding how to lose two loves at the same time in one man. It was muddied in the middle with a lot of uncertainty about Sam that made him question himself and his motives, and it ended with...confusion. "I need to find my compass. I don't know how to define myself anymore. I've lost confidence. Also, I need a sub."

He stared at the table. He was relieved to be able to get that out, to find those words, but he was appalled at the lack of emotion that went along with them. The words were the truth, but he couldn't get them out and feel anything at the same time. He'd disconnected. That was an old, ingrained defense mechanism, and he knew Clint would recognize it.

"Fair enough." Clint smiled at Scotty as he delivered their drinks. "I'll let you know if we need you."

"Yes, Sir."

"So tell me about your compass. What is your true north?" Clint carefully doctored his coffee, the motions simple, controlled, as much a routine as everything.

"Order. Routine. Balance." He picked up his wine and took a sip. "I think." He shook his head. That was as ridiculous as it sounded. "I'm not sure. With James it was clear. We had a rhythm, a focus. I don't have a focus anymore. I mean, I do, but it's like a moving target. I'm all... honestly? I'm tangled up with Sam."

"Do you regret that? Sam?"

"No." He answered so quickly that he made himself think about it again. "No, I don't regret that. He's...we're...we have something. It's just new and fragile. But it's real. I don't even regret bringing him here, though I think that may have been a poor choice."

"Why?" There was no judgment in the question, just

calm energy reaching out to him, offering him a space to work this out.

"I think Sam is a natural sub. I do. I just don't think I'm... I don't have whatever it is he needs in my toolbox. I've been taking it slow. I've been introducing him to things carefully. He does what I ask, even when I know he doesn't want to, but he doesn't invest. This is either the wrong path for him, or I'm the wrong man to take him down it."

Clint stirred his coffee, took a drink. "Tell me about meeting James, if you would."

"What? I met him here. You introduced us."

"Humor me, Tommy. You know I don't ask lightly. You met him here. I introduced you. How did you know you wanted to work with him?"

He took another sip of his wine. Did Clint bring him here to talk about James? Wasn't this hard enough without that? He sighed, looking inward, remembering what meeting James felt like. "It was in his eyes. He was curious. He wanted to know, wanted to learn. He was very direct, and he needed the connection."

Clint smiled, the look bittersweet but warm, fond. "He was, wasn't he? He was a lovely, gentle man."

"He was smart. Self-aware. He knew he belonged here as soon as he walked in the door. He felt it. I remember the first time we worked together he was so...ready. He just opened right up. We never looked back." But he was looking back now, wasn't he? He picked up his wine again, held it to his nose, let the brightness help him focus. "I miss him."

"You do. My next questions are harder. Are you ready, or do you need a break?"

He sipped the wine and put the glass down. "Go on. You've got me." That was a good hook, making him remember James that way. The way it began.

"Why are you attracted to Sam? What intrigues you?"

That was a fair question. He went with the truth, as awful as it sounded. "It was his eyes first. They were so much like James's. But they're not really, they have more gold and less brown, and they have more questions than answers." Many more. "I told him last night that he keeps surprising me. I think I've got him figured out, but then he proves me wrong. He's unpredictable. He takes risks. He's...fun." Sam was fun. Challenging. James had been...satisfying. Validating. They were nothing alike, really.

Clint's smile widened. "Next question. Would he understand if you chose someone else to work with? Another sub?"

He stared at Clint. "I don't know." Would Sam understand? He thought about yesterday and what Sam had said about fucking up. Asking him if he had any regrets. "He'd be disappointed in himself. He'd think he did something wrong. If he understood, it would only be because he thought I'd given up on him."

"And how would you feel if another Dom wished to work with him? Train him?"

"I'd be...relieved for him that he found someone that knows how to be what he needs." He rubbed his forehead with one finger, hard, like he was trying to force something out that wasn't coming. If anyone had asked him that question about James, he'd have put his foot down and refused. He'd been everything James needed. He so wanted that for Sam.

What he'd lacked in emotion earlier in the conversation, he was finding in spades now. It was white hot and it burned his ego. "I'm not wrong. I know what he needs. If I'm not up to it, he should find someone who is."

"I've had inquiries. He wouldn't lack for attention."

He hadn't realized he'd been looking down at his lap until he had to raise his eyes to look at Clint again. "If you think that's—"

Wait. No. Sam knelt for him yesterday. Sam was his.

"No. I want it to be me. It needs to be me. I want him."

"Well, then." The corner of Clint's lips quirked. "That sounds much more like my Tommy. I approve."

He squinted at Clint. How the hell did the man do that? "I hope you know what you're doing, because I don't."

"A submissive deserves someone that is passionate about him. Even the most controlled relationship deserves that spark. If it didn't exist, I would recommend that you find someone to work with. As it is, I can make some other recommendations." Clint rolled his eyes, the look uncharacteristic, a glimpse of humor that he knew was reserved for a rare few. "I've had a bit of advice from a friend."

It was comforting, that trust. It put him at ease, let him relax. "He's mine, Clint. I just can't find the right approach. He's been vulnerable, but he's also been detached. He knows what I want but not why, and neither of us knows what he wants. I ordered him to his knees and he went, but it grated on his last nerve, and even though I praised him for it, he was sure he'd disappointed me. I'm chasing my tail."

"Have you considered that Sam is a vastly more active man than you've been used to working with? Perhaps you need to decide what the endgame is you're looking for and work backward." Clint sipped his coffee. "For instance, if you are looking for, say, peace, a certain headspace, information-sharing, how do you push Sam there? Is kneeling a punishment? A boredom? You may have to make new rules—not for Sam alone, but for yourself."

"Work backward. Hm." That appealed to him, made

sense. As did rethinking conventions like kneeling. "Initially, I just need to figure out where to start. His mind works so fast, he can move six steps ahead of me while I'm pouring coffee. I don't know where to muscle in, you know?"

"I do. How many times in the beginning did I have to remind you to talk to me? No filters, just the basics? There were times I despaired of exhausting you enough for you to begin to relax." Clint's expression was dramatic and long-suffering. "Pretend you're a new Dominant. Start from the beginning. Just the basics. What do you want from your submissive?"

"Trust. Obedience. Honesty. Thoughtfulness." It was that simple.

"Now unpack those. How does he show his trust? How do you reward that? How does he not? How do you work to improve that? You know how to do this, Tommy. You're trying to add Sam into a pattern you built with another man. That's unfair to both of you. It's denying you both so much excitement."

He took a deep breath and leaned back in his chair. "I am. You're right." If he'd gone looking for a sub, he might have decided to find someone that fit that mold. But as it was, he'd met someone so different, and he'd tried to apply something that came easily, not put together something new. "You're absolutely right, Clint. I don't know how I didn't see that."

"You were mourning. The timing is harsh, but it happens. I think you can be forgiven. More than that, I think your boy would forgive you. You know I loved James dearly, but I've never seen anyone look at you the way Sam does."

"You really think so? I mean about James. Is it all right for me to...for us to do this? Are you sure?"

That was a stumbling block. He picked up his wine

again and took a sip, swallowing back the lump in his throat and pretending he wasn't...leaking from his eyes.

"I think that happiness is a rare thing and to deny yourself another chance at it is wrong." Clint took his hand, held it, and waited for Thomas to meet his gaze, those dark eyes unwavering. "I don't lie to you, Tommy. If I felt you were making a mistake, I would tell you, straight up."

He nodded, giving Clint's fingers a squeeze. "You don't know how badly I needed someone to tell me that, Clint. Someone like you, that I trust."

"I'm glad you were ready to hear it."

"It was exactly what I needed. I just didn't know how to ask until now. Thank you." He put his wine down, not even half-finished. He'd had enough.

"You are welcome. Shall we go find something wonderful for dinner?"

"Please." He stood up, smoothing out his slacks and buttoning his jacket. He felt lighter, clearheaded. He loved having something to think about. Thank God it was only Monday. He had a lot of planning to do before next weekend.

23

Thomas arrived at the club early and spent half an hour working out with a flogger and a padded mannequin. Along with his new approach with Sam, he decided he needed a new warm-up routine to get his head right and leave his week and his own anxiety behind.

He had a goal, as Clint had suggested, and working backward from that took him in several directions, so he'd just need to see how Sam was responding and take his cues from his sub. There were other things to take into consideration—their new intimacy and his own renewed confidence would change their dynamic as well.

He'd debated about his choice of clothing, finally deciding that certain trappings of the lifestyle were what they were, and went for leather pants, heavy boots, thick cuffs, and a bare chest. He was dressing for himself, not for Sam. The boots especially gave him height, made him stand straighter, and gave him swagger.

He didn't wait at the bar. He'd decided to wait in their reserved room and let Sam make the trip back himself. He was ready when he heard that knock at the door.

"Come in."

"It's just me." The door opened, Sam stepping in. "Hello there...oh, aren't you fine,"

The response was immediate, honest, and it felt amazing, as did the way Sam ate him up with a look.

His boy was wearing a heavy sweater, jeans, and work boots. Sam looked warm, cozy, and altogether too bundled up.

He crooked a couple of fingers, summoning Sam to him, and pulled his boy in, favoring him with a hard kiss. "Hello, sweetheart. It's good to see you. Is that a new sweater?"

"Mm-hmm. It is. I needed something warm and presentable." Sam's eyes twinkled. "I mean, it's not a moose humping a unicorn, but..."

"That's all right. No one rocks that one like I do." He stepped back and looked Sam over, head to toe. "You wear it well. Take it off, please. And the boots as well."

"Socks too?" Sam took the sweater off, exposing that tight little hard body to him.

He hid his grin. "Good boy. Socks too, and thank you for asking for clarity. Also, for the future, if I ask you to remove your footwear, I mean to have you barefoot. You may assume socks too."

He waited for Sam to comply and put the clothing out of the way. "I'd like you on your feet for a bit, and I know that's not comfortable for you after a while. I wondered if it might help you to use the wall, perhaps brace your arms on it? Do you have a thought about a position you could manage to hold for a while?"

"I lean my backside against the wall at work when I'm bouncing, but when I was rodeoing, I could lean against the chutes all day."

"Good." He pointed across the room. "To the wall, then,

please. However you're most comfortable for the time being. Close your eyes and focus on the room. Don't ask questions for now. I'll give you time in a bit."

Sam tilted his head but did as he asked, leaning back and propping himself up, nipples and abs going hard as his back hit the wall. Sam's eyes flew open wide for a shocked second before they closed.

He grinned. The wall must be chilly. Poor boy.

"When I say focus on the room, I mean pay attention to the senses I'm allowing you to use. You don't have sight, but you have touch, which it seems you've already discovered." He let himself laugh softly and went on. "Hearing, smell. Yes? The purpose is to help you clear your mind. Forget the subway, work last night, the men you said hello to when you came in. Just breathe and open up your senses."

He immediately gave the boy something to listen to, and paced the room in measured steps, passing first in one direction, then the other. Sam's head tilted, following him, just barely. He didn't know if Sam even knew he was doing it.

He thought about the things he'd noticed about the room before the boy arrived. The hum of the heater, the slight vibration in the floor when the subway went by underneath them, and now Sam's own clean scent. He gave the boy time, watching for signs of concentration or fatigue or just plain boredom.

He caught it in, of all things, Sam's toes. They were curling, rhythmically, slowly, over and over.

"Boy." He made sure to speak softly so he didn't startle Sam. "How many steps does it take me to get from one end of the room to the other?"

Sam's chin bobbed, his boy counting. "Five one way, four the other."

"Good boy. Do you need to move?"

That question earned him pursed lips, Sam shifting from foot to foot. "I think I'm okay. Maybe not hours, but for now."

"Very well. Were you aware that your toes were moving just now?"

Sam went pink, and his eyes opened. "Were they? I mean, I do it all the time. It's a habit I picked up a while ago."

"Boy." He stepped directly in front of Sam, authority in his tone. "Did I give you permission to open your eyes?"

"Dammit. No. Sorry." Sam shut them again. "I got distracted by my toes."

"Well, that unfortunate error brings me to what I had next planned for us. Rules." He paced away, rather pleased that the boy had made that mistake, as it provided him with a springboard. "I'd like you to start addressing me as 'Sir.' From this point forward, every answer you give to a direct question will be followed by *Sir*. If you wish to get my attention, you will use *Sir* or *Master*, your choice for the time being. When we're in this club, anywhere, I'm *Sir*. You're not to use my name. Am I clear?" He could set that question as a trap, but that seemed unfair for the boy's first time-out. "Answer 'yes, Sir' or 'no, Sir.'"

"Yes, Sir." Sam didn't look too worried; he nodded, licked his lips, but that was it.

"Good boy. Any questions?"

"No, Sir. I'm pretty well-raised. I can ma'am and sir with the best of 'em." The words could have been glib if the tone had been, but Sam didn't sound flip in the slightest. He had to grin, though. It went a bit further than just being polite. The boy would make that leap on his own eventually.

"Good to know. However, the next time I ask a 'yes or no'

question, a simple 'yes' or 'no' will do unless I require something more."

He took a few steps, letting Sam hear them. "The next rule is also simple. You don't do anything unless I've given you an order or you have requested permission. Opening your eyes is a good example. Needing to use the restroom is another. If you need something—something hurts, you're cold, you need to change position or walk, if you feel unsafe or panicked—I want you to speak up. I will always see to your needs unless I have a good reason not to, and I will be very clear why if that is the case. If you feel the need to speak more freely than I otherwise allow, you may ask permission. Everything you do will need an order or my permission. Do you understand? You may also ask questions at this point if you wish."

He could almost see Sam sorting through information, responses, worries, questions, all behind those closed eyes.

"I've confused you, have I?" He slipped his hands into Sam's. "Open your eyes."

Sam opened up, meeting his gaze. "This is tough."

"It is." Clearly the boy wasn't ready for the rule about not meeting his eyes; he'd let that one go another session or two. Or maybe forever, he reminded himself. New boy, new rules. "Why do you think I'm asking it of you?"

Sam held on to his fingers, squeezing them. "I have a few answers to that question. The first instinct is you think I'm stupid, but that doesn't make sense. You don't think badly of me." Another squeeze. "After that it's muddier. Because you want to, because that's the rules of the game, because you want me to pay attention?" Each answer was ticked off in Sam's hands.

Inside he had to cheer a little because Sam hadn't panicked about being confused and instead had offered him thoughtful, honest answers. He thought about how to reward the boy as he spoke. "I hold you in the highest respect, boy. You are not stupid. All of those other reasons you mention have some merit. Let's concentrate on the last thing you said, that I want you to pay attention. Staying present, in the moment, keeping your mind actively focused isn't easy, is it?"

"No, Sir. God, no." The relief in Sam's voice was a very real thing. "Everything starts to zoom and..." Sam shrugged, holding his hands tight.

He stayed steady and still, returning the boy's grip with a reassuring squeeze. "Obedience will be a good exercise for you, then. You'll have to keep your thoughts ordered, keep your focus on me and whatever I've asked of you. You'll have to anticipate your own needs and make sure you articulate them. You'll have plenty to think about."

He lifted their clasped hands into Sam's line of vision. "Is this simple reassurance, or are you trying to tell me you're losing your footing?"

"My balance is fine. It helps." Sam sighed softly. "It's like we're together in this."

"Oh, sweetheart." He smiled and kissed each of his boy's hands in turn. "It's not *like* we are together in this. We *are* together in this. I am thinking about you every second you are in this club. Whether you find yourself holding my hands, halfway across the room, at the receiving end of my flogger, or getting me a drink at the bar, you are my focus. I'm simply asking the same of you."

"That's fair."

That was his boy—a novel worth of thought and two words slipping free.

"So, am I to trust that you understand the rule, then?"

"Yes, Sir. I—" Sam gripped him tight. "You know that I'll fuck up sometimes, right? Not out of meanness."

"Of course. Quite a lot in the beginning, I expect. I'm not concerned with how often you slip. I'm much more focused on whether you're trying and what you learn when you make a mistake. That applies to everything, boy. Mistakes are simply human. It's how you handle yourself that matters."

He decided they'd discussed that long enough and didn't offer Sam an opportunity to reply. He'd let the boy think about it.

He looked at their hands, then into Sam's eyes again. "I want you to know that you can ask me for reassurance any time, but you have to start relying on your trust in me too. You're not giving it a chance to work for you. I can't imagine you know what I mean, but you will. Before you seek reassurance, take a second to see if you can summon that trust and let your worry go."

That would be a big step for the boy, he knew, and not an easy one.

Sam dipped his chin, the nod sure, sharp. Sam never looked away from him, trusting him to read those cues.

Surprises at every turn. The boy's reply left him breathless. Thomas squeezed Sam's fingers and returned the nod, then pulled out the most coveted reward he had in his arsenal and kissed his boy. *Nod, open the gate, and ride.*

He was so proud of Sam, but eventually he had to reel it back in, end the kiss. He knew that Sam's conviction would be tested, that it would falter now and then, and if he built this victory up too high, it could be a very long fall.

Sam blinked, swayed the tiniest bit, and he got a blinding smile. "Thank you, Sir."

"You're welcome, my boy. I'm proud of you." Gently, he

released Sam's hands, put them at the boy's sides, and stepped away again. "Why don't you stretch? Move around a bit. I need a moment to order my thoughts."

Thomas knew his next move was important, knew they needed to be done talking or poor Sam's head would explode. Sam needed different input, something physical to keep his attention so he didn't have to work so hard at it for a while.

He knew he was right when he turned and saw Sam bent in half, his upper body swaying in broad motions. Oh. That was lovely.

So. Physical work, push the boy toward the right headspace. Subspace. And if the work gave him an excuse to put his hands on Sam, so much the better. He pulled his deerskin flogger out of his kit, picked up a chair, and placed it in the center of the room. "You were stiff, hm? Feel better?"

"Yes, Sir. I was fixin' to get caught up." Sam rolled up to standing, hips swaying side to side.

"Don't wait that long next time, boy. That's what your safe word is for. Use it. We'll talk about what you need and make sure you're comfortable. Don't make it even more difficult to concentrate, all right? Give me your safe word again."

"Revolver."

Excellent—that was sure, firm, no hesitation—just like the nod Thomas had gotten. He was making a connection here that he hadn't before. Sam's eyes were on him, curious, interested, hungry even.

"Revolver." He walked to the far side of the chair. "Come sit. Backward."

"Yes, Sir." Sam settled easily, arms draped across the back. He could see the top of Sam's ink, the knotted rope attaching the barbed wire to the skin.

"Perfect. This is a deerskin flogger." He draped the soft falls across Sam's spine as he spoke, running them lightly over the boy's skin. "It's very soft, there's no snap, and the falls are wide, so the most you'll get from it is a solid thud. It won't hurt; it's not designed to. This one is a beginner instrument, meant for sensation and sound, not sting."

He rolled his wrist and let the flogger fall lightly on Sam. "Any questions? I'll allow them now, but not again until I'm done unless you use your safe word."

Sam shook his head, even as he leaned toward the flogger's touch. "No, Sir. I'm good."

"Very well. Like earlier, when you were concentrating on my steps, I want you to focus on the sound, the sensation. I'd like you to keep your eyes closed. If you think that will be difficult, I can get you a blindfold. Can you manage it? Just a yes or no, please."

"Yes." Sam closed his eyes, took a deep breath, and settled deeper into the chair.

So far, so good. He found a comfortable stance he could hold for a while and let the room go silent. He didn't want even the sound of his boots to distract the boy from the sound of the flogger. He continued to roll his wrist for a bit, letting the flogger just fall on its own, moving from one shoulder to the other and down Sam's back, covering as much skin as he could.

He liked this flogger as a sensation tool because he didn't have to worry about sensitive spots like Sam's scar. He could bring it down heavy if he wanted to, and it would make a lovely sound, but it didn't hit that hard.

He waited for the boy's skin to pink, then traded the flogger for his fingers, running them over the warmed skin from the boy's shoulders to his hips.

Sam's moan filled the air like a gift, Sam arching for his touch in a slow, lazy motion.

Rather than words of praise, he answered his boy with a hum of approval, low and gentle to match Sam's lovely display. Then he tugged the flogger from under his arm and began again, this time using the lower part of his arm to bring the flogger down, making that wonderful solid sound each time it fell.

Sam began to breathe with the blows, with him. Every so often Thomas would adjust where the flogger fell, find a new pattern, and Sam would shift, tense, then shiver. Then Sam would find his rhythm again and sink deeper.

He would be able to keep this pace up for a long while if he wanted to, but he knew what the endgame was this time. He wanted Sam deep, but not so blissed out that the boy couldn't reply to a question. Of course, it should be simple for Sam, because he was going to give the boy the answers first.

He slowed the blows and tucked the flogger under his arm, admiring the bright color coming up across Sam's skin. Placing his hands on Sam's back this time was a bit more risky, so he went with just the tips of his fingers at first to see how sensitive the boy was.

Sam gave a soft gasp, and his legs tensed, he went up on tiptoe for a second before settling down. His boy didn't pull away from him, though.

"Good boy," he whispered, leaning close to Sam's ear. "You are mine, boy. Mine. My boy, my submissive." He slid his fingers off Sam's shoulders and around to settle on muscled arms, speaking louder this time. "My boy, my sub. Mine."

"Yours." The response was immediate. No worry. No censoring. No choosing the right words.

No, it was simply—"Yours."

"Yes. Good boy." He stepped back and pulled out the flogger, draping the falls across Sam's back. "More? Or have you had enough?"

"I don't know how to tell."

That was answer enough for him. Sam was much too coherent to have had enough. "You'll know. Use your safe word if you need it. I'm going to continue."

He took a deep breath and let it out slowly, but loud enough for Sam to hear. One more round, just a little heavier, and that should do it. He brought the flogger down, using more of his arm, and raised the stakes for Sam. He called out questions between each blow, each one more intense than the one before. *Whose boy are you? Who is your Master? Are you a submissive?* Questions meant to push as much as to reinforce, to raise emotion. And just as he'd decided that the boy had taken enough, one final order.

"Tell me that you're mine."

Sam's eyes flew open. "I swear, I'm yours! I have to...up. *Revolver!* I got to move!"

Timing was everything. He dropped his flogger and hooked an arm under Sam's to steady him. "All right. Up. Come on."

Sam took a few unsteady steps, chest working like a bellows. "Goddamn."

"Breathe, sweetheart. Talk to me." He wasn't worried. He'd been watching Sam carefully. He only wished the boy hadn't waited so long. He pulled two bottles of water from a small cooler in the corner and held one out to Sam. "You may speak freely."

"Jesus. That's like..." Sam took the water. "Thank you. Damn." He sucked the bottle back. "Adrenaline rush."

He shook out his arm, making sure he hadn't overdone

it. It felt damn good. "I'm not going anywhere. Take your time, boy. Breathe. I should tell you, your back is beautifully warmed. It has a very nice, deep blush." He grinned and leaned against the wall, drinking his water and staying out of Sam's way.

"It feels awake." Sam walked himself out, pacing before he plopped down on the floor and sat. "Damn."

Thomas watched Sam for a moment, thinking about the boy's choice of words. He was learning that Sam chose them carefully, and that the boy found it difficult to wrestle what was in a wild mind and heart into conventional conversation.

"Awake." He repeated the word out loud, thinking about it and what it might mean for Sam while he tidied up the room, put the chair and his flogger away, and got them each a second bottle of water. "Can you tell me more, sweetheart?"

He set the water bottle down on the floor in front of Sam and paced away, giving the boy a good look at his boots, but not his eyes.

"I know you don't fight, but you have ink—it's like that. Tender and lit up, like everything's woke and clear."

Clarity. Something complicated and rare for Sam. It wasn't the headspace he'd envisioned for the boy, but it was valid and more than acceptable. For all he knew, this was the boy's own version of peace. Time and more work would tell.

"How do you feel?"

"Happy." That was just as simple and honest as anything, even if Sam blushed as soon as he said it, hiding in his water bottle.

"I'm very pleased, boy. You should be proud of your accomplishment today. I'm glad you're happy. Of all the goals we'll work toward, that is the most important one of all, isn't it?"

Sam gave him a half smile. "What about you? How do you feel?"

It was so tempting to answer that question honestly, completely. Certainly there was a piece of Sam that deserved to know. But this session couldn't end like the last one had. His boy needed to understand that his responsibilities continued even though their session was coming to an end.

This wasn't pillow talk. It was aftercare.

"I've already told you I am very pleased and proud of you. However, if you wish to ask a question, boy, you need my permission. Also, you've forgotten your...manners. Hm?"

Sam tilted his head, lips tightening for a fraction of a second. Then he nodded and finished his second bottle of water.

Thomas watched Sam again, reading the boy's body language. The rules were new and difficult for Sam. He understood.

"While I appreciate the acknowledgment, if you forget a rule, boy, an apology is in order." He crossed his arms and waited, standing less than a foot from his boy. "Respectfully."

Sam stood up, unfolding himself from the floor with impressive ease. Sam stared him right in the eyes, gaze sure and direct, straightforward and stony. "My apologies, Sir."

His mind raced through the scenario while he returned Sam's stare, doing his best not to reflect what was in his boy's eyes but defuse it. He'd offended Sam, which was no surprise. What was surprising was how quickly Sam's mind-set had changed. In just that quick exchange, Sam had gone from happy to angry, without so much as a breath to consider who he was talking to. As much as he hated to admit it, this wasn't a contest either of them was going to win. In fact, it couldn't be a contest at all if they were both going to step away with their dignity intact.

"Apology accepted," he said calmly, gently. "Thank you."

"No worries. My bad."

Thomas could hear the echo of hurt in those words, but the icy fury had faded. Sam nodded before stepping to the side and throwing the empty water bottles away.

He sighed and rubbed his forehead, thinking perhaps he preferred the fury.

"Was it?"

"Pardon?" Sam turned to face him, face a study in confusion.

"You were very quick to anger and even quicker to challenge me, so was it your bad? Or was it mine? Be honest."

"Jesus Christ, what the fuck do you want? You say 'speak freely,' then you get onto me for doing it. I ask after you— your feelings, just because I care about you and whether you're okay, and that's breaking the rules. You accuse me of being rude and disrespectful, and I'm *not*. I apologized. I meant it. I won't ask after you again. What else do you want?"

The benefit of the doubt? For your trust to extend to my intention? Perhaps an acknowledgment that I'm human too? But of course none of that addressed the actual fact that he'd made a mistake. And he couldn't expect that from someone riding the wave that Sam had been on. Had been, before he let it crash.

Fuck. Even an honest mistake was still a mistake.

"You're right. I did give you permission to speak freely. My...previous sub and I had an understanding about speaking freely and more personal questions. We had a...a line we didn't cross in this setting. I was holding you to an unreasonable standard, and I apologize."

Sam stared at him for a second, then walked right up to him and hugged him, hard. "I hear you. James was good at being different people when he was supposed to. Me? Not so much. I'll get it. I promise. Just be patient with me."

He accepted the embrace because he needed it and let the strength soothe him. But Sam's words made him uneasy, and he needed the boy to know that. He pulled away finally, taking the boy by the shoulders and making sure to catch those eyes. "I needed that hug, thank you. So much. But please believe me when I say that I don't need you to get it. I don't even want you to try. You're not James. You're nothing like him. I need you to be yourself, be Sam, and help me learn how this works for you. For us. I need you to be patient with me."

"For us. Yes, Sir." He saw that he'd said the right thing in the way Sam's expression softened, in the way the remaining stiffness in Sam's shoulders eased. "That's more than fair. More than."

He inhaled deeply, smiling a little at the perfect blend of leather, sweat, and Sam in the air. When he let it out, he tried to shake off the feeling that he'd failed and reclaim a little of the triumph he'd been feeling earlier. It wasn't quite the same, but it was there.

"Would you like me to answer your question?"

"I care about you, a lot, so yes. Yes, Sir."

"All right. Well, to be honest it's slightly less intense than it was when you asked, but the answer is the same. Electric. Powerful. Confident. Strong. Capable. Something they call a top's high. And so intensely proud of you. So proud it was a little hard to breathe. That last thing hasn't changed one bit."

"Oh...I'm so glad. It would suck so hard if you weren't in it too. You made my mouth dry."

"Oh no, I was in it. I was absolutely in it. What would be the point otherwise?" He hooked a finger under Sam's chin. "Tell me what exactly made you use your safe word. What that moment was."

Sam closed his eyes. "It was like a spring getting tighter and tighter, and when it let go, I needed to move or scream or something."

"Which you rightly understood to be adrenaline. Probably because I was pushing you. And you liked the flogger?"

Now Sam opened his eyes, blushing almost purple. "I did."

He cupped his boy's cheek, just to feel that lovely heat. "Excellent. I thought so, and I did too. I'll keep that one in our toy box." He winked at Sam. "Can you remember, and you might not, the difference between that intense moment and the second time I put my hands on you? Do you recall that feeling?"

"You mean the time with the weird feather or the second time you held me?"

So the feather had made an impression as well. He filed that away for the future. "Just today, sweetheart. After the second round with the flogger when my fingers were too hot for your skin. Do you remember your state of mind? How that felt?"

"Oh! Yes, Sir. That was..." Sam's lips pursed as he thought. "Nice is wrong. Warm. Like floating. Does that make sense?"

He nodded, more for himself than for the boy. "Yes.

Perfect sense, boy, and that's exactly what I was hoping you would say. That feeling, that space is really the goal. That space is where you should find you feel the safest, the most cared for. There's a place and reason for a whole range of things of course, but that space is important. Eventually we'll find a way to get you there and keep you there for...as long as I like. As long as you need."

"Can I ask a question?"

"Yes. We're..." He laughed and shook his head. "We're *actually* speaking freely now, I promise."

"Cool." Sam grinned at him. "You got the best laugh, I swear to God. So when you asked me if that was enough, should I have said yes? I mean, if that's the point, to be floating?"

"That is an excellent question, boy. Very honestly, there was no right answer to my question. I was asking to see what you'd do. I'm getting to know you. I'm learning your needs. I knew what headspace you were in—it was beautiful. I was looking for boundaries. 'I don't know' was...an interesting answer."

Interesting, because he'd thought perhaps the boy would want something more intense.

"But true, huh? I didn't know." Sam was right there, communicating, and it was heady. "So next time...since you know now and I do too, if you ask, I just make the decision and that's cool."

"Absolutely. And I will likely ask a more specific question, like, do you *need* more, or do you *want* more? And eventually you'll have two safe words as well. One for a pause and one for full stop. We have a lot to explore, my boy."

"I can think of worse things than to have to explore together."

"Hm. Yes. A wise man reminded me that the excitement is in that journey. I'm looking forward to it. But for now we need to discuss completing our scene. Once I know you're steady and back in a good frame of mind, that day's work is done. So would you prefer, as some subs do, to have a few minutes alone to get dressed and prepare for the chaos that is that bar on most nights, or would you prefer I stay and wait for you? For today, I mean. It can change each time or we can have a routine, whatever you prefer. It's your time now."

"I have one day that I get to be with you. I can be alone anytime."

"Isn't that funny? I feel exactly the same way." He looped an arm around his boy and kissed him just because he could. Of course, the boy might not want to get dressed. That sweater was going to rub in all the wrong ways.

24

God, Sam could get used to watching Thomas sleep. All the worries just dropped away, leaving Thomas quiet, at peace.

Lord have mercy, he was smitten.

Today had exhausted him. One thing about Thomas's world was the swings from high to low. The highs were amazing, the lows were devastating, and the middles were the only places to breathe.

He'd never thought that he would...hell, he would do a lot for Thomas. Damn near anything. But he'd never reckoned he would like it. How was that reasonable? Did that say nasty things about him? Did that mean he was screwed up?

He'd read James's journal, and James wrote all about what he and Thomas had done like it was a means to an end. Sam was way more fascinated by the getting there, by the climbing to the top of the hill. Once you got up, you had to crash.

He'd learned a lot about that.

254 | JODI PAYNE & BA TORTUGA

He'd been so buzzed, then so hurt that he wanted to punch Thomas in the nose. Hard. *Jesus.* So mad.

Thank God he hadn't, because Thomas was trying to figure this whole thing out, just like he was. Maybe more, because he hadn't done it before. Hell, it was like adding a new person to a Spades game. Everyone knew how game play went—not because it had to, but because that was the routine. Play your aces first, bid an extra point for a missing suit. All that. Now Sam was playing, and he didn't know the house habits.

He was figuring it—maybe not the house habits, but Thomas's.

The other thing he'd figured was not to let on when he was turned-on. *Christ.*

He'd put on that sweater and it made him shiver. From that point on, Thomas was trying to kill him. By the time they'd come back to the apartment, he'd been rock-hard and ready to...well, do what he did. Jump Thomas's bones.

Not that Thomas seemed to mind one little bit. No, sir.

His stomach grumbled at him, and he wondered if Thomas kept anything in his kitchen. He hadn't ever seen the man cook.

Surely Thomas wouldn't complain if he discovered a snack. He was empty as a worm.

He slipped from the bed and went hunting.

The office was clean, neat, sleek and shit. Sam approved. The door to the guest room was half-opened, and he peeked in.

Oh.

Oh, dear. That was not a guest room.

There were way less leather, penis-shaped things, and cuffs in a guest room. Usually bedskirts and shit you didn't want to throw away but you didn't want to put out where people could see it, sure. Paddles? No.

Okay.

Okay, whoa.

Springing wood while standing naked in your lover's dark hallway was right up there on his weird-shit-o-meter.

Snacks.

He needed a snack.

Maybe he'd get himself a peanut butter sandwich and come back and eat it on that swing. Looked like fun.

"Hungry?" Thomas's voice was so deep and quiet, he thought maybe he was making it up. Except that would mean he was also making up the warm hands on his ass.

"Starving." He pressed back into the touch, leaning good and hard, his body and soul craving Thomas.

Thomas wrapped an arm around his waist and pulled him away from the...room, then quietly closed the door. "Sorry about that. Peanut butter and jelly?"

"Sure, thanks. The door was open. I wouldn't have opened it." He wasn't an asshole. Curious, sure, but not an asshole.

Thomas led him down the hall. "Oh, no. I didn't mean it that way. I just meant I'm sorry you walked into all of that. I hope it didn't freak you out. I usually keep the door locked, but that's where I keep my floggers."

Freaked out? Totally. Hell, the immediate hard-on was way more concerning than the room. The immediate hard-on that had been totally reinforced by Thomas's hands. He chuckled at his own goofiness. "No. Not freaked. I'm sorry if I woke you. My schedule is topsy-turvy."

"Don't worry. I don't plan on sleeping much on Sunday nights. I just got cold." Thomas put a jar of peanut butter on the counter, nuzzled his neck, and grinned at him. "But I'm getting warmer. You look downright hot."

God, this was the most wonderful thing on earth—the touches, the casual nakedness, the ease. It was delicious, erotic, and he was a little stupid with joy. "I feel like a million bucks."

"Mhm. Yes, you do. Strawberry or grape, stud?"

"Grape, please." He pulled out the bread and started hunting a butter knife. Thomas put the jelly on the counter; then those cold hands landed on his back, surprising a moan out of him.

"You're like a cat." Thomas slid those cool fingers up to his shoulders and dug them into the muscles there. "You love to be touched, don't you? I mean, most people do, but you..." Thomas's thumbs slid up the tendons at the back of his neck and into his hairline.

"I..." His eyes crossed, and he licked his lips, trying to remind his hands how to move.

Thomas chuckled and whispered in his ear, "You're hungry. You wanted a snack."

"Right. Hungry. You keep distracting me." He was loving it.

"I'm so sorry. I really shouldn't get between a man and his peanut butter." Thomas pulled out a spoon and scooped out a spoonful. "You need any help?"

"You want a sandwich?" He spread peanut butter on one slice of bread, watching Thomas lick the spoon clean.

"No, thank you. I'm fine." Thomas wiggled sandy eyebrows at him, then stuck the spoon into the jar and scooped out another spoonful. "Did you grow up on PB and J? Or did you have some other go-to afterschool snack?"

"Lots of peanut butter, pimento cheese. Oh. Tortilla roll-ups. We used to fight over those." He made his sandwich and had it mostly eaten before he put the jelly back in the fridge.

"You know how I know you grew up with brothers? You just ate that sandwich in four bites." Thomas tossed the spoon into the sink and crowded him into the closing fridge door. "I remember doing that. You had to move fast in my house if you wanted to eat. Did you actually chew?"

"Possibly." He arched as his still-warm back hit the cold fridge. God, that made him dizzy.

"Ooh. You like that, like that cold wall at the club today? You should have seen your eyes pop." Thomas raised an eyebrow and grinned. "Oh, Sam." Thomas shifted him and pulled open the freezer. "You give me wonderful, evil ideas."

"What are you up to?" He stepped in closer, rubbing into Thomas's side, humming as he snuggled his cock against Thomas's thigh.

"Ice." Thomas closed the freezer. "Whoo. Cold." Thomas tossed an ice cube from one hand to the other and back, then reached out, grinning, and rolled one of Sam's nipples between frozen fingers.

"Oh, fuck." His breath caught in his chest, pecs jumping, his nipple going rock hard. He flailed a half second, hand landing on Thomas's arm.

"Yeah? Good? Hang on, lover." Thomas followed that with a warm tongue, and the ice cube itself, drawing a slow circle. The melting ice dripped on his belly, the droplet freezing, making his belly go tight as fuck.

He tried to breathe, but all his body wanted to do was feel and arch and rub.

"Mmm." The ice moved to the other side of his chest, and again, Thomas went after his frozen skin with a hot mouth.

Goose bumps popped up all over his body. *Jesus.* The ice

cube slid down his side, along his back, and around toward his nipple. He heard himself crying out, the sound seeming to come from a distance.

He kept trying to reel it in, but when Thomas would bite or slide that bit of ice or lick, he would be lost.

"Fuck, Sam. You're...I could watch you like this forever and still want more." Thomas's hand went flat, the ice cube caught between it and his abs, and slowly, slowly slid lower, until those fingers curled around the base of his cock, the heat melting what was left.

His hips moved like they had a mind of their own, humping into Thomas's fingers. Thomas stayed with him, moving with him, denying him the friction he needed.

"Thomas..."

"What, Sam?" Thomas teased. "What do you need? You're looking good to me just like this. You're fucking beautiful."

"You're driving me crazy." In the best way. God, he was having fun.

"Good." Suddenly he was off his feet, and Thomas sat him bare-assed on the cold marble kitchen counter. Fingers that had finally warmed up again slid over his knees and up his thighs. He spread at Thomas's touch, the motion instinctual, his breath coming in hard little pants.

"Look at you. You just want, don't you?" Thomas started licking and biting, moving up the soft skin inside his thigh. "Mmm." Thomas pushed one thigh wider and dove in, but that mouth didn't touch his cock, didn't touch his balls. No, Thomas latched on hard to the inside of his leg, way up close to where it met his ass, biting and sucking up a bruise.

Sam stared down, the combination of the sight of Thomas's head right there between his thighs and the sting and tug that he couldn't see fixin' to drive him mad.

Thomas finally let go and licked at the spot before pulling back to get a look. "I love that spot. I'm the only one to ever see it. Except maybe your tattoo artist. Maybe." He leaned up, grinning. "It was my turn to leave a mark."

He reached down and touched the spot, finding it hot and slick. He pressed down, loving that sweet tingle, the tiny ache.

"Like that? Looks hot." Thomas pulled him down by the back of his neck and kissed him deep, feeding him an insistent tongue as fingers fisted around him and started to stroke.

They had a rhythm—Thomas's tongue, Thomas's hand, Thomas's need meeting his head on and devouring him.

His whole world narrowed to this. Thomas's breathing through the kiss, his own, that firm hand moving, doing everything right. He was flying, like this could go on forever, when Thomas pulled away with a gasp and a grunt.

"Fuck. Fuck, I need..."

Thomas used both his hands to drag him closer, right to the edge of the counter where Thomas lined up their cocks, squeezed them together and got back to business, nodding through a long moan.

He reached down, adding his hand to Thomas's, adding his strength. He worked the tip of Thomas's cock with his thumb on every upstroke.

"Yes. Fuck, yes." Thomas looked up at him, eyes on his and also not, a little hazy, unfocused. "Give it up for me, babe. Come on."

Sam moaned, caught Thomas's lips in another kiss, his balls drawing up tight as he shot, his seed coating Thomas's cock, their hands. It wasn't half a minute later that Thomas exploded, groaning into his mouth, hips jerking against Sam's wrist.

Their kiss grew savage for a minute as they tried to kiss through panting, ragged breaths and jolting aftershocks. They clashed tongues and teeth and bit at lips and chins until they were breathing deep enough to find each other's eyes again.

Sam blinked, so caught in that gaze that he never thought he'd climb out again.

Thomas swallowed hard and stared back at him. "That was...you're...I don't even want to think about how lost I would be if you hadn't gotten in my face on the sidewalk."

"Yes." He rubbed noses with his lover. "Sunday is the best day ever."

"Sundays are everything. I want more, though. I want to be respectful of your job, of you. I know you have a plan, I'm supportive, but it's...Sundays aren't enough."

He nodded. He understood. He wanted...more. He wanted a life that wasn't at the bar. "I need to get out from under the apartment. I can't afford it, you know?"

Sam wasn't asking for money, but he was going to need help—advice, for sure, some way to figure out how to do this. Hell, help cleaning up.

"Well, you could—uh." Thomas searched his face, took a breath, and looked away, reached for a couple of paper towels and ran them under the faucet for a second. "Little sticky." Sam got a wink but an uncertain smile.

He hopped down, feet slapping on the floor. "Yeah, life's that way. Little sticky. I'm going to need your help in figuring some of this out. Maybe a lot of it. There's a lot of moving parts." Heh. Moving parts. He was funny.

"I didn't realize the rent on that place was so steep. James must have had a better salary than I thought."

"He had to have had another job. Had to." There was no way. James hadn't been living like a pauper. High on the hog? No, but not church-mouse poor like him. Sam had seen the bank statements.

Thomas looked at him, brow furrowed. "I don't know when he'd—well, I suppose it's possible but...huh."

"Hey, what do I know? He might have been super investment guy." Could have been a sugar daddy, drug running, took in his neighbors' laundry and spent hours washing it in the tub. Sam didn't know. He didn't want to know. James sure as shit hadn't wanted him to know. He bet Bowie knew. Eh, like Bowie would have had the slightest interest.

"You should...ditch the apartment and move in here." Thomas looked at him, watched him.

He tilted his head. "You'd want me here?"

He hadn't even let himself think like that, hope for something like that. It would solve a thousand problems for him, but would it solve any for Thomas?

Thomas's smile grew. "Yeah, that was maybe the most noncommittal invitation ever, wasn't it? You know how it is. I was trying to give you a polite out when I should have gone with the nod. Can I try again?"

"You always get more than one chance with me, honey." He went to Thomas, touched one arm. Things were better when they got to lay hands on each other.

"Someday I won't need a mulligan." Thomas took his hands. "Move in with me. I want you here. I want you out of that crazy building. I want more time with you. I want your company. I won't interfere with your job. I won't ask you to change a thing. But I think it would be good for us both."

Oh. Oh, wow. Sometimes Thomas knew just what was in his heart and said what he needed to hear. He squeezed Thomas's hands. "I'd love to. Yes. Please."

Thomas kissed him, laughing against his lips. "I did better that second time."

"Little bit, yeah." He grinned, melting into Thomas's arms. "Thank you for asking."

"Oh, thank you for saying yes. Just don't expect me to cook for you. I don't think I've used the stove except for making eggs for breakfast since I moved in. I know I've never opened the oven."

"I'm super good at pouring Lucky Charms. Like a master." He let himself grin.

"Excellent. And I have an ice maker, so we're off to a good start." Thomas started backing away slowly. "Back to bed? We still have a few hours until daylight."

"Mm-hmm. Bed. Together." He wasn't sure his feet were touching the floor.

homas's living room rug was covered in half-open, half-empty boxes. He dug through one of them and pulled out some books that belonged to Sam, added them to a small stack of James's books from the apartment, and headed for the office.

"Did you get that shelf cleared? A couple of the books I snagged from James are kind of tall." He stepped into his—into *their*—office and found Sam rummaging through one of the bookcases.

They were both exhausted. Neither of them had slept much after cleaning out and packing up James's things yesterday. James hadn't had much, but making the decision about what to keep, what to send home to his family, what to give away...all of that had just been grueling. Thank God for Sam. It would have been hell to do it alone. He was pretty sure Sam felt the same way.

But that was done now, and today was about looking forward, making Sam feel welcome and at home by tucking his lover's things in with his own. He'd taken a couple of days off work so they could do this without interrupting Sam's work schedule and without losing their Sunday. Sunday was...practically sacred at this point.

"Looks good in here. Oh, hey. Can you grab the top couple of books? I'm losing them."

"You got it." Sam grabbed them and set them on the shelf before reaching for the rest and putting them away. "I put the books Momma sent me away. The duffel isn't important—I can just shove it in a closet after I make sure she didn't throw any spare clothes in there. It's just my gear."

"Yeah? You mean your rodeo gear? Will you show it to me? The bedroom has a ton of closet space I'm not using if you want to hang it up or whatever."

"I'd love to show it off a little." Sam winked at him, the look playful, warm. "You'll like it. It's lots of rope and leather."

"It's like you know me. Can I tie you up in it?" He was only half joking.

"The bull rope would chafe like a bitch, but you'll like the gloves. Come and see. I'll show you what I used to do."

So charming, how Sam wanted to let him in, share with him. He followed close behind, as touched as he was curious, wondering if there would ever be a day that Sam didn't teach him something new.

The duffel was in the bedroom, and he settled on the bed. Sam sat at his feet, dragged the duffel over, and began to unpack. There were a few button-ups, a pair of jeans, three or four T-shirts, and a pair of incredibly worn Batman pajama pants on top.

Batman pajamas. He just had to smile.

"This here? This is my rigging for the broncs." It looked like...a weird mixture of saddle and chaps for a little kid, with huge D-rings on the ends.

A thick rope with a padded handle came out next. "This is my bull rope—nine/seven plait, soft tail. Not used all that much, and left-handed, of course."

"Of course." He laughed because nothing of what his rodeoing lover had just said meant anything to him but that. He slid to the floor next to Sam and leaned back against the bed, picking up some of the rope in his fingers. The smell of animal was familiar from his childhood. "What's the nine/seven thing about?"

"You see the main body of the rope? That's a nine plait. It's stiffer than, say, a five, but I like the heaviness. The tail end is a seven—more nylon, so it's softer." Sam handled the rope easily, the scent of leather stronger as it warmed in his boy's fingers.

He tested out the tail in one hand and the rest of the rope in the other. "Ah, I see." That was much more technical than he'd expected; he'd just assumed—ignorantly—that a rope was a rope. "The softer tail makes it...what? Easier to hold on to?"

"The tail ends over your wrist. I like a thicker rope around my hand, but not too hard." Sam pulled out a leather glove and put it on. Then he slid his hand into the handle, wrapped the rope around his fist, slammed his fingers closed with his other hand, and flicked the tail over his wrist like it was nothing.

He reached out and ran his fingers over the setup, feeling the way the glove fit into the handle. "That's fascinating. That doesn't hurt?"

"It's set up so you don't get hurt." Sam slid out of the rigging with a smile and kept digging. "I got my vest here. I needed this during my initiation fight, didn't I?"

"That wasn't a fight; that was a beating." He hadn't meant to snarl, but he clearly had lingering issues, even though it was...well, it wasn't *that* long ago was it? It felt like it had been months instead of weeks. He and Sam had come a very long way since that day.

"It was worth it. I got to stay."

He rolled his eyes but didn't argue the point. If you asked him right now to take a beating for Sam, he'd do it. "Doesn't make it right," he muttered and took the vest from Sam. "This is pretty solid."

"Saves lives, man. Cody Lambert invented these after Lane Frost died in Cheyenne." Sam pulled out a bunch of leather straps, set them down, then pulled out a pair of bright blue chaps.

"Such a dangerous sport." He watched Sam handle the chaps. "Oh, those are a great color." Not the black leather he'd prefer on Sam for his own favorite sport, but a great color all the same.

"Aren't they? They're a little beat-up, but comfortable on and easy to see." He pulled out tape and rosin, spurs and a neck roll. "These are all the weird little pieces and parts. Do you remember the first time I came to the club with you? When we went into that one room with the straps, the smell reminded me of this."

"The leather. I was just thinking how your rope smelled like the barn back home. Strange the associations we make." He picked up the spurs and turned them over in his hands. He hadn't missed the way that Sam held everything in his hands and the obvious pride he took in each of the pieces. Somehow, he'd thought rodeo was something his lover did for money. Fun, maybe, but still more of a hobby. But there was more to it than that. It was in Sam's voice, in the way he was so ready to answer questions. "Sam? Tell me honestly—how much do you miss it?"

Sam's expression got a little distant, but there didn't seem to be any sorrow or regret. "Compared to what? I loved riding, but the last two years I rode, I rode hurt. My medical bills were crazy. I wasn't doing good. I loved the whole rhythm of it, the ritual, knowing that I was doing something that cowboys have done for years. The rush, that's intense. Being a broke-dick cowboy that had four major surgeries in two years? Less fun."

"Less fun, still important, though, right? You just strung together something like six sentences in a row. I thought your limit was two." He cut his eyes over at Sam, giving him a knowing grin.

"Butthead." Sam reached over, poking him in the belly. "I talk all the time, but yeah. It was important to me."

He caught Sam's hand in his. "I was joking. It's not what you said. It's how you said it. I can tell it means something; that's all. I like to hear you talk about things like that." He looked at the gear and Sam and the duffel bag. "We could put some of this stuff up if you want. Display it?"

"I'd love that." Sam leaned hard against him, cuddling in without the slightest tension. His Sam needed touch more than anyone he'd ever known. "Especially the rope and the chaps."

"Of course. We can put them in the living room or the front entry, whatever you like. Were you really just going to pack it all away in a closet?"

"Well, sure. That's where it's been. I have my silver buckle from my best ride still, so when I dress up, everyone can see."

"I remember that buckle from that first night at the Italian place. All I wanted to do was take it off you." He snorted. "I was a little wound up that night. Sorry."

"Everything was hard. Everything." Sam shook his head. "Shit, I was so fucking scared. Thank God for that little waitress."

So, it wasn't just him. Everything really was hard. That was more comforting to hear than Sam probably realized. "Did she help you get home? I know I wasn't any good to you. I had to have Clint talk me off a ledge."

"She helped me find groceries and get back. I found the liquor store on my own." Sam kept holding his hand, drawing circles on his palm.

He kissed the top of Sam's head, smiling at how adorable that was and how little he actually minded that fact. "That feels so long ago to me. I know it was only weeks, but it feels so much longer."

He thought about James and how different he'd been around his late lover. His relationship with James had been like a carefully selected whiskey. They were well suited for each other; they had a certain refinement about them; they saw each other in moderation. James had his apartment and Thomas had his place. Orderly. Neat.

Sam was like whatever was on tap. Never quite sure what it would be day to day, but it didn't matter as long as it was cold and close by. He just wanted to get drunk on it. Often.

It wasn't that foreign to him, really. He just hadn't indulged that part of himself in a long while. "I know this will sound strange, but part of me feels like I've known you forever."

"Do you think that's because James and I were brothers?"

He gave that question the thought it deserved. When he first met Sam, he saw a lot of similarities. But he was looking for them. He wanted to make that connection because he wanted to feel close to James. He wanted to hold on to the lover he'd lost.

Now?

"I think that's what drew me to you at first, sure. But now, I think the answer is no. I think it's because a much younger version of me would have been so infatuated with you. I think you would have been magic to him. Like a gift. As you are to me now."

Sam's cheeks were burning, bright red and hot, expression so touched. "Thank you. God, you make me feel ten feet tall."

He needed a kiss. Nothing crazy, just a taste. He tipped Sam's face up and found those sweet lips. Sam breathed into him, one hand warm and solid on his chest.

"How are you today, babe? After yesterday. Other than not anything close to ten feet tall?" That was a tough question, actually. He wasn't entirely sure how he'd answer it himself.

"Yesterday was hard. I miss him, and...there's something about that building that's...ruined for me." Sam shook his head and smiled. "But that's not what you asked. Today I woke up with you. I don't think that will ever be less than amazing."

"You're right. It is amazing to know I get to wake up to you every morning. Even if you're still sound asleep." Sam was right about that building too. He never had gotten over the sight of James's blood in the sidewalk. And Sam getting mugged and those damn razor blade pranks? The building had a very bad vibe now. "What's left in your boxes?"

"A few more books, my chargers, the rest of my clothes. I didn't bring much." Sam shrugged, chuckled. "I didn't come here to stay. Everyone back home that's still talking to me thinks I'm crazy for coming here and moving in with you."

He knew he should say something, and soon, before Sam thought he was upset about being outed to half of East Texas, but his lover had once again managed to surprise him, and as usual, he was so proud of Sam it left him a little breathless.

Instead Thomas did the next best thing and caught Sam's eyes. Whether he understood or not, at least he would know he hadn't done anything wrong. The rest was coming, as soon as Thomas found words.

Sam winked at him, squeezed his fingers. There wasn't any tension, no stress. Sam had done what he'd done, no apologies.

"You are crazy. Just not for the reasons they think. Did you seriously...I mean, obviously you did. But...wow." He took a deep breath because his mind was racing almost as much as it had been the other day with Clint. Just for better reasons.

"I'm really happy you did that. I'm sorry that you lost some people in the process. Are your parents okay?" That had to be a big one, right? Because Sam had said his mom was counting on him to give her grandchildren. He was called a lot of things, but "Dad" was not a name he wanted.

"They will be. They're way more upset with my staying here. Bowie was cool." Sam met his eyes, head on. "I won't lie about us. I am not ashamed of you. People don't like it, fuck 'em."

"It's almost a shame you're not giving your mom grandkids. The world needs more of that attitude right there." He leaned in for a kiss. "You can leave out the bit about the flogger. That would be okay."

"Yeah, that's a bit of a challenge to explain." Sam gave it up for him, kissing him gently. "I'm still explaining it to me."

That made him laugh. "How are you taking it?"

"I'm a determined student. Maybe not the easiest to teach, but I try hard."

"If I had to guess, I'd say you are exactly as easy to teach as I am to have as a teacher. We'll be fine. Forgiving, and fine."

"Works for me." Sam inhaled deeply, held the breath, then let it go.

What a perfect opening. He wasn't quite sure how it happened, but it seemed like Sam had a way of picking up what was on his mind. He'd thought about his goal, considered his phrasing, all of that days ago. He'd just been waiting for the right moment.

"You know, while we're on the subject. Have you thought about anything you'd like to try? Are you curious about anything specific? Do you have any ideas? I want to be sure I'm incorporating things that interest you as well."

Sam was quiet for a few seconds as his boy's thoughts spun. "I still have a thousand questions. Maybe two thousand. Researching online just makes more questions."

"Well, this is a really good time to ask, because you can't get in trouble." He smiled. "I'm kidding. A thousand questions have to stem from something. What have you been researching?"

"I googled. There's a lot of...there's some stuff..." Sam stroked his fingers, petting him. "So, there's one and a half billion sites."

"At least. Which one did you decide to click?" This was good. In fact, this could prove to be gold. He could have gotten a lot of "I don't know," but he was fairly sure Sam was actually trying to give him an answer. "I promise I have clicked on them all; there's nothing taboo in this conversation."

"I started with the Wiki. Then the Urban Dictionary and Huffington Post, just for a general overview. I've watched some videos on Bing, read a few things. There's no answers anywhere, though, just more questions. It's this vast subculture that has all these layers within."

After that response, he certainly had no doubt about what Sam was meant to do for a living. The man knew his way around internet research for sure. And, like all internet research, looking up "BDSM" produced a bottomless pit of link surfing. But there was one thing Sam hadn't mentioned, or perhaps wasn't ready to admit he had gone after.

"I believe we have already discussed how limitless the combinations of wants, needs, and desires are in the lifestyle. Unless you get a bit more specific in your thinking, you won't even find suggestions. You've read a great deal, it seems. Did you click on images?"

"I did. They were very sexual—some were erotic, some were porn. So I know that...okay, this is awkward, and I swear I don't want details, but you said you and James had separate rituals and rules for things. Is that how it works for you?"

"We did. I'm hesitant to be too specific, because I want us to create our own rituals and rules, and if I've learned anything from working with you, it's that what works for me is something I am having to reevaluate."

He knew what Sam was asking, or the gist anyway. But the question was, unintentionally, loaded with land mines.

"James and I had very specific boundaries and practices that changed whether we were at the club, here in my apartment, at his apartment, out in public, and so on. With regard to intimacy as lovers, that was reserved for the bedroom. If we wanted to set goals, push boundaries, work on headspace, that sort of thing, we did that at the club. And if we wanted to meet somewhere in the middle, that's what my playroom was for. And each location had a set of rules as well."

"Did you have a manual?" The words popped out of Sam's mouth, and his eyes went wide. "Oh, God. I'm sorry. That was rude."

"No." He laughed, probably more delighted than Sam was ready for. "But talk to Clint sometime. He asked me the same question. It was like a signal. I'd say meet me in the playroom, and we both understood what was expected. He'd pull me into the bedroom. That was clear as well. I understand that it sounds outrageously restrictive, but James found peace in understanding the boundaries. It made him feel safe."

"Yeah. He kept everything in boxes. He always did." Sam looked down at their hands. "I'm not that way. I'm way simpler."

Simpler. Sam. Sam whose mind moved at lightning speed. He wasn't about to assume he understood what Sam was telling him.

"Tell me what you mean."

"James had teacher-James, fighter-James, Vegas-James. I'm just Sam. Here, at work, at the club, online—I'm just Sam. I guess, in that, I'm more like Bowie."

He nodded along as Sam talked about James. That was exactly the man he'd known. And while he understood conceptually what Sam was telling him, what did being "just Sam" mean in practice?

"If we go back to your question about intimacy, about sex...are you suggesting you might prefer not to have those sorts of boundaries? That you'd like to try integrating our various roles?"

"I don't want to do anything to make you uncomfortable. I worry about you, about your heart."

His heart. It might be a little bit broken and a little sore, but it was healing steadily. His heart was one thing he wasn't worried about. It was the only thing he knew had a clear path. "Don't worry. I think my heart is safe with you."

"Yes." That was pure confidence. No question, and it made Thomas smile. "So, would you want to...how did you put it? Integrate? Would that freak you out?"

"I want to try anything that interests you. Anything at all. I'm interested in what 'just Sam' might bring to the table." He was interested in trying out some of his favorite toys in the bedroom too.

"I think that..." Sam pursed his lips, censoring himself. Thomas waited for a second, then pressed his hand firmly against Sam's chest, and the words just popped out. "I think that I am interested in the sexual aspects with you."

He smiled. Every bit of him, every little nerve ending was interested in what Sam, what his *boy*, had to say. He leaned in, lips close to Sam's ear, his voice a rough whisper. "So, what you're saying, my own, is that you'd like me to tie you up and fuck you. Or...perhaps flog you until you come?"

Sam's eyes went wide, the scent of sudden arousal like a drug. It was heady, addictive, and absolutely nothing compared to the husky sound of "Yes, Sir."

Oh, fuck.

The rush was so intense it made him light-headed. He licked his lips and swallowed, his cock stretched in his jeans, and a groan escaped from deep in his chest, loud and involuntary. "Good boy. On your feet."

He helped his boy to his feet, or to be fair, they actually helped each other. "Clean up in here and just stand right where you are and wait for me. I'll be right back."

He might have gotten an acknowledgment, but he didn't wait to hear it. He didn't need to. The boy was moving instantly. He headed for his playroom, knowing exactly what he wanted; he would just need a moment to select the right tools.

He returned with his hands full to find Sam waiting exactly as he'd asked. He looked his boy over eagerly and laid everything out on the bedside table. If this was going to be a regular venue for their activities, he would task the boy with finding a small chest he could keep a few things in.

"Strip, please. Don't rush, but take everything off." God. He couldn't believe how gravelly his voice sounded, even in his own ears. The boy had him high already. He was going to have to take a few breaths and find his focus for what he had in mind.

The T-shirt went first, baring that perfect belly, hard nipples; then Sam eased off his borrowed pair of sweats, taking the tighty-whities with them. Sam folded everything and set it aside, giving him a view of that ink, of Sam's tiny ass.

So fine, and all his.

He picked up a pair of cuffs and stepped in front of his boy. "You are lovely, boy. You're breathing, yes? This will be much less fun if you forget to breathe."

He shifted the padded cuffs from one hand to the other, letting the short but thick and heavy chain jangle, the metallic sound bright in the quiet room.

"I'll try to remember that." Sam shivered, eyes fastened on him. "No locking the knees; no passing out."

He allowed himself a bit of a smile and took a breath himself. "Show me your wrists, please. Palms facing one another."

He waited for Sam to comply, then began fastening the cuffs on, thick silver buckles standing out against the stiff black leather.

"We're going to revisit safe words first. 'Revolver' is your full-stop. You use that word when you've had enough, when you need something immediately. Yes? So, if I hear 'revolver,' then the cuffs come off, the scene ends, and I see to your needs. No hesitation. However, there are many instances in sexual play, and when tools that offer sharper sensations like cold, hot, and pain are in use, that a yellow light rather than red is more desirable. A pause button you can use when you just need a minute to breathe, to regroup. Or to decide if you need to use your full stop. Do you understand?"

Sam nodded, eyes on the cuffs. "Yes, Sir, I do. That makes a lot of sense. I like that. What about you? How do I know if you need something from me?"

His smile grew wider—he couldn't help it—and he gifted his boy with a light kiss. "I so appreciate the instinctive ways you care for me, boy. The way you think about my needs. It's something many subs struggle with. When offered everything they need, it's easy to get lost in that." He closed the buckle on the second cuff, letting the full weight of the chain hang between Sam's wrists. "I am not the one in cuffs, sweetheart. I can ask you for what I need. I can also *take* what I need."

He let that sink in, pacing away a few steps. Oh, he could get used to the sight of his boy in cuffs. They suited him beautifully, highlighting the innate strength, the corded muscles.

"Do you have a word for me, boy? For your soft stop?"

"Is *yellow* okay?"

"Couldn't be simpler. It's fine, boy." It was what James had used, but there was no need to say so. The word was as common as subs were. He knew many who used the stoplight convention. "Up on the bed, shoulders on the mattress, and that lovely ass up nice and high. I don't care where your hands are for now—be comfortable."

He raised an eyebrow when the boy didn't jump to it, but he knew Sam was working out what he meant. "Questions?"

Sam offered him a quirky grin. "I'm trying to figure out how not to face-plant."

"Mm. Good luck with that." He leveled the boy a stern look. "Go."

Sam wrinkled his nose, but he moved, climbing up, balancing himself on his knees as he moved the pillows, then used that stunning core strength to ease himself down, hands then elbows. Show-off.

"Oh, now that is a nice view." He walked past the bed and gave the boy a swat on the ass. "That's for not using *Sir* when you answered my question." But really it was more because he couldn't keep his hands off his boy.

Sam wiggled, muscles twitching, but that was it. "Sorry, Sir. I'm still trying to figure those details."

"Not to worry, sweetheart, I understand." For now. But he'd earned the right to that title, and he expected it to be used. He pulled his little bottle of warming lube off the nightstand and the little beginner's butt plug. He showed the plug to his boy. "Isn't this adorable? And it's the same color blue as your chaps. How wonderful is that?"

Sam shot him a look, half-shocked, half-unbelieving; but

that melted into amusement. "What the hell are the chances of that? I-I got nothing. Sir."

He laughed—his boy was so much fun. "And I have a treat; this lube isn't cold. We can try the icy one next time." He stood at the foot of the bed and ran a hand over Sam's thighs, before he reached between them to tease Sam a little, rolling the boy's balls in one hand. "Honestly, boy, this view. It's a shame you can't see it the way I am."

Sam's blush climbed up his thighs, then spread. Sam rolled for him, moving in his hand, dancing for him. Always in motion, his boy.

With his free hand, he poured out a little of the lube, right over Sam's hole, letting the warm start to kick in before spreading it with his fingers and letting one slip right inside. Sam groaned for him, the sound raw, sliding right out. Thomas watched as his boy first pressed down into his hand, then back up onto his finger.

"That's a good boy. Feels good, right? It should." He slipped his finger free, slicked the plug, and started working it slowly into place. "I only have one hard rule for this session. You are not to come without my express permission." He gave the narrow plug one last little bit of pressure, and it seated itself with a pop.

Sam gasped, pushing up on his hands. "Fuck!"

Surprise.

"Isn't that lovely?" Thomas reached over his boy's back, put a hand on his nape, and gently pushed him down. "Do you like it?"

He grabbed a towel and made sure to wipe the lube off his fingers before picking up the paddle he'd chosen. Wouldn't do to have it slipping out of his fingers.

"It's weird, Sir. Foreign." Sam wiggled, side to side, body testing the toy.

Thomas imagined so, but he knew it didn't hurt, probably wouldn't make much of an impact if Sam hadn't been so focused on his hole. His boy had no idea of things to come. His thuddy but light little paddle and a couple of nice floggers he'd choose from, depending on how the boy was responding.

He drew the paddle through the air so his boy could hear it; then on the second swoop, he swung it into the softest part of one lovely butt cheek. It hit with a thwack, and Sam tensed, muscle going rock hard.

He ran his hand over the spot. "So, this little paddle is just to warm you up a little. Everything is new for us, so I want to know what you think of new things. Like, dislike...I don't know yet is also a perfectly fine answer." He brought the paddle down on the other cheek, but a little off-center, so he nudged the boy's plug along with it.

Sam clenched, trying to protect his hole, and that moved the plug inside him, making the boy roll his hips. The third smack was easier, and Sam relaxed into it.

Once he knew his boy was breathing and not fighting the blows, he stretched out the full length of his arm and started up a rhythm. One side, then the other, like a tennis volley, over and over until his arm felt warm and Sam's ass was blushing pink. The occasional, not at all accidental, nudge to the plug seemed to be more appreciated as time went on as well.

Sam was silent but not still, moving for him, responding to his touches, breathing with the blows.

Patient, not complaining, not all that interested. Not the boy's cup of tea. And not his own, to be honest, if he wasn't getting a response that kept his dick interested. Still, the pink was pretty, and his arm was warm, and he knew Sam enjoyed the flogger.

He slowed his blows, made them lighter to let his boy know that he would be stopping soon, then tossed the paddle on the bed. He placed both hands on Sam's pink cheeks. "Good boy. Not your favorite toy? Not your favorite position? Both?"

"It's...cold, Sir. The other felt like—like a part of you."

"The flogger? It's my favorite tool." Was it that obvious, or was Sam just that perceptive? "I've brought three to try, but I need you to see if you can stand for me for a bit. Roll to your side, then onto your back and I'll help you up."

He could get a chair, as well, and might need to if the heavy cuffs and standing proved difficult for his boy. He was considering renovating the playroom a bit to make it more Sam-friendly, but for now he didn't really want to take his boy in there. He wanted to keep it all new, and he and James had never had toys of this nature in the bedroom.

"Oh. Head rush." Sam laughed softly as he turned and stretched, reaching up for him. "It's weird, moving with something inside me."

"It should be more than simply weird; it should be distracting. And since it's not, we'll use a bigger one next time." He winked at his boy and helped him off the bed, standing close to make sure he was steady on his feet. "For now, it's nice to look at, and that's good enough for me."

They'd lost a little of the tension they had earlier, but he just knew his boy would float on at least one, if not the combination of his floggers, and they'd get it back. He slipped a hand around Sam's cock, which he was gratified to see wasn't entirely disinterested.

In fact, Sam seemed more than willing to get that desire back, pushing into his hand with a soft moan. Perhaps his boy wasn't as unaffected as he seemed.

"How do you like those cuffs? I like the heavy chain

when I can't really restrain a sub—this room hasn't ever been used this way. Maybe I'll have you add some tie-offs and tethers near the bed, boy. Would you like that?" He was slowly leading his boy to an open section of wall, literally by his balls.

"They feel...intense, heavy. Like—" Sam's breath caught in his chest, whether from his fingers on Sam's balls or his own censorship, Thomas didn't know.

He pushed his boy's back against the wall, caught his eyes, and since it had worked earlier, he pressed a hand into Sam's chest. "Like?"

"Like you have me. Like I don't have to worry." Sam sucked in a deep breath, right there with him, so present.

"Comforting." So interesting. "Good boy." He gently turned his boy to face the wall. "Let's find a comfortable position for you." He helped Sam raise his hands and place them flat against the wall, showing him how he could brace his forearms as well if the chain got too heavy. "Will that do? Is this something you can hold for a bit? I can move you to a chair of this gets too hard."

"This is solid for me. Good. Thank you, Sir." Sam wiggled, settling himself deep in his feet, the stance sure, thighs spread, rosy ass exposed for him.

"Good boy." He took a breath and went to get his floggers, tugging off his T-shirt as he went. It was warm in the bedroom now. He laid two of the floggers down close to the wall where Sam would be able to see them. The third was the same tool he'd used the other day, and the one he intended to start with now. "Words, please."

It took Sam a second. That head tilt was one hell of a tell, letting him know that his boy was trying to get it, not defying him. "Okay, right. Revolver and yellow, Sir."

"Excellent. Good boy." He rewarded Sam by letting the

falls of his flogger swing between the boy's thighs and gently lick Sam's balls.

Sam sucked in a breath and went up on tiptoe. "Damn."

Mmm. Yeah. Damn.

"You'll remember this one. It's exactly the same as the one I used the other day. I have two more. I won't say much about them, but you can assume they get gradually more intense. They're right at your feet, if you didn't see them."

He shook out his arm and got started, this time beginning with his simple, consistent forearm swing, the falls landing on his boy's shoulders. God, this was so easy, so comfortable. Sam was the perfect height.

Sam groaned softly, the sound sweet as hell, filling the air. Oh yes. His boy responded to the floggers, to the way the falls wrapped around his body. That suited him just fine.

"It's like a familiar friend, isn't it? I love how the leather gets softer as it warms. You can smell it if you pay attention. This one just loves your skin. Hugs your shape." He spoke just loud enough to be heard over the solid thud of the flogger, and rhythmically so he didn't interrupt the boy's concentration.

"Love the smell..." Sam began to move with his blows, offering him little sighs, low moans.

He could just do this, keep after the boy until Sam's skin got hot and red, until Sam couldn't stand it anymore. He'd like to see that. Sam would probably love it, but today he wanted more.

Thomas wanted to push his boy, listen to him respond, learn what turned him on. What got him off. What got them both off.

He stopped suddenly, wanting his boy a bit off-balance as he switched one flogger for another. This second one was made of stiffer leather and had narrower falls. He paused, standing close enough to Sam's back to feel the warmth coming off the boy's shoulders. "My boy. Mine."

Sam leaned, entire body trying to reach for him. "God, yes. Yours."

He let the boy have what he wanted, meeting Sam halfway and allowing the boy's back to press into his chest. He rocked his hips forward as well, jostling the little blue plug with his own stiff prick, making sure Sam felt him.

Sam cried out, fingers curling against the wall, hips rolling in a couple of hungry thrusts. "Oh shit, you're magic."

His boy's words made him grunt, made him ache. "I'm going to let you feel my flogger, boy. My arm. And I'm going to make damn sure you feel me for a couple of days."

"Please." The single word echoed between them, ringing with honesty.

"Oh, my boy." He stepped to arm's length. He knew these whips so well, had used them so often that he knew just exactly how far away to stand. All the same, he tried out a couple of test swings, letting the ends graze Sam's pink skin.

"Yellow and revolver." He said the words out loud for his own sake and his boy's, to remind Sam this was for both of them, that Sam was not alone. Then he looked at Sam's back, made sure he was clear on where he wanted to hit, and brought the flogger down on target, twice. Once on each shoulder.

Sam bit out a cry, hands leaving the wall, the chain going taut.

Fuck. His boy was so beautiful.

"Good boy." He wanted Sam to hear him. He gave the boy a breath or two to make sure there wasn't a safe word coming, and when he was confident he wasn't going to hear one, he gave his next order. "Count, boy. Every stroke, out loud. One, Sir. Two, Sir. Tell me you understand."

He needed the feedback, the sound, the words to make sure he was reading Sam well, that he didn't push the boy too far. He didn't want to hear "revolver" today. He and Sam had plans.

"I—" Sam cleared his throat, licked his lips. "I hear you, Sir. I hear you." Then he blew out a sharp breath, sucked one in.

"Good boy. Make sure I hear *you*. Steady now." He took another breath and laid down four strokes in a row, two to Sam's shoulders and two more to his rosy ass, listening to his boy carefully.

The first two counts were clear, the third one husky, and the fourth one almost inaudible, Sam's hips curling in before rolling out.

He tucked his flogger under his arm, stepped up close behind the boy, and rested his hands on Sam's hips. "Breathe. If I can't hear you, you're not breathing." That wasn't always the case, of course, but he wanted his boy to hear his voice, and even he needed to remind himself to breathe from time to time.

"Good—good timing." Sam moaned for him, arching like a cat under his hands. "God, your hands. I was fixin' to—"

He slid his hands around to Sam's stomach, stepping even closer. "Which one? Yellow or revolver?" It was good to know he was reading his boy well. It was so important to get that right, if nothing else, in case his boy ever let things go a step too far and couldn't articulate that. They both had learning to do.

Sam's groan was pure, unadulterated pleasure, his boy

snuggling into him, rubbing them together. "*Yellow*. I just needed to breathe a second, needed you a second."

"Good boy. I'm here. Tell me how you like my flogger." Someday he'd be able to ask how his boy liked his arm, but that was a step deeper than his boy was ready for yet. James had only gotten to the point of being able to read his state of mind by how he was hitting a year or so ago. Sam would figure it out faster, he knew. The boy was just more in tune with those things.

But James had been very quick to figure out the power exchange dynamic. It had been apparent to his former sub right away. Thomas had a feeling that it would take Sam much longer to realize—or at least to use—his own power and leverage.

"Mmm...it stings more, but the burn after is...deeper. It's harder to, I don't know, not ignore, but it's more than the paddle."

"A flogger isn't one hit; it's many at once. It's more specific and longer lasting than a simple flat paddle. There are more complicated paddles, of course. Good boy. I'm pleased by how you're processing." He dropped a light kiss at the base of his boy's neck and stepped away again. "You're stunning like this. You color up beautifully."

He got hold of the flogger again and ran his fingers through the falls, swung it in the air. "You called the time-out. You will let me know when you are ready to begin again."

Sam wiggled and settled himself—it wasn't quite bracing himself for the flogger, but it was more than standing.

Thomas didn't mind waiting. Patience was a huge part of his responsibility to his sub. Sam hadn't turned down his flogger, and that by itself was exciting to him, energizing.

While he was waiting, he gave the instrument some thought. Four was plenty in a row the last round, and now Sam's skin was buzzing. He wouldn't get four again. But he'd get two, and maybe he could get two out of his last one. His fingers itched to use the more advanced flogger, but he had to be careful not to push Sam too far.

"Are your hands getting heavy, boy? You're welcome to make yourself comfortable."

"Good idea." Sam leaned, braced his upper arms against the wall, and stretched. "Oh...damn, that feels...oh..." That sound was pure sex. "I'm ready for you."

Sir.

He thought it, but he let it go, remembering what Clint had said about redefining convention. His boy was absolutely obedient, and squarely in the right place with his intention.

He grinned, glad Sam couldn't see him. The boy was also hot as hell right now, and part of him was ready to just toss the flogger and get on with it.

"Very good. Count, boy." He allowed his need into his voice. He wanted the boy to know. Just two and he'd see what was next for them. He eyed Sam's back, intending to make these two count, raised his arm, and swung. His breath caught as he watched the neat red welts rise for a second and fade almost as quickly, leaving hot skin behind.

Sam panted, muscles rippling, moving like water. It made Thomas's mouth dry, the way he could see proof of Sam's response. The little motions never stopped, offered to him. "Jesus, I'm on fucking fire for you, Sir."

"Yes, my own. Patience, soon you'll get your reward." And he would have his. His cock was trying to tear a hole in his jeans.

But Sam wasn't asking for a break. The boy's words were still crystal clear, and that sent lightning up his spine.

Thomas marched toward his boy, dropped the flogger that was in his fingers, and picked up the heavy one, its black and white falls plentiful and narrow. The handle in this one was weighted, balanced to help it land exactly where and how he intended. He slid a hand down Sam's side, a second of comfort, and moved behind him, at arm's length one final time.

"You asked me earlier how you could know my needs. I need this, boy, and I believe you're ready. I believe you might need it as well." He took a deep breath, watching his words reflected in the set of Sam's shoulders. "Breathe. Just two and you'll have what you want...what you need from me."

"Yes, Sir." The words were rough and raw, gravelly and aching with need—their hunger. Sam took a deep breath, held it a long second, then let it out.

"Good boy." His words were so quiet he wasn't sure himself if he'd even said them out loud. He gave the flogger one more test swing, but he didn't want to make Sam wait. He lifted his arm and brought it down twice, first on his boy's left shoulder, then his right, the effort making him grunt.

Once again, he watched the welts rise, only these didn't fade right away. These wouldn't fade for a day at least.

"Oh, fuck!" Sam's hoarse cry made Thomas's balls draw up tight, the pure, honest hunger in the sound meant for him and him alone. "*Please*. Help me."

He was already moving, reaching for Sam to steady him. "Right here, sweetheart. I'm here." He lifted his boy right into his arms and carried him to bed, then helped Sam to stretch out on his stomach. The boy's back needed care and was too sensitive for sheets.

He shucked his jeans and briefs, taking a rubber out of one pocket before tossing the jeans to the floor. "So proud, my own. Fuck, I want you."

Sam arched, hips rolling up in an offer old as time. The movement made Sam shiver, hands fisting in the sheets. "Sir. Yours. Need you like breathing."

His fingers were shaking as he forced himself to breathe and carefully remove Sam's plug, but that was the very end of his patience. Those gorgeous red welts covering straining muscle almost pushed him over, but as he took hold of his boy and sank in deep, he knew on their own they could never be enough.

"My boy. Sam! Oh, fuck." He didn't have restraint, just raw need, but he gave it to his boy without a second's hesitation.

Sam took his need and fed it back, meeting his thrusts, slamming toward him. His boy was a flame underneath him, threatening to set them both off.

They rocked together until he didn't exist anymore. His need was Sam's; his purpose was his boy. He wasn't even sure he was breathing. He took Sam's cock in his hand, worked it through a tight fist and growled the word, "Mine."

"Gonna. Yours. Please." Sam's body rippled around him, muscles gripping him so hard he could barely breathe.

Thank fucking God. He should technically have given permission but he couldn't get air in, let alone words out.

The strength of Sam's climax forced a cry from him, and he froze, arched over the boy's back as he came in searing, blinding waves.

He was lost. Flying. His blood roared in his ears, and tremors rocked them both as the haze of need slowly lifted. Finally, when the room came back to him and he could breathe again, Thomas dropped a kiss to Sam's nape, grunting as that little connection caused Sam to clench around him.

"Fuck, babe." He shifted and rolled, stretching out along Sam's side. *Jesus.* He was completely wiped out, but he needed to get some ointment on his boy's skin, and he had to stay focused on whatever else Sam might need from him.

He kissed the edge of Sam's shoulder and reached up to carefully take the cuffs off his boy, then ran his fingers over Sam's wrists to make sure they hadn't chafed or bitten into the skin. They were well made and trustworthy, and apart from sweat and pressure marks from the weight of the chain, the boy was fine.

He sighed, annoyed with himself for not thinking to bring his aftercare kit from the playroom as well. "I'll be right back, boy. I won't be far. I will hear you if you call for me."

Who knew if Sam would, but the extra assurance wouldn't hurt in any case.

He slid out of bed, shaking his head, thinking that would help clear his mind, but it didn't. He washed up and went to get his kit, trying to understand this strange headspace. He felt relaxed and sated like a lover but proud and protective like a Dom. These things hadn't coexisted with James, and he wasn't entirely sure he knew how to process that.

With James, when a scene in his playroom was over, they were just Thomas and James. Their roles in that room, he realized now, had been play, and they fell away that easily. He didn't regret that. Those scenes almost always ended with kisses and thank-yous and beautiful, affectionate moments between lovers.

He made his way back to the bedroom and looked Sam over, realizing at last what made them so different.

Sam—his boy, his lover, his friend—lay in his bed. In

their bed. It had become a place where everything they were together was welcome. The strange feeling in his mind was the place where the clarity of his role as Sam's Dom and the desire of his role as Sam's lover overlapped.

Then he knew. He knew what this emotional space was called, but he was afraid to look at it head on. He wasn't ready to say it out loud.

"Mmm...you okay? You look a little dazed." Sam would know; his boy looked utterly blissed out.

"I am. Fine and dazed. I feel fantastic." A little raw mentally, but physically everything was better than right. He pulled the ointment he'd been looking for out of his kit. "Your back needs a little attention, sweetheart. How do you feel?"

"You ever been outside after a hard, heavy rain? It's like that." Sam had to work so hard to express his emotions, like he'd never been taught how.

He knew exactly what Sam was saying, though. Maybe it was telling that he didn't seem to have words for that either right now. "I like that smell in the air after a hard rain."

Damn. That wasn't going to help Sam connect the dots.

"Yes. The way that you can breathe too. You got a way of driving the storms out."

Oh. He smiled. "That's beautiful. Thank you, sweetheart." He very gingerly spread on the ointment, mostly just covering the spots where the skin was angry or weeping. It had a nice anesthetic in it, so it should cool the sting for a while. "I'm sorry I didn't take your cuffs off right away. I'm so conditioned...you said 'help.' I didn't hear a safe word. I'll be more attentive next time."

Sam chuckled softly, fingers dragging on his thigh. "I needed you so bad, I was fixin' to scream. I didn't even notice the cuffs." Sam's voice dropped to a near whisper.

"Except they helped me a little. I wanted to jack off then, but your hand...God, so much better."

"So much better. And truthfully, I liked seeing them on you anyway." He finished up. Sam was in fine shape, and this probably wouldn't even hurt tomorrow. But the skin was going to pull like hell at work later. "I need a kiss, sweetheart."

"Oh, yes, Sir." Sam pushed right into him, laughing as their lips met. Sam kissed him like there was nothing else on earth he would rather do than hold Thomas, give himself over wholeheartedly.

He laughed at first too, Sam's happiness spilling over, but then a sudden, deep ache seized in his chest and he found himself clinging to Sam, that kiss like an anchor, like if it let go he'd just be lost.

Sam held on tight, hands smoothing over his skin, fingers digging in and finding his sore spots. Comforting him. Loving him.

Breathe. Just fucking breathe.

He sighed and rested his forehead against Sam's. He felt like he should apologize, but that would make what Sam was doing seem like pity, and it wasn't. He didn't know exactly what it was, but Sam wasn't feeling sorry for him, Sam wasn't thinking about James or Texas or vengeance or anything but them together. He owed that to Sam as well. "Thank you." There was more, but that was the best he could do at the moment.

"Yes. Thank you too. God, you're beautiful to me." Sam kissed him, every few words. It would all seem an affectation, but the honesty, the sincerity rang from Sam.

He returned the kisses and just let himself believe it because it was exactly what he needed to hear. "I'm just so... relieved. Grateful that—" He swallowed and shook his head, then leaned back and tried to give Sam a smile. "You have to go to work soon. You should get some rest."

"I do, but if you don't mind company, I'll just love on you a while. I'm happy as a dog with two tails."

"I definitely want the company. I'll take every second I can get." He tilted his head, searching Sam's eyes. "I'm happy too."

"Good. It would suck if you were all grr...argh... orgasms." Sam's joy shone from him.

Thomas laughed, which actually felt pretty good. "I am very pro orgasms. I could have them all day. Would you like another?" He grinned back, eyebrows waggling.

Sam cackled. "Lord, I think my balls are empty. That was...whoa."

"You were stunning, Sam. You don't...things are new to you, that's obvious, but you don't behave as though you're new to this. You didn't seem nervous. You're curious in such a genuine way."

"If I get nervous, it'll be in the middle of the night at work when it's dead. I'll have hours to stress whether I'm doing all this right." Sam dropped him a wink before his expression got serious. "I believe in you. You said I just had to be honest, so I'm doing my best."

"You can't do it wrong. You and I are reinventing what's right. It's...liberating. And terrifying."

"Well, sure. That makes sense. You got all this pressure on your shoulders, all this expectation."

"Mm. Right. Pressure and expectation. You wouldn't know anything about that, would you? I think you might be projecting a bit there, stud." He grinned so it didn't seem unkind. But Sam had been the poster child for trying to make everyone happy. He did feel some pressure, but only from himself. He had a sub to take care of. "I'm just trying to be a...a good person." If nothing else, he could at least say that.

Sam nodded to him, so serious. "I hear you."

He nodded back and took one of Sam's hands in his. "How the hell are we ever going to top this afternoon?"

"Well, honey." Sam grinned at him, lips drawing up. "There's always Google."

READ the next book in the Cowboy and Dom series now!

Interested in learning more about BA's cowboys and Jodi's gentlemen? Want free fiction and news? Join our newsletters!

What's Up with Jodi
https://readerlinks.com/l/2317334

Spurs and Shifters
https://lp.constantcontact.com/su/A9CRUzp/baandjulia

Hey, y'all!

We want to thank you for giving First Rodeo a try. We hope you enjoyed the story and are looking forward to the next book in the series, Razor's Edge.

If you can spare a few minutes to post a review at the retail website where you made your purchase, we'd very much appreciate it!

Don't forget to "like" our Facebook pages and groups to keep up with all the news--new releases, sales announcements, giveaways, sneak peeks-- and of course the rodeo pictures, coffee memes and just general fun. We'd love to have all y'all!

Yeehaw and thanks for reading!

BA & Jodi

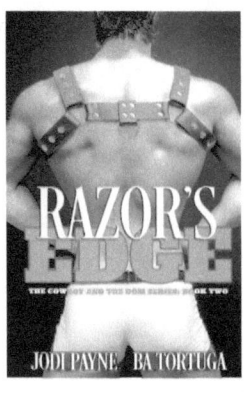

THE COWBOY AND THE DOM

Book Two: Razor's Edge

Razor blades left by a murderer remind Sam and Thomas of James, the man they lost to violence...and that his killer is still out there, always watching them, biding his time.

Their carefully built relationship also teeters on the edge of a knife. Sam's efforts to be a full-time sub to Thomas fail time and again, and Thomas must learn to accept the fact that Sam isn't James, but a different man with different needs. Through jealousy, confusion, arguments, and stress, they struggle to reconcile their massive differences and learn what it means to be a *them*.

But a misunderstanding might be the last straw—or the opportunity the killer has been waiting for to take Sam out of Thomas's life once and for all.

Read Razor's Edge now!

ABOUT JODI

JODI takes herself way too seriously and has been known to randomly break out in song. Her MCs are imperfect but genuine, stubborn but likable, often kinky, and frequently their own worst enemies. They are characters you can't help but fall in love with while they stumble along the path to their happily ever after. For those looking to get on her good side, Jodi's addictions include nonfat lattes, Malbec and tequila any way you pour it.

Website: jodipayne.net
Newsletter: https://readerlinks.com/l/2317334
All Jodi's Social Links: linktr.ee/jodipayne

ABOUT BA

Texan to the bone and an unrepentant Daddy's Girl, BA Tortuga spends her days with her basset hounds, getting tattooed, texting her grandbabies, and eating Mexican food. When she's not doing that, she's writing. She spends her days off watching rodeo, knitting and surfing Pinterest in the name of research. BA's personal saviors include her wife, Julia Talbot, her best friends, and coffee. Lots of coffee. Really good coffee.

Having written everything from fist-fighting rednecks to hard-core cowboys to werewolves, BA does her damnedest to tell the stories of her heart, which was raised in Northeast Texas, but has heard the call of the high desert and lives in the Sandias. With books ranging from hard-hitting GLBT romance, to fiery ménages, to the most traditional of love stories, BA refuses to be pigeon-holed by anyone but the voices in her head.

BA loves to talk to her readers and can be found at http://batortuga.com/ and her newsletter signup link is http://bit.ly/BAJulianews

AVAILABLE FROM JODI & BA

The Cowboy and the Dom Trilogy

<u>First Rodeo, Book One</u>

<u>Razor's Edge, Book Two</u>

<u>No Ghosts, Book Three</u>

The Soldier and the Angel, a Cowboy and Dom Novel

Sin Deep, a Cowboy and Dom Novel

East Meets Westerns

(single titles)

<u>Wrecked</u>

Flying Blind

Special Delivery, A Wrecked Holiday Novel

Temptation Ranch

The Merry Everything Series

<u>Window Dressing</u>

Cowboy Protection

The Higher Elevation Series

<u>Heart of a Cowboy</u>

<u>Land of Enchantment</u>

Keeping Promises

Bigger Than Us

The Triskelion Series

Breaking the Rules

Making a Mark

Making the Rules

Les's Bar Series

Just Dex

Hide Bound

Wholly Trinity

The Lone Star Series

Tending Tyler

Roped In

The Collaborations Series

<u>Refraction</u>

<u>Syncopation</u>

Puzzles Series

Cryptic